LAGUNA CANYON

CALIFORNIA

1916

To Judy
with Best wishes

Philip Dashtey

Many Americans these days tend to know the old West more as a story than as the wilderness it was. My western adventures all happened before gasoline. I never saw an automobile until I was almost forty and that first car sounded like the devil's work. I guess time makes every man a stranger if he lives long enough.

Before the great buffalo hunt killed off the herds, I saw prairie wolves running in packs, antelope stare from the rims, and wild geese arrowing the sky. There was room enough to ride for weeks and never meet a soul.

I have to say civilization can bring a conquering emptiness. Guess there's a contradiction there, evident up in Los Angeles when I ride an electric trolley, see a motion picture show, or just continue making the *white man's sign that walks by itself,* as an Apache once described my handwriting. God knows what he'd call a modern radio, a biplane, or that fool who drifted over in an air balloon last Fourth of July and fell into the sea. Word is that war over in Europe isn't going well for the allies but President Wilson appears determined to keep America out of it.

Looking back I understand why it's old folks who can see around corners. Recollecting strains more than my scribbler's eyes. Sneaking up on a vanishing past can be tricky as stalking turkeys over dry leaves. I tend to forget names although features of landscapes fifty years ago come to mind fresh as bread.

I'm not that old a buckaroo but I seem to have outlived everybody I knew worth remembering. It is a great comfort that the sweetest presence of all remains. When an evening wind whispers in the willow tree Dahlia planted by our bedroom window, I know it must be her.

Dahlia was literally a stepchild of the *Almanac*. Though raised to speak Spanish and sequestered in a strict household, she secretly studied English largely by memorizing and reciting passages from a fragmented King James Bible and from an 1850 Robert Thomas's *Farmer's Almanac*. Both our conversations and our gardening profited from Dahlia's cloistered education. Typical of her early speech were facts she shared when I was watching her wrap fruit tree scions to store for spring planting. *Señor Thomas's book say that Spain has more apple trees than any country. Why? Is because the Spanish eat an apple an plant the seeds from their mouths. An is true a cow givest best milk in the morning than in the end of the day, an carrot juice in the churn make butter more yellow, but is better to feed a cow the carrot to make the cream yellow?*

Occasionally Dahlia's memorized wisdom, when halted by some intrusion of logic, initiated a tricky question.

I have watch a chicken peck. A peck is not so much. A bushel is very much. How come four peck make a bushel?

There was a determination accompanying Dahlia's curiosity and insight acquired from a life spent in virtual solitude that gave her a quiet, deer-like grace. I sometimes felt a need to reply to Dahlia's invocations of farm wisdom or Biblical aphorisms with a quote of my own, but seldom did. My Quaker family held that silence is a teacher closer to god. Consequently, lacking any wisdom that dealt with chickens, I answered her question with silence.

Dahlia's response to my retreat was to provide another fragment of *Almanac* commentary: *Silence is sayeth to be a gift with no trouble an a treasure without enemies.*

In the years we settled along the canyon, Dahlia's appetite for books expanded, as did her grasp of spoken English. Although our times of intimacy continued to be enriched by her memorized fragments from the Song of Solomon, Dahlia swore she'd never again enter a church.

A lot has changed since we settled this spot back in 1873. The Tongva peoples have either died or been pushed onto *rancherias* out in the desert. I haven't talked with a Tongva in some years. The original Californios are long gone. My neighbor Secondino Mora, one of the canyon's last Spanish settlers, died twenty-six years ago. The old man still used a raw cowhide as a front door to his adobe.

Mora lived the *Golden Age* of the vaqueros even after he was cut loose in 1833 from working free-range mission stock. He remembered seeing a thousand horses race through this canyon when the hills were overrun by wild cattle and a man mounted his horse just to walk twenty feet. Mora could whittle a saddle tree and rawhide it tight as skin. I topped and broke plenty horses under his direction. He rigged those spooked mustangs so they'd quick rein to a cowboy stop. Anyone who doubts cowboy culture has roots in California is plumb bankrupt of vaquero history. In 1879 I helped George Rogers build a school. Lagonas was becoming a destination for folks from Los Angeles, though nowadays it's rare to hear hooves or wagon wheels.

When we settled here Laguna Canyon was just an old Indian trail a handful of homesteaders pushed ox carts along. Used to be common to hear a lion scream from the big rocks above the road. Mostly hear rattling automobiles now, with drivers beady eyed as mice in an owl's claw.

Hitting the beach, folks tend to brake their Model Ts and gawp at the pretty view. Many people aim to stick. Can't say I blame them. This coast is a charm. Sweet breezes, avocado and citrus orchards, an ocean to harvest. A climate more kiss than weather. I guess it's my proprietary rights makes me act the grouchy old-timer listening to newcomers act like they were first at the rail; they're often accompanied by a slick agent hungry to show off a scrubby hillside lot.

This cabin occupies a prime flat and remains the cozy nest of embroidered pillows Dahlia made it. When we lay claim to this piece, the area was still called Lagonas and there was no push to file papers and no one to care if we didn't. One day Jim Irvine rode down here and allowed I'd fixed up a nice spot even if it was likely I'd squatted on a boundary of his land. Never saw nor heard from the man again. Turned out they fixed the town limits just inland from my place so it's likely I might yet get to pay taxes. Can't complain. About all this little flat on the southern edge of the old San Joaquin Rancho cost me was love and sweat. The ground is nicely silted by centuries of erosion from Irvine's big pastures above the canyon rim. We are sheltered from the wind too, with enough dead and down to keep a fire burning longer than I will.

It's been a year since my wife collapsed into her flower bed. White hair spread like silvered water, those brown features among the petals. It broke my heart to hear her struggle for breath at night. She had planted corn flowers, daffodils, iris, and tulip bulbs in concentric circles, somehow keeping track of their bloom times so they blossomed in a harmony of colorful flourishes. It was a garden Dahlia spent most of her time with. After all, she was a perfumed flower herself, and plants were the sweetest family she ever raised.

Can't say that anticipating mortality makes a man prepared. Both of us knew our time together was growing short.

It was a bright summer morning. I was sitting on my usual bench, gossiping with a gray squirrel that comes around to filch cushion stuffing, when I heard that part moan, part sigh, a sound I recognize enough to know few people make it twice.

I gathered Dahlia up, lay her out, and tucked her in our bed as though she were asleep. My wife lay so peacefully it took me awhile to accept that she had gone. Holding vigil alongside her, memories gathered as though our life together called its audience to share my grief.

I sat alongside her a full day before surrendering to the hard truth that it was time to carry her body to its final resting place. I lay my wife to rest, directly in the ground, exactly as she had wished. A coral tree we planted ten years before shelters the spot. Come September scarlet blossoms and an inscribed granite slab marked her grave.

DAHLIA ALITA YOUNG, 1850 – 1915
Fallen petals her children
their ground her beloved pillow

For weeks I wandered through our home and garden in a hypnotic state, finding loss more a presence than an absence. Small wonder I still talk to willow trees.

From this desk it's a good mile down the canyon, through the eucalyptus groves and across a salt flat to the beach. A man might watch waves hours on end mesmerized as when he started. I guess part of becoming Californian is allowing the sea to show us how to make peace with shifting tides.

According to today's *Farmer's Almanac* the moon will bring a high surge. The scenery will be a picture: pelicans gliding north, oyster catchers skittering the foam. Another California day, though, a sea will come in overly deep to pry mussels so there is just too much bait and too much tide to tempt this child to go fishing. Plenty reasons to stay home and get more pages done. Certainly been a distraction putting them together. On a good run though the story keeps writing itself. *No beginning no end,* somebody said. So help me, there's a world of truth in that idea.

At times, forsaken by my own solitude, I start talking to the dead. More company in my memory than comes to visit anyway. Thinned out some tubers yesterday, transplanted every one as though they were Dahlia's. Keeping my promise just as she always prodded me to: *Fix a good breakfast my beloved. Keep writing. Don't need a map to follow your heart.*

I don't, my love. More ink on these fingers than blood on the trail that guided us home.

> *I've learned the art of alchemy*
> *by nature I've been told*
> *the moon turns earth to silver*
> *the sun turns earth to gold*

o

My father was a wanderer with dreams of moving west. He started on his journey in 1851 and that September I was born on the trail. Before and during those wagon-train days, my mother, from Quaker roots, insisted we find our own truth. She pushed me there by speaking it herself. She also worked on wayward speech, correcting my language as if reining in an eager colt. Miles from civilization she would lecture on *the proper use of words* even if only a stray cloud was listening.

Were she alive, Claire Young might have raised her brow catching an earful of my past trail companions' ruffian talk, and been equally at a loss to see our only reading material was written on a prairie sky. She liked voicing Emersonian phrases which flew over my head, such as *the infinitude of the private man.*

Nonetheless, some of her efforts must have stuck. Hearing me complain that a cattle boss's order for me *to bed em down early* was ambiguous, a fellow cowhand observed, *Kid, you sound like you fell from a high-toned background.*

High-toned is a long throw from the tree. My folks were hardscrabble survivors either scratching poor ground or foraging the country for wild meat. I recall torn britches, scabby ankles and many a missed supper.

My father, Augustus Young, worked hard curbing a tongue that could be loose as his wife's was mindful. A Pennsylvania coal miner turned settler, he'd barely saved a stake to outfit his dream of moving farther west. He'd parented three children, a boy and two girls. Both girls died of smallpox before I came along. My mother claimed I was the very spit of my father. True, I had his bony features, thick yellow hair, loose-limbed lankiness, large hands and big ears. But my eyes are hazel like my mother's and tend to pause observantly, whereas father's gaze was restless.

My mother said a Mennonite midwife helped deliver me in a Conestoga wagon west of St. Louis. I was named Devon, Devon Everson Young. The snows were soon due, so she persuaded my father to settle where we had stopped and not turn back to seek work on the St. Louis levees, where a cholera epidemic had taken several hundred citizens. He finally gave in and we settled nearby, initially helping a local farmer.

We ended up staying in that Missouri bottomland country for twelve years, long enough for my father to recover from a bout with smallpox and for his benefactor to provide him a decent reward in return for years of faithful work. I was homeschooled by my mother, who took her Quaker teaching more than seriously and in my father's opinion over-educated me. Hunting and farming provided the rest of my schooling.

In those days hardwood stands along the Missouri River were a rich source of mast. Consequently bear, deer, peccary, turkey, and immense colonies of passenger pigeons thrived; a northern flock and a southern flock's arrival were separated by maybe eighty miles. Each great flock took a full day to pass overhead, the great ongoing sky darkening of wings of Biblical proportions.

Unfortunately, once they landed, the impact of a nesting flock hit like a plague. Dense colonies covered forty square miles, nests loading tree branches to breaking point. Pillaging hawks, owls, crows, ravens, possums, vultures, foxes, raccoons, and weasels grew fat on squab. My father saw a man drop thirty birds with one shotgun blast. At one time, a bushel basket of pigeons brought five cents, less than the cost of lead to shoot them. Many settlers knocked down the roosting birds with long poles and fed them to their hogs.

We tired of gathering, plucking and eating what had become an infestation of birds. Worse was having to wade through their sticky droppings. The woods were transformed into a ghost forest of skeletons coated with lime. Life had been sweet for the wild turkeys until ten million passenger pigeons eradicated the acorns. Walking pigeon-guano miles under those gloomy, nest-shrouded glades, I never imagined the great flocks could ever run out.

As part of my father's work hunting for his employer we ranged far afield. He taught me the ways of game, how to build a hide, stick to a faint track through a variety of country, and make a decent shot. He said I was naturally quick and had me practice flipping three nickels off the back of my hand until I could catch one at a time before they hit the ground. Years later, wandering the Southwest, these skills proved valuable. My father liked to claim my good hearing was due to *ears that stick out like barn doors* adding, *and you see well in the dark because your ancestors hewed the devil's coal hoard.* I remember his pickerel grin when he lit his chalky pipe and reminded me, *Don't forget lad, it's a miner's shovel warms a mother's kitchen and makes hell a coal scuttle colder.*

Augustus Young was a compulsive man who, his wife claimed, *traipsed headlong into strange country as if he knew where he was going.* Though ultimately profound, my mother's influence seemed less adventurous. Although I neglected some of her grammar I absorbed her honesty and self reliance. I believe what I see, hear, smell, touch, and taste, and assumed these qualities were inheritance enough to guide me through. How was I to know fortune delivers both malevolence and love?

°

In 1861 we acquired a new wagon and team and left Missouri. Crossing onto open plains during an early frost, our wagon train craved fresh meat. Against our scout's advice my father elected to take his Sharps rifle and range ahead alone. After three impatient days and no sign of him, the wagon master announced, *Ma'am, I'm of the sorry opinion your husband has gone an got his self scalped.*

When nobody on the train could convince my mother that her husband wasn't going to return, at her insistence a breaking plow was harnessed and a crew of men hastily built a sodbuster cabin in a nearby grove.

My mother had bartered our yoke of oxen and harness for forty dollars, three days of labor, enough chimney piping to draw smoke, four planks for a door, three buffalo robes, a barrel of lamp oil, and a few handy offerings gifted us by the two kindly women. Those four planks about broke the bank. Sawyer wood was scarce out there on the grass that only three years before had become the new state of Kansas.

We carried in our goods and remaining furnishings, hung schooner canvas against the inside walls, and began trenching a drainage ditch around our hut. We were blessed those immigrant men who pitched in hailed from decent sod themselves. The house was barely a foot higher than my head and scarce bigger inside than a wagon, but its walls were of well layered sod three feet thick.

Our wagon was hauled into place before our door and unyoked. We'd traded our ox team knowing the animals would likely starve. That box wagon helped break some nasty blizzard winds that winter, at least until we finally burned it, spokes and all. Many a freezing night I'd proclaim, *We should have kept and roasted those oxen.*

After the men had cut a tidy frame and hung our door they laid in some flat stones for a fireplace, hoisted a jug of whisky all around and were soon off to their wagons and away. A crack of whips and heave of shoulders against their yokes and the wagon train disappeared into the distance of a suddenly lonesome prairie.

We sorely missed my father. He'd been a hard man in some ways, especially in his manner of teaching me. He had patience for only the proper use of tools, the care of a hunting rifle, and the ownership of truth. A sharp word and his warning eye fixed me firm as a wedge in a log. He was equally quick to swing me on his shoulder or surprise me with a useful gift. Any small softening of his voice swept the whole of my world toward affection. As for my mother, her grief endured and I noted a growing fatalism and lingering silence where cheerfulness had once been her way.

The wagon master who declared my father scalped was a prairie newcomer and possibly prone to overstatement. So far most talk of *wild Injuns* had proved to be campfire exaggerations or yarns left over from eastern Indian wars. The Osage people in Missouri had been friendly. Their villages were surrounded by fields growing squash and beans which they traded with us freely. I realize now there was only one game I played with those Osage kids and it might be called "prepare to be an Indian." Maybe the great white fathers back in Washington were paying attention to great things, but in that teeming bottomland the Osage attention to the smallest signs of life joined them irrevocably to the earth. The Indians' mindful focus rubbed off on me. Insistent lessons in alertness were not always delivered politely whenever I failed to spot a few deer hairs on a branch or neglected the use of nose, ears and eyes. My woodland stealth acquired another level of silence. Father had taught me how to hunt an animal but those Osage taught me how to become one.

We anticipated my father's own country sense would guide him home. My mother insisted she had seen more than one man ride into the wilderness, get lost, and return after weeks of wandering. But we'd entered a strange and expansive country, and had been warned of tribes increasingly hostile to incursions by white settlers. The rumors about Plains tribes were of a barbaric people whose skill with the bow was matched only by a stealth directed to scalping men, women, and children. We kept our one rifle loaded and daily scanned the horizon as long as weather permitted.

Realizing amongst our silences that we were prepared neither for the best nor for the worst, we set to busily scrounging prairie turnips to eat and what became a veritable mountain of buffalo chips to keep us almost warm. We leveraged some leftover sod upon our roof and extended the ditch from all corners of our cabin for runoff. Remembering a requirement forgotten after being so long on the move, we heaped a low sod corral nearby and dug a trench inside to serve our outhouse needs.

For a few weeks the weather alternated between frost and scattered sleet, but soon the big snows came and silenced the world. Drifts piled so deep we floundered through them. Walking out a distance, we were relieved to note our snowed-in sod retreat melted into the whiteness of its trees.

Nights, lulled by the hush around me, I'd startle at the merge of moaning winds and howling prairie wolves.

Nightly there was the sullen smolder of our fire and my mother's breathing punctuated by the utterance of her dreams. I was glad for the buffalo robes. One folded beneath and one on top, along with a cocoon of woolen blankets, kept us reasonably warm. Yet there were nights so cold we fed the ever-hungry fire and coiled fully clothed in our beds. During particularly cold snaps my mother would wrap a heated stone to warm our feet.

On such days breath frosted the room, our drinking water froze, and we lay awake long shivering hours.

There was no window to our cabin. Our only grace if we had any was the extra lamp fuel my mother had bartered. She managed the oil as though doling out life itself, and rationed enough reading light throughout our ordeal to stave off inner darkness.

Often as the weather made possible we'd shuffle into the morning snow and venture to an edge of our cottonwood grove where, gazing from its rise upon an unbroken reach of whiteness, we felt marooned by its impossible scope. Although sometimes careless of our obvious tracks and the smoke rising from our chimney, we constantly feared we'd be discovered by hostile Indians. Luckily we never encountered any other humans. And in this realization knew that most likely we would never be found by anyone else, my father included. It was not wild Indians but the long winter that came close to finishing us.

I was regularly sent to collect water from the creek until there was only ice to bring back and melt. One morning after a two-day snowfall we couldn't open the door. When we finally dug ourselves out, snow-laden cottonwood trees seemed winged as prairie angels. Fortuitously, beneath them a cow buffalo holding a pack of prairie wolves at bay stood panting. I retrieved my father's rifle and my mother urged me to finish the struggling animal. At close range I aimed below the shoulder and dropped the cow with one shot.

Using our only large knife and the same axe we used to split wood, we worked at skinning that lone cow. We left the stiffening hide, cut into ragged patches, where it lay.

The prairie wolves constantly circled our butchery as we hastened to slice the meat into manageable chunks and strips.

After feasting on fresh buffalo liver we set to work fashioning a smoke box of our wagon's tool chest. Using green sticks to make racks we cured some of the buffalo meat and kept the rest to let freeze. I recall hacking at that meat and heaving slabs onto our roof barely out of reach of the same wolves that had chased it to our bellies.

I also remember my mother's shadow hunched over our only soup pot. Days became a monotony of starting buffalo chips, waking in a hypnotic half-sleep to tend their fire, or frantically pushing outside to scrape a heavy snow from the roof. Our reddened eyes stung perpetually. Every necessary foray outdoors required a drama of coats, boots, wet feet, and ferocious shivering. As our lamp oil dwindled, gloom, silence, and acrid smoke became a second skin. The closeness of that sod box still haunts me, even if it did grant me better vision in the dark.

With little but her books and small conversation to carry our minds over a long winter, my mother developed the habit of speaking to me as more a man than an only son. Marooned in our ocean of shared solitude

I grew familiar with the confused blend of hope and hopelessness that defines grief. Some nights I could not separate my dreams from the reality of my mother's despairing isolation.

I also learned complaint is no friend of the spirit, and that there are canny means of survival. Born to a frontier existence, my mother had brought along herbs and medicines, including dried cranberries, which she claimed protected us from scurvy and other bodily disturbances.

We never fell sick, though both of us grew thin on a scant ration of biscuits, corn mush, beans, and buffalo meat boiled in the same sooty snowmelt we drank. Overall it was my mother's resilience and determined optimism that nourished me as much as our scant provisions.

Some mornings we stayed put under our frosted robes and watched our breath make clouds in the gloom. It was a heroic chore to get up and light a lamp and blow the fire back to life. Enclosure and famine gave us owl eyes. The distances between our words began to lengthen in seeming direct proportion to our shrinking supply of fuel. Even on our first joyous foray onto spring's thawing prairie we walked hunched, whispering like hunted outlaws.

The new sun soon straightened our backs.

Having long accepted the grievous truth that she was widowed, my mother decided to join the first passing wagon train. By now our goods were reduced to her books, a few tools, a saddle, a rifle, and the few clothes we owned. Fortunately my mother also had most of our remaining stake cached in a leather pouch and figured it was more than enough to buy our way ahead.

The days after my mother assured me *good weather means the possibility of another wagon train* were longest of all. I'd scout eastward along the thawed wagon ruts hoping to spot the white canvas of prairie schooners heading our way. They never came.

For two more weeks what had been an encompassing blanket of flailing snow became rain. It seemed our sod cabin, having withstood the wintery tempests, would now be washed away. Despite our best efforts to plug its chinks, the sod leaked streams of muddy water. We were filthy and sodden as the moldy canvas shrouding our walls.

When the rain eased off and the sun came out, my mother handed me a bar of soap she'd hoarded all the way from Indiana and suggested I take a turn in the grove's gushing creek. My hair had developed a population of its own. Seeing me scratch, my mother dug into her mysterious hoard of goods and handed me a flat, corked bottle of amber liquid. *Let me rub some of this in your scalp son. Best to use this concoction before you scratch yourself bald-headed. Forgot I had it. It kills lice and their eggs.*

What is it? The fumes made me suspicious.

Some fellow's attempt at snake-oil whisky.

But it's intended to be drunk!

Yes. But your father likened it to coffin varnish. Forgot I had it.

When she poured that tonic on my head, ice, then fire, sent me running flat out to jump in the creek. It was chilly hopping around in that rushing melt water but more than the critters in my hair needed washing away. After months of enclosed gloom it was past time to scrub my bones.

While we were enclosed in our sod refuge through that endless winter, my mother's eyes had been my only mirror, and in their reflection I also saw something darker that could not be washed away.

°

An early migrant train finally showed up, a slow-moving party of ox carts following rutted evidence of the Santa Fe Trail.

My mother and I walked out to greet the lead wagon. After the party had parlayed then negotiated for what seemed an eternity, we were taken on as paying passengers. For a charge of one dollar a day we could walk or ride alongside anyone willing and share their food on condition we would be of whatever use the elders commanded.

Rumor had it the outcome of recent battles had not favored the Union forces. Most able-bodied men from our immigrant train's home state had long been pressured to join the fight. But these Mormon converts who'd quit Ohio had turned their backs on the war, determined to join kin who'd settled farther west years earlier. Two of the younger men were veterans. One had lost an eye and the other an arm, both wounds acquired at Chancellorsville.

Apart from these two ex-soldiers, who were more receptive, our hosts were an unyielding bunch in their determination to recruit converts to their fold. My mother's refusal to forsake her Quaker roots did little to endear her companions. We walked behind their high-wheeled wagons in banished silence. To this day I steer clear of insistent believers no matter their stripe.

For two months, covering over six hundred miles, we continued across the sunburnt prairie without serious incident. Even youthful eyes developed a crow's-feet stare. Ox teams set the pace. Each day was like another, walking, walking until the mind became lost in absence and blisters toughened, assisted by greasy liniments applied to boots and calloused soles. As the prairie's shimmering distances expanded our voices grew quieter. Each night camp evolved into a whispered community of abrupt conversations.

When we reached Wagon Mound, where wagons made the big swing south toward Santa Fe, Mother saw an opportunity to quit the train.

A cavalry detachment had bivouacked below the Wagon Mound rock. Its superior officer rode over to inform our train of a call for school teachers down on the Pecos River. My mother, determined to secure such a timely and suitable post, decided we'd join the column, and we continued south toward Fort Sumner.

The army wagons were lighter, employing harness mules rather than yoked oxen, so we sustained a brisker pace than had our previous company. The soldiers were at least polite to my mother, the only woman on the trip. We mostly rode instead of walked, and slept and ate right well. An army ration of salt pork and beans was constantly embellished.

The soldiers were not adverse to shooting Indian sheep and claiming the meat to be antelope, though they did bring plenty of jackrabbits and game birds, which they threw at me to pluck. The troops were a diverse and often coarse mix, held in check by an Irish sergeant and two junior officers, both frequently drunk.

The soldiers were in the habit of filching supplies which were intended solely for delivery to Fort Sumner. Supposedly we were an escort ordered to protect wagon goods sent out to the frontier. These supplies were also rifled by Captain Joshua Lawrence, who helped himself to cigars and liquor. His men were none too shy either about liberating the occasional sack of coffee or twist of tobacco.

I was told Fort Sumner, our destination, was an outpost raised in the New Mexico Territory at Bosque Redondo a spot named after a grove of big cottonwoods. There, Kit Carson had volunteered to oversee the settlement of a Navajo tribe he'd conquered and marched into captivity. Carson had a reputation as a bold Indian fighter and scout who had led expeditions as far as California. Although he was a man of few words and polite in the extreme, my mother observed he was remorseful for attacking those Navajos up in Canyon de Chelly and destroying their orchards. But she also questioned if any clear-eyed version of history would reveal which was more savage, wiping out whole tribes or the greed that licensed white men to do it.

Consciously tight-lipped about a thing or two, my mother had seen plenty blood along the fringes of the Eastern frontier. She'd turn a narrow eye upon hearing the usual disparagements of "bloodthirsty savages." *A sadly disrespected people,* she'd claim, *deserving of better treatment than a string of broken promises.*

Even young as I was, from my perspective Carson's "remorse" did seem too late an apology. Carson had lived most of his wandering existence among Indians but this did not slow him from brutally uprooting the Navajo tribe. I saw Carson a time or two. A surprisingly small, intense man with straight blond hair, Carson had been first to raise the Union flag over New Mexico. Most men spoke of Carson as fearless, honest, and loyal. He was also a natural born killer who pursued vengeance as a sacred calling. His wife was said to *possess a beauty of the haughty, heart-breaking kind.*

I heard much later that Carson's views toward the tribes softened, though too late to amend for the capture of an entire people. My own allegiance was already sealed.

My cohorts were all Indians, and soon the fort soldiers began to treat me like one too.

Except for the few Navajo who'd escaped to live in the mountains, Carson's captives were forced southeast on what became infamously known as the Long Walk. Hundreds died. Sequestered within a forty-mile-square boundary with Fort Sumner as its center, the tribe existed on maggoty rations provided by an often indifferent government agency.

The imprisoned Navajo numbered around eight thousand. This encampment consisted of a great scatter of hogans surrounding the fort for some distance. I recall witnessing a circle called by Chief Barboncito that involved the entire tribe. This medicine wheel was so wide the people on its opposing sides were barely visible. At the center of this immense circle crouched one terrified coyote held by two medicine elders who placed a turquoise stone in its mouth before setting the animal free. Something of great portent was to be determined by the direction in which the released animal headed. The coyote ran west, which to the joyful Navajo signified they would soon be going home.

In the fort my mother spent more hours doctoring malnourished children than following her commanding officer's stern edict: *You, ma'am, must endeavor to educate these red devils to decency and save them from barbarity in the name of godliness through the fortuitous intervention of our ill-afforded generosity and civilizing intentions, which you will find stubbornly unappreciated. Likely you will meet considerable resistance but you must persist with the full weight of my command at hand, ready to enforce strict discipline at any hint of discontent.*

The government promise, to provide their Navajo captives *eight thousand sheep and a million pounds of corn* never came close to fulfillment. Numerous Indian children were taken into slavery by predatory ranchers, and disease eventually eradicated a quarter of the tribe. What remained of native livestock soon over-grazed the area and starved, forcing Navajo into cattle raiding, a practice for which, if caught, they were summarily hanged.

My mother's life was isolated. By regulation enlisted men were forbidden to address her, officers were not permitted to mingle with school teachers, and the nuns made it clear her assistance to Navajo children was not sanctified. Given the corruptions of an idle garrison and random, often brutal oversight by bored and resentful troopers, my mother's allegiance soon drifted toward the "red evils" she was paid to civilize. Her patients were her only company. Several Navajo women chose my mother's simple doctoring over the fort hospital, where several who entered never returned.

Seduced by my mother's opinions and by any opening that offered escape from the fort's military strictures, I developed a youthful affinity for anything Indian.

I began frequenting the hogans and grew my hair long enough to wear Navajo style in a pony tail bun folded at the nape of my neck. I'd observe warriors painting snakes on the soles of their moccasins to increase their stealth and watch them daub lance tips with a mix of rattlesnake blood, cactus pulp, and charcoal, taken from lightning-struck wood, to empower their accuracy.

The tribe had been granted a collective herd of sheep, though well short of the number the army had promised. The youngest boys who tended these found it increasingly necessary to shepherd the flocks farther afield, as the region was relentlessly grazed down.

Local youths were also required to help in the husbanding of squash, corn, and beans, which granted a meagre return that made the tribe even more determined to hunt in defiance of Bosque Redondo's edicts and miserable rations.

Perhaps a bit inflated by my experience surviving a solitary winter on the open plains, I shared my Navajo friends' will to roam but had to wait until the elders according to their custom, enabled such a special privilege for a *bilagaana,* a white man uninitiated to the spirits and decorums of the land.

The Navajo were justified in their desire to break out. The Pecos water was alkaline and many children died of dysentery. Their chief, Barboncito, claimed this sickness was a sign from the Great Spirit that his tribe *was never supposed to live west of the San Juan River.*

Despite disease, virtual imprisonment, and doomed efforts at viable agriculture, it was clear these people still intended to embrace a meant life … one of spiritual intention. Retrospectively, though I spoke little of their tongue and perhaps naively embraced more than I understood, Navajo ways gifted me an elemental outlook that endures to this day. I accept that there is only air, earth, fire, water and the kinship of all living things, and that forgoing these gifts makes us strangers upon the Earth.

Although some say Navajo means *people who work the fields* and the tribe was expected to plant traditional crops, the hardpan Pecos River country offered desolately poor ground where corn barely grew above two feet. In the face of such privations, the Indians continued to defy General Carleton's mandate that they *forget the old life and reconcile to the new.*

The "new" also heralded extermination of the great bison herds, death by smallpox, measles, influenza, and dysentery, all caused by the oppression of white men disrespectful of the centuries Navajo people had existed in harmony with a land they considered sacred. The "new" also heralded treaties frequently ignored. Many white-man assurances proved to be empty promises. I nurtured no illusions that my adopted kin were saints, and in due time witnessed Indian barbarity too, but in Bosque Redondo the evidence favored my opinion that justice was on the red man's side.

It turned out that my urge to adopt Indian ways was insufficient to adapt me fully to tribal morays. I had none of the Navajo's old ways to forget and too much of my own roots to remember. Nevertheless, from what I recall of years among the tribe, I determined it was the better of two choices to become part Indian rather than succumb to Fort Sumner's enforced hierarchy.

As a buck-skinned youngster thinly tethered by my mother's obligations toward Fort Sumner, I sought liberty among other captive sons. Indifferent to tenets of military settlement I found adventure in rebelliousness and was eager to chase every impulse to its source. My cowboy sidekicks called this *playing out your string.*

Almost fifty years later I read many a story describing characters caught between two worlds. I figure as a new native son of these quilted American states I am several ways immigrant by dint of my Irish lineage and by the influence of the American landscape partly witnessed through adopted Navajo spiritual values.

What of this earth is not immigrant? Trees? Animals? Birds? Seeds? Clouds? All are visitors. The Lakota called the Little Big Horn River the Greasy Grass. I recall one of their poems that eloquently captures the temporal fragility of all living things:

> *All day we lay out by the Greasy Grass,*
> *the Earth is all there is and the Earth will not last*

My own youthful freedom was not excused of tragedy. An Asiatic cholera outbreak reputedly brought down from Fort Harker had killed over three hundred soldiers and Indians and soon infected Bosque Redondo.

After barely a week of fever the epidemic claimed my mother, although I believe she also died of a broken heart. I stood vigil at her bedside day and night. Before she drifted from delirium into unconsciousness my mother accepted death as stoically as she had faced life. Characteristically accepting of her fate, my mother had me read Emerson to her, interjecting commentary whenever she thought any fragment useful to me.

Most fixed in memory is her spoken gratitude for *the gift of you, my loving son, who so completely fulfills a mother's most profound expectations.* Even as I witnessed the light fade from my mother's eyes, their lingering affection helped strengthen my spirit.

Although now on my own among the Navajo, I was far from being viewed as an orphan. The fort's business carried on as though a deceased schoolteacher's contribution to its youngest wards was by convention a service to remain largely unnoticed. Conversely, in recognition of my mother's kindness to their children and women folk, the Navajo built me a hogan on the fringe of their settlement.

I stayed on at the fort until just before Kit Carson died in 1868. Shortly after Carson's passing came news that General Sherman was to visit Bosque Redondo. Sherman, after listening to Chief Barboncita, allowed the Navajo to return to their own country, the Dinetah. The government's attempt to create a viable reservation in Bosque Redondo had been an abject failure. As for my liberation, my mother had left me her books, a new Henry repeater rifle and seventy-five dollars owed her by the army. This inheritance provided me a start.

The Navajo, or Dineh, which translates as "the people," were usually reluctant to share their customs with the *bilagaana*. I was fortunate to find a measure of acceptance among the tribe and to be given a name. I have big ears, so I was nicknamed Gha-Tso which is Navajo for Jackrabbit. Later I was given another permanent name: Gaagii Hasleen, or Crow Man. Nobody else called me that after I left Bosque Redondo, except my sweetheart, who used it as an endearment, whispering *haaasleeen* into my ears.

I was never abused by the Navajo until events caused them to see me as bearer of bad medicine. On the contrary, though barely subsisting on rancid government hand-outs, those people were solicitous. I fostered their kinship and their traditional medicine. What little I picked up of the Navajo language I enjoyed speaking. More useful was to learn from the Dineh how silence enriches the presence of all things.

Containing a curiosity bordering on awe I did my best to be respectful and alert, maintaining a polite distance outside the circle of any tribal gathering. Having spent my early youth wandering green hills, rivers, and woodlands, it seemed a similar exploration to roam among people as a local shadow.

Used to living at a distance, one day I was apprehensive when a young Dineh led me toward one of the bigger hogans. Inside, one of three elders directed me to sit crosslegged in the middle of a sand painting. The sand painting represented a circle with four stick figures forming a cross within it and what looked like four birds forming each corner of this design. It was discomforting to step onto what clearly had been time-consuming work sifting various colored pigments with such complexity and precision.

I'd peered into such ceremonies before and later discovered that to the Navajo a sand painting is *a place where the gods come and go*. I had no idea why this painting was prepared for me. After an elder had smoked me with a sage bundle, all three sat and began to shake their rattles and sing. Soon this steady chant fused into one sound.

I became pleasantly at ease as their chanting washed over me. When the men fell quiet I was directed to walk out through an opening representing the spirit hole or door of the sand painting. The elders then swept away all evidence of its creation and explained that the intention of this ceremony was to bring my spirit into balance.

After this healing initiation Navajo youths began to invite me on their trips below the Pecos River. The Indians also taught me to respect their Blessing Way, a cornerstone of Navajo spiritual practice that rests upon Hozho or balance and embraces their belief that all living creatures are our relations. I began to see these beliefs reflected in the respectful ways of the Navajo people. I was told life is a manifestation of the Ye'ii, the gods who created the Corn People, Snake People, the First Man, First Woman, and various sacred images often woven into rugs and sand paintings.

Acquiring some facility with Navajo speech and acquiring an Indian name caused me to be perceived by the fort's soldiers as gone crazy native. My appearance, choice of companions, and vagabond behavior had a price. Besides facing the strictures of the resident Fort Sumner nuns who worked to *thrash the savage out of me*, I was at times randomly whipped by army pickets.

Along with my Navajo brothers I continued to wander far afield. Despite being disciplined for *failing to know better*, I challenged Brigadier General Carleton's commandment that for me and for the Navajo *severity was the most humane course*. My response was to flout my appearance as a long haired renegade in a deer skin breech clout and high top moccasins.

Embracing a renegade identity began to wear thin given that, despite my open embrace of Indian style and the benefit of acquiring some Navajo friends, I was never going to enjoy full acceptance by the tribe. A day would come when I'd have to set out on my own lick. Occasional cattle drives that passed near Bosque Redondo on their way north provoked the possibility I might join up with one. With my mother's silver dollars and her Henry repeater I imagined myself acquiring a good horse and setting out to become a top cattle hand. My confidence was not altogether blind ambition. Hunting hungry can steady anyone's sights. Lean years potting rabbits and prairie chickens had honed me to a dead shot. I also believed myself capable of riding anything on four legs. In those years, fostered by prairie skies, I had a mind open as the rivers and stars.

That spring in New Mexico down on the Pecos River I was barely sixteen. The fort surgeon had ordered my mother to be wrapped and taken out for burial. Two soldiers lowered Claire Young's remains into a trench, filled the hole, hammered in a flimsy cross, doffed their hats, and walked away. There was no reading or any hint of ceremony.

Sawyer planks were always scarce; consequently my mother's grave had been given a burial marker hastily fashioned of wagon boards and horseshoe nails. There were several other hastily dug graves in the allotted ground for none-military personnel, many of these burials entirely unmarked. Closer to the fort the army had its own tidy military cemetery with a picket fence and a flag waving over white crosses on neat graves tended by a buffalo soldier who had only one leg.

There were no native graves, and none of the Navajo who had appreciated my mother witnessed her funeral. The Navajo view death as unclean and remain secretive about how and where they abandon their own dead. Usually an individual is carried outdoors to die; otherwise others have to smash a hole in his hogan and abandon it forever. Only four chosen men are supposed to conduct a burial and they do this naked, except for their moccasins, then quickly dispose of any tools. No one mentions *the one who went away* ever again.

According to Navajo belief, a long time ago Coyote Old Man decided Earth needed death. That lop-eared trickster craftily brought mortality into the world because he was afraid that without it the two-legs people would overcrowd the Earth. The first human beings originally placed a hide in the water and if it floated this meant people would live forever. However Coyote Old Man threw rocks onto the hide when the human beings weren't paying attention and it sank. Ever since the Navajo have seen death as a nasty trick that they view as unclean.

For my part, even witnessing my mother's corpse I was too young and too shaken to comprehend the impact of mortality. I stood a long time in the wind whispering over her burial while that one-legged grave tender watched from inside his army outfit's tidy cemetery.

Perhaps just as Coyote Old Man intended my world also foundered that day. My mother had been a loving and patient guardian who encouraged my kinship among the Navajo with amusement. She never scolded me after I'd disappear days at a time or was hauled into her quarters by some army picket who'd caught me sneaking past his post.

Her steady brown eyes saw through me. She fed me discipline, books, and affection, faithfully sewing my clothes even if they were becoming more buckskin and moccasins than woolen breeches and homespun shirt. I told her everything I ever did, disappointing her was worse than any lash I endured from a cavalry soldier or willow switch the nuns used to urge humility into my renegade soul.

I'd grown, *an inch or two taller than your father,* my mother said, *a fine looker at near six foot with that yellow hair of yours thick as oat straw. Guess when you quit wearing it long as an Indian I'll get to trim it neat again. Got your father's handy hands and direct ways too though you speak a lot nicer and quieter, and your manners show there's pride in there, honesty and goodness shining through.* I recognized her hazel eyes and small bones as mine but had my father's big ears and a broken nose, acquired when I was pitched from a borrowed colt I'd attempted to run bareback over a farm gate. My father's own broad nose had been re-arranged *more than once,* he'd say with a smile.

I was industrious at being my mother's son. I kept her army rations supplemented with birds and small game that she kept simmering in a cook pot and walked many a mile to gather wood. When the ground swallowed her up, it was as if I was made of lead and had ice in my belly. I felt lost to any place, family, or kinship that had offered refuge.

After the fort's hasty burial detail left I spoke over my mother for a while, then pulled out those wagon staves and took off for the river. I burned that cross on the bank of the Pecos along with a yellow certificate a soldier handed me requesting *name of deceased, place of birth, time, date, and cause of death.* The only place my mother lived was inside me and of a time that was forever.

Wanting to respect the Navajo blessing way I dutifully removed everything except my moccasins, jumped into the flooding Pecos River, and let its waters carry me where they may.

The current took me well downstream before I crawled onto a cut bank near a grove of cottonwoods. I lay there in the weeds heaving tears, oblivious whether the noon sun blinded or warmed me. I was lying there in my misery when I heard a rustle from the willows and a black bear and two cubs shambled out.

That mother bear was in no mood for grief. She started out sniffing scent and the human she smelled scrambled up the nearest cottonwood, a scrawny one, hopefully high enough to get beyond her hooks. I wrapped myself around a limb and held on for dear life.

That bear *wuffed* twice, rose on her back legs, and started shaking the tree. Leaves, bark and dead branches scattered everywhere. I could smell that critter's musky fur and sour breath as she pounced repetitively against my cottonwood. I hung on with all four legs hoping a lull in the people-hunting proceedings might allow me to scramble higher.

There must have been a nest above me because a whole family of pink nestlings fell down and the bear quit pounding the trunk, scoffed up those babies, lost interest in me, and wandered off.

I clung to my perch until my own limbs quit shaking and that bear seemed well out of range. Shinnying down I heard a squeak and spotted something pink elbowing stubby wings in the leaf-strewn grass. This wrinkled

foundling naked as me sprouted nubby blue pinions;
the rest of him was a yellow-rimmed beak, bald head,
and rheumy slit eyes.

It took me some hours to walk back to the reservation
cradling that fragile chick. Seeing my naked condition
an army picket let me pass without a word. Back in my
hogan I fed my orphan some leftover corn mush and
we both slept through the next day.

I was medicine-savvy enough to figure some connection
existed between my mother's loss and the appearance
of a fledgling bird. Exactly what the meaning of it all was
I had no direct idea other than a sense that our joining
was somehow meant to be.

I named the bird Shash, which is Navajo for "bear." I started
out feeding Shash with a hollow straw, shared morsels
of whatever I could snare, mostly rabbit or prairie dog
meat. Not at all fussy, Shash gulped down anything I
placed in his craw: salt pork, spiders, scorpions, lizards,
grasshoppers. He was constantly ravenous.

Watching me feed Shash, one of Charles Goodnight's
passing trail hands told me that cowboys hated ravens
and crows because they were notorious for pecking
eyes out of newborn calves. I took the hint, and to the
obvious delight of my pet crow started bringing him
gifts from slaughtered sheep, or eyeballs scavenged
from trapped or hunted game. Shash devoured these
delicacies eager as a carpet bagger slurping prairie
oysters.

He feathered up dandy and grew into a shiny iridescent crow with a range of exclamations from warning squawks to lofty *klook klook* opinions. Shash liked to nod his head to a whistled tune and was particular to *"Turkey in the Straw."* He'd turn perky, side stepping up my arm to inspect a song with that beady stare his kind must have stolen from a canny old miner squinting through darkness for hints of gold.

I assumed Shash to be male by the way he behaved around women. He'd fly up around ladies doing aerial somersaults, fall as though about to crash, then abruptly return to perch on my shoulder pleased as a bachelor sashaying from a fiddle dance.

He stuck by me day and night, either perched on my shoulder, my saddle horn or roosting on a branch I rigged above my blankets. The only constant light inside my hogan was a diamond glint from his eyes. Anytime he heard footsteps he'd start to prancing as though the sky was about to fall. I'd lie reading by an oil lamp with Shash roosting nearby. When I talked to him he'd lift his wings and strut around on that saddle pommel, hanging on every word.

I felt blessed to have someone share my hogan, especially another orphan. He was tidy too. Crow droppings are a regular chalky event but he'd peck up his excretions, fly them outside, and deposit them neat as a housekeeper. Most impressively he'd follow me on longer jaunts, sometimes flying higher than I could see before re-appearing no matter how far from Bosque

Redondo. He had plenty chances to quit me. Even when he heard a flock announcing a roost down along the river Shash stuck around.

Having an antsy black bird perched on my shoulder had unanticipated social consequences. I had no idea that the crow is viewed as a witch's helper among the Navajo and they believed that touching crow feathers causes an eruption of boils. Shash's antics didn't help to ease their suspicions. My crow developed into a full-fledged rascal who openly disdained everybody except young women. He seemed to distinguish Navajo girls from every other human by their hair, which to his eyes possibly resembled a nest. He'd make nasty rattling noises around soldiers, Navajo men, and dogs. Everyone in the tribe was skittish about approaching us, even the young women, who he liked to flirt with by crow-hopping around their feet or swooping close to their bundled hair.

When we'd show up at the gates of the army post to get my rations, the line of Indian women quickly opened a gap. Seeing Shash on my shoulder, even the nuns, or "black robes" as the Navajo called them, crossed themselves and gave me a wide berth. I took this as indication that my crow proved to the nuns the devil perched on my shoulder, which explained why they'd quit lecturing me about hell fire and salvation. Contrary to their superstitions, ultimately I was to receive a crow's mortal blessing. Although it came about that the Navajo banished me from their camp and the Bible swampers chased me out of their holy corral, Shash stayed on my shoulder until the end.

°

As long as I can remember my mother greatly appreciated Ralph Waldo Emerson's essays. She liked to remind me during our long prairie winter together that Emerson had declared *a friend is one before whom I may think aloud.*

Luckily at Bosque Redondo besides Shash I acquired four Navajo friends. I understood their language enough to accompany them on forays below the Pecos River or, as they announced, to *tal-tso-go intas-se-pah,* which means "anywhere we take a gun. "

In truth we lacked guns, because the army forbid them to the point of imprisonment, so we cached hunting bows and picked them up whenever we got free.

Cha'Gee, Bluejay, was the accepted leader of our bunch. Cha, as we called him, was always peering over the next rise and talked a streak for a Navajo, although this was only a tad more than the other silent three. His eyes were sharp and always busy.

Ha-Thali-Tso, Big Singer, though sullen was an excellent tracker. Big Singer had made all our arrows and was always on the prowl for flint, though his best arrowheads were hammered out of iron.

Shash-Yaazh, Bear Cub, was the most wary and liked to scout our forays, often circling back and watching for signs. I suspected Cub was the youngest among us. He stuck close to Big Singer when he roamed with us.

Then there was Ne-Tah, Fools Them, full of jokes and renowned as a long runner. Ne-Tah was tall and leggy and seemed to be carrying an inner secret that made his eyes dance. All of us appeared close to the same age although year counts didn't seem to matter much to the Navajo.

These young bucks hoped to acquire warrior names by accomplishing some brave deed that served their tribe. Sneaking off the army enclosure was an opportunity to exhibit a bold indifference to Fort Sumner and its oppression by bringing home fresh meat. Whenever we returned every detail of our journey was retold around the fire.

We foraged farther afield along the lower Pecos where red rock cliffs offered tributary creeks and thin cover for a sparse deer population. The more fertile high desert hunting country was farther north and west, below Santa Fe where pinon, ponderosa, juniper, year-round water, and a variety of feed, offered attractive cover to elk and other game and lately, to white ranchers. The local country available to us was harsher, drier, emptier or at least that was our experience so far.

It was late in August when in early dawn we waded a shallow crossing and followed a drying feeder creek toward a spot where we'd previously seen deer tracks. Shash flew out of sight which was fine with my fellow travelers. It was a hot day and the country was treeless except for broken copses of willow and weedy grasses along the vanishing stream beds.

We moved at a steady jog until the wash opened up to sporadic watering holes, many of them pocked with coyote and bird tracks. We reached the farthest spot south we'd ever scouted and decided to lope a little farther toward a stand of cottonwoods shimmering in the near distance.

Closing on the trees, we skidded to a halt. Big Singer pointed to a trail of prints made by unshod ponies and lifted four fingers, whispering *lii an'ayeh*, saddle horses. We ducked toward a cut where the tracks led into some willows and suddenly heard a voice. Peering over a rim of the creek bank we looked across to a grassy flat touched by a reedy perennial pond. Below us a circle of eight Indians sat listening to a chanting elder shaking a tortoise-shell rattle.

We were instantly afraid. The men were obviously Apache, the very name denoting *enemy*. Their dress was sufficiently known by us to see they were Chiricahua and well outside their range. Each man wore high-top moccasins a long breechclout, a cloth bandana, and left his hair unbraided. Bows and spears stacked outside their circle, their faces streaked with white mud, the warriors were raptly attentive to their medicine leader.

Before our presence was detected Bluejay made a run for it, fortunately, as it turned out, into the brush. Why we didn't hightail after him is any fool's guess. The rest of us, choosing haste over caution, ran back along the creek bed straight into four Apache outriders coming down the wash. These warriors began herding us with their lances. Making us drop our bows they escorted us toward their waiting clan, who by now stood ready to deal with this intrusion.

While we were held at lance point the Apache with the rattle kept on chattering. This character was wildly hostile to our interruption. He kept pointing to the ground, making slashing signs, and shaking his head, which sported a chinstrap skullcap with antelope horns. He also wore a cougar skin draped over his left shoulder and loosely cinched around his waist. His eyes were looking past us, far-seeing beyond four captives who'd broken his medicine circle.

The Chiricahua were constantly on the prod, raiding below the Rio Grande to take horses, cattle, women, children, and whatever they could loot. Too often their targets woke up to a raiding party helping themselves to a pueblo of soon-to-be-very-dead or captive Mexicans. The Chiricahua continued this pillaging even after having been mercilessly reduced in numbers by the Comanche.

Cunning and fond as they were of guerilla tactics, the Chiricahua were equally attached to medicine rituals such as the one we'd interrupted. Killing us in the middle of a power journey could be tricky. All human beings had two souls, a good one that went into the sky and another not-so-good one that, if insulted, might stick around to exact revenge upon the living.

A killed Chiricahua enemy would be politely disfigured and blinded so his spirit couldn't find its way back among the living. The cougar skin fellow before us staring into his choices maintained a stone face that impressed me as permanent. His thin lips appeared to have been carved by the slash of one quick blade. I grimly observed that he likely blinked, at most, once a week.

Standing quietly and staring hard ahead, I feared my breathing time would soon be over. Having heard nightmare stories about that Chiricahua skill at prolonging torture, I hoped this bunch were in a hurry to find another ceremonial spot. These Apache were painted for medicine, not war, but as sworn enemies they were stubbornly dedicated to killing Navajo.

The medicine man made another short speech then watched approvingly as the rest of his group discussed how to best finish us off.

It didn't take long before they started in. They picked Big Singer first. Immediately he began singing his death song. Pierced by three arrows, the youth swayed a bit before collapsing when one of the Chiricahua swiftly moved in and cut his throat.

They massacred my other companions the same way. I was stricken by terror witnessing those braves fall singing, but the spirit of their dying even more than my horror transfigured this final act of their youthful existence.

Witnessing the assault I struggled to accept my turn. *If it be the end take courage, witness its hour, its instant,* I murmured, holding to my father's reminder *to face danger head-on and die fully awake to it*. But fear and slaughter crowded this intended clarity with a blur of contorted faces, singing voices, and spouting blood.

The traditional Navajo boys expiring around me had been taught to make every day *a good day to die.* My philosophy embraced the hope that the morning sun declared every day a good day to live. Sorrowful to conclude the journey of a life taken much for granted, I slowly bent to sift a last handful of dust.

Straightening up, the Apache with the rattle flicked my ears. Looking into my eyes, he lectured his men in terms close enough to Navajo for me to savvy that he'd decided I was Ghat-Tso, a jackrabbit.

In response the whole bunch lifted their bows, vying for the coup of finishing off a big-ears white man.

The braves gathered around to choose who would do the job. They haggled until finally the elder selected two braves to shinny one hand over another up an arrow shaft, a game won by an eager, squat Chiricahua with a scar across one eye.

Right away the winner stepped up and notched his bow. I was headed out of my trembling body when Shash landed on my shoulder. That scar-faced Apache lowered his bow and stumbled backward. The whole bunch behind him froze.

Standing tall and feigning innocence, I watched the Apaches listen to their chief gesticulating a blue streak. He seemed stumped for an explanation how a white boy Ghat-Tso at the point of death had summoned this ghost bird. The medicine chief rattled at the sky, then at me, then back at the sky. The sky didn't talk back, neither did I, neither did the hunkering braves.

I gathered enough to grasp that they believed Shash allied me with the powers of a shape-shifter, because they kept muttering *ant jihzhing* which is Apache, and, fortunately, Navajo too, for "witch medicine." I realized they were spooked by my crow for the same reasons the Navajo around Fort Sumner were. One afternoon, walking alongside me through the fort gates, a Ree cavalry scout had grinned when two passing Navajo averted their eyes from me and Shash. *Look like these pony tail Injuns think you friends with shape-shiftin bird an too scared to fixum an you too. Navajo think you got witch poison can backtrack arrow an camp in shooter's liver. Damn shooter plenty bad medicine now, nobody look at him, no squaw cook him, no make push push too. Tribe say, big time adios, witch shooter, you go take skookum horses, ride long time from us way over too much mountain. Sum bitch shooter never come back. Guess you walkin okay round here, yellow hair.*

Right now it appeared that Ree scout had been right, because no matter how much that medicine chief harangued them, not one of his spooked Apaches had the sand to finish me off. They stood around in sullen knots while Shash hopped from shoulder to shoulder injecting a few testy squawks.

Finally the frustrated elder ordered his braves to gather up their weapons and medicine shields. They were moving out but before they did he took out a sage bundle, knelt in the dust, drilled his fire stick into its kindling, and lit the dry leaves. I hunkered, kneading sweat into what I believed would be my last handful of earth. After the old man smoked his bones with sage he started working his painted rattle again, which aroused Shash to clatter in perfect imitation and startled the old man into dropping his sage bundle.

He poked around, lifted a sachet out of his medicine bag, and emptied its contents into his hand. Shoving these in my face, *Yi'yaa!* he insisted, *Yi'yaa!* which was close enough to Navajo for "eat" to tell me I was to swallow this offering of red mescal beans. As an alternative he mimed a pulled bow aimed at my heart followed by a chop across his throat.

As part of my Navajo education I'd been warned to recognize dangerous plant allies, particularly mescal beans. We'd been cautioned that ingesting the little red devils offered a poison path deadly to all save the initiated. I could see by the fire in the old guy that he wasn't about to lose face and his gesture of slicing an invisible knife across his neck convinced me that eating his ghost food was my only choice.

As a prayer I lifted the beans to the sky and gulped them down. Shash flew off my shoulder and glided out of sight. The medicine chief whispered *gaagii* in my left ear then, as though having exchanged an important transaction.

I stood there a long time in front of those squatting Indians. They appeared highly focused and, waited expectantly holding their bows and lances. I began wondering what they were so damn interested in because, unseen to them, my rippling cramps and nausea had developed a serious revolution that was strangling my innards with a bitter bile even as another wave of nausea

peaks
WHOA
I begin feeling fine because
increasingly I am wandering
bare foot
buck naked
out of the woods, picking my way around elk droppings
toward a small lake rimmed by green green reeds and rushes
and a red wing black bird warbles
warmth through my bones
I am in some
HUM BELLY HUMBELLY HUM HUM *talk-to-the-world-place*
becoming
beauty all round
beauty above beauty
everywhere a beauty roping me with rainbows
under a cloudless
blue blue day
trees throwing strands of light YES THE WORLD SPROUTING
skeins of light
setting me to seeing how I am pieces of everything
and right now wading into a silver shining mercury lake
so slippery to slip naked into and swim belonging in water
water, telling me all over how much I am of water,

a naked river man
among millions of millions of water droplet forevers
gliding, slipping under the surface
toward a busy coot's little black-centered red eye
stopping to share effortlessness
interrupted by an arrowing wavelet surge
of spiky white chin whiskers
sprouting a beady-eyed grin eyeball to eyeball
an otter offering invitation to chase
OVER HERE OVER HERE TOO
until with the flip of a tail she vanishes
and water becomes the regular
drowning possibility
splashing to make shore
waking spitting water on a flat rock
sprawled headlong
under the beak of a bird
a boss crow big as me
standing proud on two knobby knees
with inky unreadable eyes
and a great hand RIPS A BLACK HOLE IN DAYLIGHT

and the crow croaked *gaagii* and flew into me, and wings settled into shoulders feathers became skin and springy crow legs tricked ankles into growing flat feet and a cracked voice inside wanting to name shiny things and there I stood feeling as nonchalantly hungry about picking over rancid wolf kill as a child takes breakfast when something else started feeling hot, sandy, and uncomfortable and I vaguely considered I might be headed exactly where it turned out *I am.*

Returning from that mescal-bean world I found the Apaches had departed after staking me down with rawhide thongs. My brain hummed loud as trapped bees. That Apache medicine man had unloaded years on me and I had to catch up to them by listening to a brain harvest of questions for slow hours, for slow weeks, and I worried that his voice was holding my brain hostage to a slow lifetime.

How can someone all at once feel himself to be another man? The same man yet another man. A man much older than the one he was minutes before? Or maybe it had been months, seconds, decades, in another place altogether? How can a world a man awakens to hold another world within the same world he knew hours before? Same crevices, same rock, same cottonwood, same sky, same coyote prints, same creek bed, same quail tracks, same vinegary pony shit, same sagebrush, same hands, same cracked big toenail, same sun-bleached shirt, same creased pants. Same, same, same knee swatting, head-shaking same.

Gaagii, crow, was what that Apache medicine man had whispered in my ear. And I awoke to learn that he had transferred more than his whisper to my trial. Those mind-plundering seeds had implanted something lurking within me. Perhaps that plant doctor knew mescal beans can steal souls long enough to add centuries to their host's journey across the dust.

The effect of that Apache elder's medicine continued to manifest unpredictably, arriving with the physical sensation of being pulled between myself and a powerful other presence.

Such was my mental shuffle between panic and tranquility as I lay recovering in the sand, my eyes closed, my arms and legs pegged down.

I have since read of tribal elders keeping vigil over a collapsed mescal visionary taking his journey *across the slippery rocks* to seek answers to drought, famine or disease. Traditional remedies exercised in an attempt to revive a disembodied seeker would occasionally fail and all that would remain for the living to do was to abandon their shaman's corpse to the wilderness from which it came.

The Apache had gone but it turned out I had surfaced to much more than I desired to know. Still experiencing flashes of hallucination, I lay dozing in a quiet spot along a river when I became possessed by the throaty words of a disheveled figure in a fringed coat festooned with colored strips of cloth, beadwork, copper medallions and fetish objects, among them rib bones, rodent skulls, and bird claws. His face, covered by a shriveled rawhide mask with its slit mouth and beady eyes, evoked a primitive figure from long ago.

The man's shaken rattle was all too reminiscent of the Apache medicine man's rattle that heralded the loss of my Navajo companions. My disembodied state was attracting weird visitations and this one was on the hunt for something he saw in me: *I am Ust Orda a kam from Tamir Shayha the mountain that leans against the sky where like you I heard voices from other worlds. Golden hair, you have eaten a magician's poison and lived and so attract other wanderers hungry to ride your soul. Long ago I lost my way back across the slippery rocks yet my people still seek my return, singing through the winter night, brother, we need your sorcerer's sight that guided you to the world where demons eat their own hands, there where the ravenous ones rend our horses for glee, there from whence you always return to divine our sickness. Come back, come back, our untouched girls will be generous after you tell us why the herds have not returned, nor the rain, nor the ermine, nor the white geese. Ust Orda listen, listen the sun is rising here but your body is so cold and still. Come back, come back. O sleeping one with golden hair, young friend hear me. I seek an opening in your ribs, entry to the human world where for a kindness you might invite me ...* abruptly a crow shadow eclipsed the image rousing me from another of several invitations from which I'd awake wondering if I was fated to host such fugitive voices with no one to teach me what to do with them.

My head on fire, tongue dry as lizard rock, body caked in dirt, I lay lie arguing with my legs, angry because they wouldn't listen, wouldn't stand up, and when they didn't, I remained tied to the desert sand. And afterward I'd wonder about the intent of that Apache elder with his tortoise-shell rattle and red beans. At times his transmission struck me as an insight passed on from the wild-eyed stare of ancient outcast men and I was cursed to be an echo of its loneliness.

I recall my involuntary convulsions, sputtering tongue and a great serpentine hum of voices then an agonizing constriction, relentlessly pressing to abrupt release that revealed my ankles staked by rawhide thongs. It was my own shape I had found, discovered like a new country unsure if it was a human or a mountain range, unsure if I could absorb the thrum of coursing blood whose sensation was flexed muscle, whose frame was splayed arms, whose bilious furry tongue lisped … *thuwhaat … watt … water, water.*

So as though hurled from some great height I fell relieved to touch desert gravel, tiny aggravations of shin-pricking rocks, my sight welcoming a sky's layered reefs, sun fans streaming earthward fierce as an eagle's stoop.

Those Chiricahua had pegged me down with rawhide thongs and driven a lance between my legs with a cluster of black feathers fluttering from its haft.

Surfacing into wakefulness I imagined a familiar voice but it really was Blue Jay standing over me surrounded by mounted Navajo who'd come to rescue their kinsmen, who still lay where they'd fallen. The Apache had arranged broken arrows all around me all pointing away from the staked body of someone they believed best left for the elements to kill.

Painted for war, the Navajo walked their ponies and made talk. It was decided that Blue Jay cut me loose though he was quickly told to throw down the lance that had been thrust between my legs.

As the Navajo war chief signaled Blue Jay to drop the lance something fell from Shash's beak onto my stomach. It was an eye. A human eye.

Seeing this nasty omen the braves kicked their ponies and shouted *Chindi! Lizhini Chindi!*, meaning "Witch! Dark Witch!" A check of their slaughtered kin revealing that Big Singer was missing an eye hastened their departure.

A clutch of impaled feathers, Shash was much reduced, his eyes thin slits, his spidery feet stiffened, his feathery rainbow flash gone. Why had he taken Big Singer's eye? Maybe to bring an offering? Shash's final theft had cost him. Likely one of the Apache had speared him on the ground, because his bloody feathers were smeared with dust.

Having looped their dead's ankles to catch ropes, the Navajo burial party trailed their kinsmen's bodies away. After painstakingly picking loose my rawhide knots, I flicked the glaring eyeball off my stomach.

I cradled Shash and wept like a broken child over my lost companions. Scraping a hole under a willow tree I buried Shash and Big Singer's eye and arranged flat stones in a winged pattern over the spot.

I felt beholden to the fate of the murdered Navajo. I had followed each youth's last song lifting toward the sun. Certainly my life was spared but as much of it as I'd ever summoned had shared the certainty of death. I was weighted by grief and gratitude and guilt, burdens I had no idea how to honor.

As for Shash, his kind had rescued me from a bear, loneliness, and Apache arrows. Since his burial day, venerating his kinship, I take heed of the omens of birds. Whether I am mulling the purpose of my life or divided between a choice of its direction, suddenly there they are, the crows swooping alongside, reminding me that wherever I am going they have already been.

o

Heading back for Bosque Redondo I followed the prints of the Navajo ponies who'd gone ahead.

Hours later, after wading the Pecos River, I discovered that a big hole had been knocked in the back of my hogan and a circle of stones placed around it with a small pathway leading from the opened side to the outline of a horned toad scratched in the dirt, a Navajo sign declaring me either the equivalent of dead or, at best, a troublesome ghost. Footsore, parched, and increasingly disoriented, I was a walking shadow of myself.

Over the next few weeks I was restless. It was good timing those Navajo had concluded it was in their interest to turn me invisible although I admit they were too damn good at it. Nobody spoke to me. All Indians averted their faces and some were in the habit of waving sage toward any direction they saw my tracks.

One day some boys threw rocks at me and shouted *Gaagii! Gaagii!*, which in their language sounded like a raven's croak. A passing elder warned these boys that in abusing me they were inviting a curse. To further emphasize my banishment, when I took my usual route to the river I found a cluster of owl feathers pricked grotesquely into a stick character sketched in the dust with big ears drawn on just clarify its message. I was familiar with the belief that, to the Navajo, an owl is a bearer of nasty omens.

Pretty soon, however, these tribal beliefs ceased to penetrate. I'd taken to lying awake sweating and having nose bleeds. Unable to sleep, I'd hear the voice of Gaagii the crow spirit that Apache medicine man had lodged within me. When Gaagii took over his power was seductive. I'd resist his presence yet want it at the same time. I ate little and bathed even less. Surrendering to impulse I'd gallivant down to the Pecos to sit with my legs in the river, repeating a crazy song or a cackling string of private lingo.

"Devon Young" gave way to a raggedy loner who talked rivers to tree people and sky people and especially to lizard people. He'd lost the boundary between his body, wings, branches, and cloud critters and everything that talked back. He'd fly ecstatic races along the riverbank's rocky terrain and survive bad landings his body covered with bruises, leaves, burrs and thorns. He was often unsure if *he* had truly been flying. *He? I? Me? Are my feathers black? Is that mine, that body, far below? Maybe it belongs to someone else? Looks like it fell from the sky.*

I'd find myself miles from Bosque Redondo with no idea how I got there. Drifting back to my hogan through that great silent country I made a friend of darkness.

I felt free in darkness; it had no walls. I might have blown away like a dust devil if my behavior continued. I bathed in dust, slept in dust, ate dust. I picked up any likely pebble to speak to and got answers. I detected mysterious whispers in all things around me. Staring at a horizon I'd feel myself and distance become the same emptiness.

I was easily alerted. A sage wren's trill, even the abrupt presence of my own hands could startle me. Conversely, I became recklessly emboldened, drawn to tightrope fallen logs or tiptoe along a cliff edge feeling power in holding a fine balance on a great height. I could burst into bubbling laughter like escaping quail, happily muttering, *Crow Man, now you know you need nowhere, nowhere to go, here is where you are going, here, here is where you belong.*

I'd stand high and mighty on an overlook and shout *bidziil bidziil,* Navajo for "he is strong," my arms extended transfigured by the sky, allowing the landscape to spread my wings. Solitude liberated me to smells, touches, tastes, and enclosed a mystery with no boundaries beyond sunset and sunrise.

I might have travelled permanently in that babbling world and become a long-fingered hermit with bark skin and wild hair, wide-eyed with crazed wisdom and baffled wonderment. I was becoming a skeletal nomad who smelled like the ground and wandered among the Navajo staring as if faces were distant stars. Or perhaps I'd just fade away and become a river, a castaway seed, a cathedral of bones, another lost speck alone on the plains. Whatever transported my body and to where made little difference because there was no me to care.

The cavernous interior of those medicine beans as big as night is a croaking presence of the crow that never sleeps. One night I woke up shivering under moonlight reaching for me with blue fingers. Studying my skinny arms and stepladder stomach I determined to become human again. In one breath civilization offered a convenient surrender.

Stepping into the cold morning my befuddled skull struggled to arrange a new map. I had been carrying around a talkative pebble and dropped it. I was starting to think, fiddling with thought like a fragment of something broken off. Impatiently I concluded *who needs thinking anyway.* Maybe this other man can emerge easily as washing your face. Maybe, after months of being crazy as a three-headed road runner, stringing two simple ideas together made me cocky.

Wandering back through Bosque Redondo my see-through way of looking intensified. If I looked sideways at people colors silhouetted their bodies. I saw how a human travels his own country, carries his own baggage, and talks to his own lives. I trusted the degrees of radiance of this visible anatomical cloak as evidence of what they were carrying from long ago before they, like me, were captured by their skin.

I had become a walk-on human, someone re-entering this life carrying a piece of someone else. Some days this piece looms a bigger presence than others. Some days along the trail a lone crow approaches with his cocky, *aw-shucks* sashay, just to squint sideways and confirm that he remembers me. Some days crows surround me, scolding as only crows can scold, before they fly off. Deep within the flock's departing chorus I hear Gaagii's beak hard at his work of ripping darkness into wings.

o

Despite my spate of *loco* shenanigans I slowly became a shade more human, or at least something that might pass for it. No matter what came next I was confident that the country camped inside me was a companionship of rivers, mountains, and plains. Maybe it is dangerous to have been kidnapped into another life, but it was fine by me if someday I was to become a grasshopper, a piece of flint, a grizzly bear, a cavalry captain, a river rock, a jumping mouse, a bleaching skull, an abandoned saddle. *Sooner or later,* I liked to chuckle, *maybe a soul gets a shot at being everything.*

I ducked out through the hole smashed in the back of my hogan, wandered down to the river, and took a cold swim. In early October the river was chilly. I wrestled around in the current until, huffing, I staggered ashore, ambled toward the fort, and walked into the surgeon's dispensary.

Dripping wet with my ribs showing and greasy hair plastering my shoulders, I asked a flustered orderly for a set of clean clothes.

The fort surgeon was sent for. In wire-rim spectacles and a stained surgical apron over his blue uniform the captain smelled of whisky and cigars. Looking me up and down he was in an irritated hurry to dismiss my interruption. *Almighty blazes, what's he doing in here? I've seen more meat on a crutch. I heard some heathen white boy went Indian. What's your name son?*

Gaagii Hasleen.

Say again?

Crow Man.

What?

Whats what?

The surgeon slapped my face. *You need to learn how to address an officer of the United States cavalry. Now what is your goddamn name and what in hell are you doing entering this post filthy as a Comanche blanket?*

I lost my feathers.

Feathers? Holy bejesus. Where's your folks?

Long way over big mountain.

The boy is touched in the head. Orderly, escort this sorry business out of my sight. Git him some decent cover. My guess is savages stole his senses. No telling what else, probably used him foul ways to boot. Doze him four tablespoons of Jalap and might as well add in twelve drops of Calomel. When he's done emptying, wash him up and take him over to the chapel. Maybe those starched sisters can whip some wheels back on his wagon.

The orderly had me climb into a horse trough and scrub with a bar of gritty lye soap. In company supply the quartermaster threw me a bib shirt, a used set of breeches, sloppy knee-top boots, and a cut-down cavalry belt.

Before I could get dressed both cavalry soldiers grabbed me. One poured an evil-tasting potion down my gullet and, smiling at my growing pallor, pointed toward the company latrines where I splattered my history into an abyss.

The way those bluecoats grinned reminded me that *there's been many a child earned his bitter medicine.* My father had offered this cold comfort when I came home bloodied by a farmer who, seeing I'd scattered his haystack by playing in it, chased me over and under from everywhere except his heavy hands.

Basic cavalry post doctoring is elemental: *clean out one end or the other, otherwise amputate, bury, shoot, or imprison.* When that gut tonic cut in I was soon ankle dancing toward the latrine. I had to roost in that nose-holding dark a long time before my lower forty's trial was concluded due to loss of further evidence.

Squatting on that splintery halo I conjured up a plan and sashayed out of there feeling lighter. I had buried my mother's seventy-five silver dollars and kept our Henry repeater oiled and safely hidden in my bewitched hogan where no Navajo dared go. Temporarily I was willing to become the post's whipping boy. No matter how much they foisted their rules upon me they'd never get deeper than my first layer of thick skin.

When I stumbled out of the company bog the duty soldier declared me *worm free* and offered that *a young buck like yourself ought look to signing articles in the United States cavalry. Mebbe git yerself on as a drummer. Steady rations. A mount an full rig. Ain't nobody mess with yer backside on this post neither.*

I grinned as dumb a grin as I could muster. Much of what I had learned of the military was written in the eyes of Civil War veterans or imprinted on my backside by local army pickets who were all too handy with a quirt. For me and many other settlers witness to crowded cemeteries and one-legged parades, soldiering had lost its shine.

I headed for the schoolhouse. Arriving dewormed and absent of my pet crow and moccasins, I was a white boy in their eyes again and the nuns were on me like tar. They spooned me a bowl of molasses porridge and started right away arranging me a campsite in heaven.

Over the next weeks each time the nuns scheduled a baptism I took off to talk to my primary religious advisor, the Pecos River. Soon dismissively diagnosed as recalcitrant and mentally unfit I was assigned to cleaning the officer's stable. This chore was fine with me. Horses talked sense. Watching a stable hand in serious confab with his mounts convinced the fort surgeon that *the savages' abuse had pushed me too far north of my ears.* I willingly acted knot-headed in the interests of solitude and the grub the one-legged buffalo soldier delivered to my stable, sustenance usually only a maggot shy of the same barrel meat the government rationed Indians.

So there I was stuck, between nowhere and nowhere else. I slept in the hay, took the army's grub, accepted their haircut, shoveled horse muck, hummed in my fractured lingo, and itched to join the first trail outfit that passed through.

As luck had it an outfit showed up. Jim Kennedy, following the trail broke by Oliver Loving, had pushed his own herd across the Llano Estacado and, fording the Pecos, bedded his longhorns down a mile above the fort.

I took to hanging around Kennedy's camp and acting polite. Angling for a job I offered to ride whichever rank horse any bored cowboy figured might offer me a bucking challenge. Those trail-gaunted fellows, having survived six waterless days, were pretty worn out and wide open to any entertainment. Watching a big-eared kid volunteer to break his fool neck riding green stock offered those cowboys a handy opera.

I chipped a tooth and bruised my ridgepole a time or two hanging onto those catamount ponies. Showing my stuff to whooping Texas cowboys, I'd jump in the saddle and keep scratching even after one of those boneyards bucking six ways to Sunday threw me in the dirt.

Taking notice that I could stick in the saddle and jump smartly back on board when I didn't, Kennedy's trail boss was entertained enough to allow that *you might as well be paid for working so dang hard to break your fool neck.*

Even feeling rickety after riding a dozen rank ponies and swallowing maggoty years of abuse in Fort Sumner, getting hired for half a dollar a day as cavvy boy alongside a herd of longhorns offered a promise of shining times. "Cavvy boy" represented the lowest rung on a trail crews ladder.

My daily chore was to ride herd on the "cabbalada" or remuda, either term applying to the outfit's collection of horses and mules. Cavvy boy was viewed as a beginner's job but it offered work in the saddle and that was my ambition at the time.

When we headed out I was gifted a Green River knife, a bedroll, and saddlebag of plunder some snake-bit cowboy didn't need because he'd been put to bed with a pick and shovel. I didn't trouble to inquire as to the late owner's name. Unlike the superstitious Navajo, a practical cowboy figures, even passed on from the dead, a bedroll and knife deliver the same purpose.

I also had dug up my mother's silver and rounded up some decent boots, a broke in four-by-four-hat, two homespun shirts, and a set of spurs. The range boss practically gave me that cottonmouth-bit cowhand's pistol, a five-shot Navy Colt conversion re-rigged for new-style ammunition. An ex-confederate soldier, observing my new weapon, pointed out, *that's a handy piece you have there. Don't matter how much speed or guts a feller lays claim to, bullets beats balls every time.*

Kennedy himself walked me toward the remuda and told me to pick out any mount carrying his brand, the

Lazy D. There was a decent mix of green broke and seasoned horses. All around us the longhorn cattle seemed antsy even after having crossed the Staked Plain on sparse grass and no water. I dapped a loop on a big buckskin, threw on a saddle, tied on the yellow-boy rifle scabbard, and lit out to check my prospects working the stock.

Leaning that cowpony into an easy start and rounding those mules and horses into a tight bunch felt like a brand new day.

o

There were thirty-seven horses and mules in Kennedy's remuda. Five of his regular cowhands had their own string run in there too. The cow boss insisted every hand, regardless of whose horses he rode, saddle up a fresh horse twice a day.

I'd never had the opportunity to make peace with so many horses. Working so regularly together the distance between myself and every horse I rode shortened to an easy lean or click of my tongue.

Moving alongside a big drive my chore was to keep the horses bunched. For everyone else work meant relentlessly pushing two thousand or so tail-flicking butts as far as they walk toward sundown. Now and again afoot, I learned to keep an eye peeled for a crazed longhorn still eager to kill one of us two-legged nuisances who'd chased him out of the Texas Breaks.

Kennedy's cowhands represented a rough breed. Outsiders like to disdain Texas cowboys, not always humorously, as *the lowest form of life*. The Lazy D bunch did prove a hardbitten crew, some slow to an opinion, others quick to take offense. On the trail most were easy going. Every man could sing night rider ballads to calm Kennedy's restless herd. Generally the men were politely direct and expected the same in return. Only two were quick tempered and one of them, perennially morose, kept to himself.

Trigger-happy at the end of a long push, Texans had a reputation for acting like raiders when they galloped into a town. Some of our crew were Confederate veterans. They tagged me a Yankee despite the fact I was too young to have fought the war. Several looked for any opening to declare their lone star homeland enduringly free. With so much Confederate and Union blood still seeping into the ground, it was a good idea to avoid discussions around issues of victory or defeat.

Kennedy's cowboys had all been up the trail a time or two and would swap hair-raising yarns. Their trips between south Texas and Kansas cattle towns had hardened them with its hot, thorn-ridden country, rattlers, rustlers, crazy weather, and hostile Indians. Exposure to danger had bred in Kennedy's Texans a wry fatalism tinged with sparks of suicidally infectious bravado.

Nightly hovering around cookfire embers the Lazy D's shadows would lean on darkness and talk to the fire.

It was a teaching to be entertained by the yarns and imprint of a country that shaped the American cowboy.

So far this drive had been peaceful. We kept an eye out for renegade Comanches and saw none. Word had it Indian troubles were breaking out throughout the entire Southwest. These reports proved to be overblown.

By calculation our third night up the trail was my nineteenth birthday. I shared this with no one except the Crow Man inside me. As a present I wanted Gaagii to leave me be awhile. *It's time to join the human beings,* I muttered. Feeling privileged to be the greenhorn of Kennedy's crew I was a rapt listener on the edge of any circle. I realized how the necessary habit of a prairie whisper had softened western speech. Broad gestures and a loud voice around a fire could draw arrows, so it was healthy to keep still and talk low in the throat. In Indian country I learned to hunker motionless as the quietest rock time ever chiseled.

A steady routine taught me how to get along and soon I was lifting my reins confidently toward the next horizon. I ate my share of dust clear up to the Kansas line. Overall, even though he taught me more than a few basic rules of Texas etiquette, Kennedy opined I lacked the maturity to qualify for full pay.

Approaching the border weeks later we encountered a high-wheeled cart accompanied by three Comancheros. This crafty breed of mestizo traders, who provided whisky and guns among the Comanches in exchange for hides, stolen cattle, and American captives, warned us the whole state of Kansas was up in arms over diseased cattle crossing into their territory. Apparently an army of Kansas ranchers had encamped on the border prepared at all cost to stop tick-bearing herds from infecting their stock.

Tick fever or not, Kennedy wasn't about to quit. He asked his whole crew to take a vote to turn east or push on. Going ahead invited trouble but every one of those Texas boys voted to back Kennedy and his trail boss. Turning their backs on a troubled Kansas border was too much of a surrender for armed Texans still whistling "Dixie. "

I eagerly offered to throw in with them too but Kennedy insisted his lead hand pay me off. I protested, assuming whatever lay ahead was part of the job we'd all hired on for. I believed I had enough sand to acquit myself as good as the next man. I'd been practicing that Navy Colt on cactus paddles and prairie thistles and voiced as strong an allegiance to the brand as everyone else.

Kennedy would have none of it. Judging me *too green to fight with seasoned men who've been up the trail with him to hell an back*, Kennedy told me, *Son, I won't see you pull leather on Kansas Yankees and be turned outlaw to both ends of a country's feud* and silenced my objections with a nod to his trail boss.

The man had me cut out two horses, explaining *Thar's plenty grub in this gunny-sack and water for a week to straddle whichever one you make your pack horse. Thar's cricks after that and likely plenty to hunt. Jest back-track our trail. If you spot smoke, afore riding up to it, make goddamn sure it comes from a*

wagon train or a chimney. Consider yerself a lucky sum buck. James
Kennedy has seen a share of trouble. Take my word he's looking
out for you. I'd say gittin two Lazy D mounts beats a shot to the
brainpan by some riled-up Yankee on the Kansas line.

Leaving that morning two horses, a sack of supplies, and
many miles richer, I felt well provisioned yet banished
as when the Navajo had turned their backs against me.

Soon I was riding herd on a prairie sky and camping
alone, counting stars my only company. The third day
out my route was blocked by migrating buffalo. The
herd took well into the night to pass by. The plains were
home to millions of these crook-backed oxen but I'd
never seen this many. I was told the animals tended
to gather in herds so immense their distant rumble
preceded a flood that darkened the earth.

I'd been dubious listening to a Montana trapper describe
One buffler herd I seen covered fifty square marl. Nother up on the
Missouri reckoned above two million head though countin ain't a
justice bein as their numbers kept on comin long after we quit guessin.
Strike me if'n them varmit wolves wasn't lopin along in herds too.

The herd I watched was countless enough to earn my
amazement. Its thunder shook the ground for hours. I
held my mounts on a short rope and hunkered down
at a respectable distance to watch even as darkness
fell. I couldn't see the other side of the herd. The wall-
eyed stares of the nearest buffalo inspected me even as,
head down, the animal charged toward some relentless
destination. Their cloven-footed passage, so native to
the long grass prairie, was a glory to see. Had the heavy

animals not been so impossible to domesticate no doubt their kind would have outnumbered cattle being shipped to eastern markets. Many animals, shot for their hides, were left to rot. Choice buffalo cuts sold for two cents a pound if a fat cow could be dropped close enough to customers for the meat to remain fresh.

It would bring a reigning silence to the West when the great herds were shot out. Drifting back to that day I feel that herd rumbling through my bones and it sobered me to realize such a holy bounty could be so swiftly extinguished.

At daybreak I awoke in my blankets to the empty plain as though buffalo had been shaggy ghosts stampeding dreams. Straggling cripples and sick calves scattered across the landscape, harassed by swooping ravens and pitiless hamstringing wolves.

That afternoon I caught up with a military supply train and was welcomed to accompany its wagons down to Albuquerque where I hired on for a teamster carting supplies up into Taos. The company included forty troopers armed with breech-loading rifles. Every stop we circled the wagons. A Comanche war party, following their usual practice, usually refused to chance frontal attack against entrenched and well-armed military detachments. Our next camp was made under a full moon known on the plains as a Comanche moon. The moonlight lived up to is name of enabling Indian predations when, despite our vigilance, they ran off five of our horses.

The army's Indian scouts had dropped three fat buffalo cows and the cavalry officer had decided to camp another night and prepare the meat. I was quickly set to work helping to pull hides. The whole company was soon gorging on steaks three Kaddo squaws roasted in pits. Sweet and greasy, buffalo hump, known as "puddin meat," made gluttons of us all. I watched two buckskinned civilian teamsters, face-to-face over one fire pit, devour its contents until, bellies bloated, they rolled aside moaning in the grass.

Late in the day the soldiers lashed their wagons onward and I rode along stringing my pack horse and calculating Kennedy's pay added to what I had left, which amounted to forty-eight dollars. I planned on selling my cowpony and purchasing a better saddle horse.

In Albuquerque my new teamster boss, Nap Boudreaux, an ex-trapper, proved mean enough to corral bears with a switch. He claimed to have *Dipped his trap stick up in Montana's Musellshell country until the beaver wuz all played out.* He'd also hunted bounty scalps to sell to the army. The man boasted of *Tradin more fur than any man alive, killin a heap o' griz, an peelin scalps off injuns, young, old, an dang few of em already dead.*

Boudreaux insisted we address him as cap'n. The way he cussed would sizzle bacon. A sideways look at my boss's hulking shadow sobered me. It was a dull red, perhaps a sign all those scalps had stained his murderous soul.

Needy of help, Boudreaux had gruffly taken me on. It was around a hundred and fifty miles to Taos, a deal of it uphill over rocky country. Navigating red rock arroyos and scrub pinon, Boudreaux aimed to make fifteen miles a day. It was a hard push. We had to crosshaul wagons carrying three thousand pounds of freight over broken ground and sometimes through ice and snow. There was supposedly a bonus paid for winter hauling, which the other wagon drivers and myself never saw.

Making seven roundtrips in just under four months we foundered five oxen, whose ration of feed was minimal. Every day Boudreaux also insisted we bullwhip the wagons for too many hours. His teams were bound to play out as were his men. I tended to bite my tongue at Boudreaux's callousness. In way of letting off steam I regularly practiced with my .44 Navy Colt whenever we'd done unyoking those big-wheeled ox wagons. Ammunition at forty cents a box motivated me to keep my target practice focused.

On my last spring trip up from Albuquerque the country around Taos was the prettiest I'd ever seen. The town was overlooked by a mountain with a swathe of sagebrush prairie sweeping northward cut by a deep river canyon that hadn't been bridged. Taos, an Indian name that means "red willow," had plenty of trees, creeks, and fertile bottomland where, earlier, Spanish settlers built adobes and even a few fancy haciendas.

Overall Taos struck me as being very peaceful and very pretty, with its dappled leaf-shadows and low, blossom-hung adobes. The center of town was a short dusty street dominated by a hotel where we unloaded watched by settlers, local drunks, and Pueblo Indians.

Commerce was picking up. Drummers, settlers, ex-trappers, disbanded soldiers, and assorted fortune seekers trickled into town. The road into Taos on the way up from Santa Fe wound between huts occupied by dispossessed Indian women and naked begging children. North and west of town the Españolas had developed productive land, sedimentary arroyos more than valleys, into tidy farms. The creeks and irrigation that made this possible had been excavated into a maze of ditches complicated in ownership as a prairie dog town. The folks in Taos, long before gringos arrived, tended to consider the water and, in fact, the whole region as theirs and viewed the United States as an invader.

Despite rumors of silver and land for the asking, water rights were the true gold of that country. Rights had all been claimed and the Españolas were as possessive about irrigation ditch systems as wolverines over fresh meat. More men were shot in feuds over water than got ventilated over liquor, women, or cards. I would be out on the rolling sage country and suddenly come upon the greenest little rancho seemingly sprung from nowhere. It was a treat to witness the tidy agricultural techniques and productivity of those small farmers and to enjoy the tamales and tasty fixings their women produced. Clearly on that high sagebrush plateau water, red dirt, and sunshine did the trick.

That morning after payday we were supposed to swing Boudreaux's teams back down to Santa Fe. We'd finally come to words over the way he ordered me to abuse his stock. Loyal to his oxen more than to his greed, I quit. I'd already traded up to a better horse and planned to seek other work. Nap Boudreaux would have been thorny to face. Luckily when I rode out my drunken boss lay passed out like a hill. Whoever pours destiny out of a boot isn't shy of imagination.

I'd happily anticipated doing anything better than getting paid to abuse oxen for Nap Boudreaux. Inside a week I was hired by Mr. Lannis Owens, owner of the Dobe T. which at the time was the only free-range upstart cattle outfit fringing Taos. In the beginning the work was straight forward enough. I drifted the sagebrush checking on scrub stock and water holes, or was sent as a loaned outrider to some of the local ranchos.

Ultimately, the way things eventually panned out at the Dobe T, when it came to arranging a future I didn't know shit from honey.

o

My father liked to say, *If there's trouble left behind it's planning an ambush down the trail.* Trouble, in the form of a pursuit, was certainly following me now.

I'd been working at the Dobe T for almost two years when I fell in love with Dahlia de Belardes, only daughter of a widowed Española patriarch. Risking her father's wrath, we met secretly. Sorrowfully our romance was discovered and Dahlia, after being publicly chastened, was taken somewhere far away from New Mexico. Tormented, yet determined to track down my sweetheart, I compounded my troubles by winning a Dobe T poker game. My good luck against Rusty Cuellar resulted in a gunfight and the sheriff's posse hot on my trail.

Making my escape up that mountain, I tried to resist looking back. Any posse would be easily winded chasing a fugitive with a good lead and a well-nursed horse. I had too short a life to be measuring the distance between getting born and getting strung up in a cottonwood tree. Common sense soon slowed me to a walk.

Northern New Mexico offered plenty of open country. More by habit than plan I'd galloped out of town on the west side, following Willow Creek past the granary and haciendas that face the pueblo where it squares up against the mountain. In early morning gloom the air was tinged with smoke and one sneaky coyote trotting ahead of me veered toward the creek. Having that critter cross my trail felt like *hello, bad luck*. I spurred my horse past a sleepy buckboard heading in for market and then it was *adios, Taos*.

At the Blue Lake crossroads I headed up the canyon, slowing to a steady walk as the trace grew steep. In an hour, suddenly captive of light, I kicked into a canter. When my horse began to blow I slowed her to a natural walk and reined off, weaving through brush close to the rushing creek. I can still smell the dew and hear a posse of imagined voices pricking my back. I felt stretched to my core by the pull of a lynch mob at my back and the determination to follow my heart and find Dahlia.

There was no point in trying to be shy and attempting to cover my sign because any Pueblo tracker could easily pick up wet prints. I figured to make it past Cimarron and head onto the big open, where I'd have the pick of three directions. Once there, I knew that if I doubled back south through Las Vegas I'd run into a lot of people connected to Taos so dropped that idea. There was plenty of thick cover northward up through Raton Pass into the Spanish Peaks which was an appealing route but might also be the posse's most likely guess. I decided to chance heading east out onto the plains. Given the Indian troubles and lack of supply, the plains were a risky proposition for a quickly assembled and ill-equipped volunteer posse.

The time had come to find out what sort of bottom there was to Saloon, my horse. The mare had proved agile around cattle but I'd never pushed her any distance. When she'd nuzzled up to me in that corral below Ranchos the owner hinted she was *a sight hot-blooded but broke in easy as a dog.* Saloon could whirl on a dollar and now she was proving to have heart, too.

That country on the way up to Cimarron was game rich. At Summit Meadows two elk spooked back down the creek bug-eyed and trotting with heads thrown back. The big herds were already drifting higher and I saw pebbly scat churned into sandy crossings below antler rubbings ribboned on low branches. Picked off a limb, elk velvet smelled of sour blood. There were plenty quail chuckling along in the grass, prairie falcons dropping, nibbling jackrabbits, a fox sunning on a rock, arrows of snow geese beating north across a big sky. Too pretty a place to have to see on the run.

It was plain to any eye that this park country was untouched. Deer, a lot of them, continued nibbling even as we passed close over frost-heaved ground that seeped spring's gravely flood. We walked past black bear and a cub scrounging a stand of aspen. Measuring each another, me from the saddle toward that piggy squint with camas roots hanging off purple lips, I advised that old girl, *you never looked at so much trouble.*

Mid-day came on warm enough to sniff creosote sap. Gnats zithered in swarms. Inhaling the sun smell off boulders as we rocked uphill, the air tasted sweet enough to remind me how existence might taste without it. The confluence of fears that drove my getaway and longing to hold Dahlia in my arms again seesawed me between disembodied desperation and an exhilaration I'd never felt in my life. A surplus of imagination didn't help.

I saw my own ghost rising like white smoke departing a body dangling from a noose and swaying in the Taos Plaza. I'd seen enough of the town's civic obligations to know that, even though confident I'd be brought in, a sheriff's swamper would still be sent to print WANTED posters to pass out as souvenirs of my hanging. The mayor and judge would dust off their usual speeches to satisfy a plaza crowd who commonly agreed that a hanging resolved any problem.

Executions provided an entertaining satisfaction for the community. Given how private vengeance was often dispensed by a bullet in the back, the occasional exercise of public justice threw a bone to the illusion of law and order. New as I was to local hangings, on the fringes of a crowd I detected that many a citizen felt satisfied it was someone else's neck feeling the weight of their ass. Given such direct experience with Taos's law, I looked back more than once on my way up that slope.

I made Cimarron, passed the Aztec mill, and headed toward Shwenk's saloon. The place was hugely empty. I swung onto a stool at the long bar, its wood sweating liquor from the previous night's rowdy mix of drifters, cowboys, horny teamsters and frail sisters.

Shwenk's was as quiet in the day as it was boisterous at night. A solitary Jicarilla barkeep slid me a plate of tortillas and some stringy beef smothered in a soupy *atole* that tasted burned.

The Indian eyed me, nodding as he waited until my food was finished and I'd downed a glass of watery *horchata*. The saloon was so quiet he could hear me chew. The place had an echo and the barkeep's boots squeaked.

The focus that barman gave me while I wolfed my grub was part of his job. Cimarron remained lawless except for the iron rule of its boss, Lucien Maxwell, when and if he was around. Very few local arrivals slipped past the watchful eyes of a Maxwell-hired hand.

When the Jicarilla barkeep asked my destination I lied: *Down the valley to find work.*

The barman had studied saddle drifters, many young, rawboned, and hungry. I fit the mold but tried to appear affable even with my pistol rigged for a quick cross-draw beneath my steadied smile.

I glanced across the floor that lead up to a balcony where sporting women took their paying customers. The barkeep, thinking he spotted an interest, thumbed me suggestively upstairs. I grinned, lifted my empty glass, and turned it upside down.

The place was still untidy from gambling and boot-heel dancing. There were a few tilted chairs and a faro wheel that had stopped nowhere lucky. In one corner a dealer lay snoring in his cards. I drifted my eyes over the wheezy floor boards and squinted at Shwenk's gaudy canvas of undressed belles sprawled against backgrounds of plush curtains and velvet furniture. Studying one naked lady I saw she had two fresh bullet holes in her most prominent offerings.

Cimarron was doing well, and with evidence of gold in the region big money was moving uphill. The town was known as a magnet for trouble. I recall a newspaper headline declaring, "Cimarron is quiet. No one has been killed here in almost three days." In truth the whole territory was beginning to jump. Spring had been promising. Meltwater gushed into the *madre acequias* around Taos where farmers plant the lush bottomland and the Dobe T herd was flourishing. It was even rumored a railroad was pushing into Kansas, maybe as far south and west as Santa Fe.

Now that the war between the States had been settled only Indian troubles were holding back a flood of wagon trains. The Army was eager to run the renegades back onto reserves but were having a rough go of it. A Yankee sergeant waving greenbacks had tried to recruit men at fourteen dollars a month to join the fight. None of us working down in Taos for the Dobe T rose to the bait.

It didn't help that a few weeks previous a column rode into town with half its troopers dead or wounded. Word had it Comanche braves were marauding all across the Indian Strip, and, besides, many of us took the Army's presence as proof that everyone chomping on President Johnson's coat tails was about to move in, bringing more government, more taxes, more people, more law.

Growing up in Bosque Redondo I'd seen plenty bad blood between bored troopers and half-starved Indians. In Taos my sympathies leaned toward the Española and Pueblo communities more than bluecoat army recruiters flashing paper money and bad manners.

The Dobe T hands slept in a low-roofed log-and-adobe-chinked structure with two front windows and a stove off to one side. Seven bunks were built into the walls. There was a bench around a table and four chairs staked out according to first hired. A small back room served as kitchen with a wash basin, storage and racks for slickers, boots, and tack. Infrequent inclinations to bathe were served by an outside pump. At the owner's insistence our bunkhouse was kept tidy, but neatness did nothing to erase its musky blend of sweat, tobacco smoke, saddle leather, and hot coffee.

Although Mrs. Owens frowned upon her husband's workers drinking liquor, pay day usually meant there'd be a jug of Taos Lightning and a card game initiated by Rusty Cuellar and his glued-on shadow Joey Lomitas. But it had been increasingly difficult to seduce more than three Dobe T boys into a game, given that Cuellar ran a suspiciously consistent winning streak.

Under the dim light of the table three cowboys ponied up and I watched Cuellar fleece all of them out of their money. More out of irritation at Cuellar's inflated cockiness than belief that lady luck had invited me to the dance, I decided to sit in. In the previous hour Cuellar had won thirty-one dollars so the losers stood around anticipating Cuellar would clean me out too. I paid in my two bits and Cuellar dealt both of us five cards, discarded two, dealt himself two more, and raised me fifty cents. I anted up and called. Cuellar turned over two pair, aces and twos.

Two pair, bullets and ducks, moccasin boy, Cuellar grinned as he spotted the lousy hand I'd attempted to bluff him with and raked in the pot. The watching cowboys shook their heads as Rusty dealt me another hand. I watched him flip the deck with a confident gleam as his stubby fingers slicked the cards. He paused to take a drink, juggled it in his mouth, and swallowed with a drill finality.

Rusty Cuellar's lidded eyes sunk under protruding brows, and his carved lips were pinched to an unpleasant grimace. He was in the habit of checking his holster as if to assure card players its pistol was always handy. I noticed he either tightened his lower lip against his teeth when he looked at his cards or rotated his neck, adjusting himself to what I guessed might be a disappointing hand.

After wagering back and forth for over three hours, our shares of the pot were little changed from where we'd started. Each of us had been bet down to our last dollar and then had recovered our losses. The Dobe T hands, including the cook who had moved closer to our game, continued exchanging nervous looks.

Our contest had fallen into a studied ritual of gathering and showing cards with every call, accompanied by Cuellar's profane expressions of victory or defeat. Cuellar's red hair, parted starchily down the middle, had become mussed into a spiky nest as Rusty's comments grew increasingly provocative. Winning or losing a hand, I held my tongue. We'd progressed to fifty-cent bets and occasionally raised one another in dollars. After winning a five-dollar pot, I waited for the next deal. Cuellar stopped shuffling, took another slug of rotgut, and challenged *You got the sand to pony up a dollar ante an play dollar raises?*

I nodded.

That nod mean in or out? Scared to talk les'n I get to call your bluff behind that fake dead man stare?

To which Joey Lomitas chimed in, *The kid got nothin but nothin Rusty. He jus grabbin the apple hopin greenhorn luck won't buck him off.*

Rusty dealt me three fours, a jack, and a two. I discarded the two and Rusty slid me an inside jack that completed my full house.

Rusty adjusted his neck, discarded, and gave himself three cards.

Raise you five was my play as I looked him square in the eyes.

Fold. Cuellar responded. *Lessee what you got.*

Got to pay to see them I said, though deliberately allowing Cuellar to glimpse my full house before I raked in the pot.

Cuellar's irritated response was to raise the ante. He pushed in ten dollars. Leaning across the table, Cuellar flipped me my cards. *Time to play for white meat an find where the eagle shits, moccasin boy. I hear you got some Ranchos señorita callin yor donkey out of the barn. Lessee if these poker ladies lay down that easy for you.*

I pushed in ten dollars and picked up two queens, an eight of spades, a three of diamonds, and a six of hearts. I kept the queens and the eight. Rusty dealt me another queen and an ace. He took two cards and raised me five which left him only two dollars. I raised him five and called. Cuellar snapped over a nine of clubs, a spade ace, then grinned as he revealed his three eights.

I showed my hand. Spotting my three ladies and what he figured should have been his fourth eight. Rusty abruptly stood up. *Cheatin sonbitch, you play me brown.*

Watching Rusty's eyes narrow, I guessed it polite to let him finish staking out his claim over bad luck before scraping up my winnings.

You think I never seen nobody cheat? Where from you slip that inside eight? Cuellar violently swept aside the cards, money, liquor jug, and all.

Holding my seat while scraping liquor off my shirt, although my face was burning, I responded evenly, *Never cheated anyone and damn sure never played a crooked card.*

You lyin sack of shit, you been ropin me all night, cabron. Come in here playin green an all the time you was a card mechanic figurin to clean out this bunkhouse an weasel our pay. What you think, Joey? Mebbe hogtie mocassin boy with a piggin string an make him a gorl.

The silence in the bunk house deepened another notch. Although threatened and scared, I resisted dropping a hand toward my holster. Fear had initiated a cool focus and beneath it a simmering Irish righteousness. The spittle-lipped bully was running a hot iron over me in front of the whole crew. If I backed down, the outfit would reckon I was either a cowardly cheat or too puny to pull my own hat off.

Rusty Cuellar was known to rile like a wet rooster over petty things. Rusty ran cover for Joey Lomita's yellow streak and liked to act the honcho whose bullets and opinions declared the same punctuation.

Pointing an accusing finger Rusty bent down, gathered a handful of scattered cards, and threw them in my face, *What you got now yellow hair? Nother eight?*

Joey Lomitas continued to chime in, *Lessee you show Rusty where you hide the estra card 'till the pot gets rich.*

Admit cheating when I wasn't? My father taught me that *even a half man deserves the whole truth.* How many men had Rusty scared away from speaking their truths?

Having finished kicking over chairs Rusty was loudly hunting support, but each man kept studying his boots, all except Joey Lomitas, who nervously scuffed his feet like a centipede with chill blain. Sensing things were quickly heading south, I remained warily prepared for the developing show.

Under the weight of uncertainty's strained silence the bunkhouse shrunk, and after Rusty quit scouting faces he settled on staring me down. So did the rest of the Dobe T bunch. Maybe I was too dumb to recognize the election taking place because I stood where eyeballs meet on that frosty trail that leads only toward one solution.

It was anxious Joey Lomitas who was feeling most suspended from his partner's stare down. He swaggered into the mix to prod my chest, announcing, *I tink, Rusty kick your flaco ass.* Rusty sighed as though volunteering to execute this necessary chore. *Mister Owens doan wan no card cheats aroun his place. I think I take care of this for him. You an me. Outside.*

Luke, our white-haired cook, a sometimes sober ex-mule skinner who had a face so creased he needed a map to shave, chimed in that he'd make fresh coffee, suggesting we set down and let things cool off. I openly appreciated this idea. Despite his excessive culinary affinity for bacon grease, the old-timer had shown me a kindness or two.

Outside as the boys waited, the hopeful cook again piped up that *everybody aught drift back inside and have coffee* and suggested *Hell, Rusty, why not just split the fool pot with the kid.*

By now Rusty's face had grown dark enough to slow down a bat, and the cook's cheery idea didn't bring any light. *Shut up Luke*, Rusty spat. *You stinkin coffee an your burn bacon belongs on a gut wagon.*

Without ceremony Rusty started throwing punches. I took to ducking like a chicken on thrown corn. Admittedly I was spooked. When it came to a full-grown fight I was a first-timer. Previous scraps were more like barefoot square dances, scuffles with settler's sons my age. The ground was muddy but squishy under both of us. Rusty was wearing heeled boots that sucked into the wet ground and I was in Navajo moccasins that skidded but didn't sink.

The Dobe T boys formed a half circle in the early light. The air was cool and the dawn quiet enough to hear Cuellar's haymaker grunt over the cluck of waking chickens and nicker of cowponies in the nearby corral.

By the size of my opponent's overhung belly he clearly wasn't on the outs with his beans and was huffing hard as a winded bronc. I was spry and skinny and my adversary's roundhouse swing promoted further spryness. I hoped against hope that maybe he'd tire and keep swinging wild so I could allow one of his punches to graze me, fake going down, and see what came next.

While I was concentrating on evading him, Rusty staggered and fell in the mud. Seeing a possible conclusion, I offered a hand to help him up and declared a clumsy conclusion to our fracas.

Rusty rose as if to shake and went for his iron.

Cross drawing was pure instinct. Consequently the first thing I knew was that Rusty lay in a heap beneath an acrid spiral of powder smoke. Things happened so fast I didn't connect his fall to my actions at all. He'd collapsed on his face, revealing the fist-sized exit hole in his shirt the .44 slug had made between his shoulder-blades.

Intending to help him to his feet, I rolled Rusty onto his back. His legs kicked briefly then, with slow, rattling exhalations, his eyes froze to a glassy stare.

I was breathing fast and trying to deny the abrupt evidence of a man shot dead. But reality arrived with a revelation that the body at my feet would never again contain Rusty Cuellar. Shocked into my own mortality I feared that from this moment on I was banished from the human circle.

Flooded by so much weighty information my thoughts raced to find a solution to their horror. Sure, it had been either Rusty or me. But even an act of reflexive self-preservation didn't let my conscience off the hook. Hearing Gaagii's ragged laughter glide out of his darkness I holstered my still-smoking .44.

Meanwhile, Joey Lomitas rushed forward, watched Cuellar heave his last gasp, and then took off toward the corral shouting *you cheatin pendejo you shoot my fren!*

I stood with the old cook, the only man in the bunch square enough to step forward. The rest of my shadow audience was jumpy and one of them advised me that I was *in big trouble* and that *sure as eggs Joey Lomitas has gone fer more of it.*

Luke pushed me toward the bunkhouse. Hurrying to help gather my getaway rig the cook tried to stuff a fistful of poker winnings into my shirt. *Don't let this thing paint you, son,* he advised. *Rusty's been asking for it. That weasel Lomitas will likely throw in with the posse that gets onto you.*

Around Taos, wherever there's blood, there's kin. I suggest you grab distance and don't waste time covering tracks. Those Pueblo boys can hunt down a whisper in a prairie wind.

I quickly changed my muddy moccasins for boots and hightailed out of there without much mind to any direction. I should have picked up more of that poker take. The money I'd just spent at Shwenks left me with four dollars and ten cents, which made it a mighty long way to somewhere.

o

Paying the barkeep in Cimarron, I considered what sort of lead I might still have over my Taos pursuers. Much of the ground I'd covered would leave an easy trace. I had attempted to break up my trail but soon quit because the ground was too wet. Better to keep nursing my horse and risk the posse spotting me. After piling up the canyon my pursuers would be too blown to catch up. True, sometimes horses in a bunch feed one another's speed but they can bottom out together too. I doubted that any posse-man's motivation to catch up matched my ambition to save my own neck.

I estimated the time it took for the sheriff to round up men, dig up some Pueblo trackers, and get on my tail gave me at least a two-hour lead. Pushing out from Shwenks and swinging into the saddle, I surveyed the high timber that cast feathery shadows toward the direction that stretched beyond Cimarron onto the plains. Open country was my ally because distance determined how well a rider was prepared to keep going. I was willing to chance it, figuring that a posse without supplies would balk at the prospect of chasing someone onto the prairie.

The Dobe T boys, including Joey Lomitas, who was certainly chasing me now, knew my gunfight with Rusty Cuellar climaxed a mix of sorry events. Payday had come with its musical clink of silver. I seldom gambled but when my first romance was disrupted, I felt heart scalded enough to try to beat the devil with his own cards.

Gunplay, and unpremeditated instinct on my part, had left Rusty Cuellar lying behind me like a distant mountain range. It was mostly the image of Rusty's dead body that kept me leaning my mare into a canter as I followed the trail among scattered rock outcroppings that opened toward Wagon Mound.

Last summer I'd considered working the hay higher up around Chama, rejecting better pay down in the valley for the sake of seeing some new country. I'd begun to cache a few dollars in my saddlebag. Over four months I'd saved to buy Dahlia a gift because, I'd sing to myself, *beauty shines brighter than silver.*

Only miles out of Cimarron and on the run from a vengeful posse I wondered just how far ahead I'd have to look to see Dahlia. As I kept on through the dark I heard an echo of offered advice: *Son, the reason men honor love,* my mother had said, *is because love looks up rather than down.*

Switching rein fingers I decided to let my mare nibble awhile, then I re-saddled and walked on. The stars glimmered purple light. Sentinel rocks seemed witness to everything I'd done and was about to do. Deeper than fear of my pursuers was my belief that destiny was influenced by honor and affection, dignities I hoped might protect well-intentioned men.

I began to nod off sporadically, waking abruptly to urge my horse. No matter how I replayed events, back at the Dobe T Cuellar's corpse was never going to get back up. I thought of other final stares I'd seen: my mother's, those of my butchered Navajo sidekicks. Every life that had passed through mine had bequeathed an accompanying familiarity. But, regarding Rusty Cuellar, I felt empty as a church on Saturday night.

To escape the emptiness I ceremoniously revisited the day I'd first met Dahlia. That wintery afternoon I'd been sent to flush out three steers that habitually strayed along the river below the local sheriff's holdings in Ranchos.

It was chilly. The cottonwoods wafted their sapling clusters with a few remnant yellow leaves. Frozen cattails in the sinks were flattened into baskets. My reins were hard and my chaps frosted stiff. A pair of old-timers pitching hay into a corral above the Little Rio Grande beckoned me. When I waved back they signaled an offer of a drink. I pushed the strays across the icy creek and headed them homeward. A hot drink sounded good.

The men dropped their pitchforks, walked into their hacienda's front yard, and hunkered next to the sawed remains of a big cottonwood tree. A willowy young woman emerged from the adobe to shake out her hair. She wore a white shift embroidered with blue flowers. I stared at her shape, sculpted by the winter sun, and at her shining auburn hair as she gathered it. She glanced hesitantly back at me before going inside.

I was leaning against the big cottonwood stump when she returned to hand out corn silk tea laced with honey and mescal. Her shift was shrouded now by a white woolen shawl. She walked lightly toward us holding her head high as though delivering a hospitality more than a womanly service. There was a quietness in the woman's face. Her almond eyes were dark and contained the stillness of someone a long time alone, a shining absorption of realized intelligence. Her quickening glance took me in.

As the señorita three-fingered me the steaming mug I detected a private courage enhanced by grace. Her fingers were long and she lifted them to her lips briefly after she offered the tea. Self-consciously I nodded, *gracias, señorita*, too hastily to conceal my glimpse of her imprisoned life. Besides seeing her beauty I'd seen a translucent truth, and she knew it.

I figured this prime river-bottom location, the well-tended size of the hacienda and its hired men indicated that the girl's family was well established and likely prominent in the community. I'd already witnessed how Española landowners exercised intentions to maintain control of their old world culture. Just observing Taos grandees taking a drink in a local cantina their attitudes seemed calculated to remind both kinsmen and strangers how rules are kept and if necessary, enforced. Conventions of Taos aristocracy sprinkled public conversation with masculine salt. Every important hombres simplest declaration was given weight, even if its implications were thin as bath water. Just looking with interest at a man's daughter could get you knifed in the dark or, if the patriarch were rich enough, in broad daylight. But I remembered Thoreau said, *Love is as much light as it is flame.* At that moment in Ranchos, I was all flame.

o

Every attempt I made to deny that I was smitten with Dahlia just encouraged another losing argument with a lightning bolt. Maybe I should have known from the start that, given the weight of Taos history and my lowly status within it, Dahlia de Belarde's smile was intended to remain as close to me as the moon.

Local origins were no secret. The whole place sprung from a native style reflected in the way many adobe structures, new or old, appeared built to vanish seamlessly into the ground. As for Spain's signature, it prevailed in the mannerisms and speech of the local men who considered themselves mostly related to New Mexico's original Spanish conquerors.

One afternoon, after selling some Dobe T steers, Mister Owens stood me a fine mescal at Taos's fanciest place, the Hotel Saint Vrain. Appreciating the smoky liquor I returned a few times to have a drink on my own. In the evenings the bar was illuminated by a stone fireplace and close to its hearth, captain's chairs were reserved for local elders. Seated in their customary circle the men roosted familiar as old birds admiring their rookery.

Nursing a cup of mescal I occupied one of the side chairs frequently enough to be accepted as just another polite listener. Made from the *corazon de tobala*, the heart of the agave, the drink had a subtle kick. I determined, after three cups exactly how much was required before a hinge fell off my gate. Often an Indian elder from the Taos Pueblo would enter, offer each guest an unspoken clasp of the hand, and abruptly leave.

The Saint Vrain served as a mercantile by day; by night it was a hotel for stage passengers boasting four upstairs rooms and its saloon bar. The entrance lobby's floor-to-ceiling mirror was said to be the only one in the territory. Local Tiwa Indians intending to walk in just for a quick glimpse stood transfixed as if their own image was about to leap upon them. When first making my way into the place I paused to study a stranger's reflection, my own. Prominent cheekbones and a straight nose reminded me of my father. I was surprised to see my image loom so grown, and to observe creases feathering a weathered stare. Gazing too long into the mirror created a gap between myself and my image, a ghostly sensation as though my body had been set adrift.

Seated to a side of the flickering room and nursing a distillation the barkeep served as *solamente mescal natural*, I'd listen in on the Saint Vrain patriarchs pronouncements. My ear detected a force to their Spanish, a language seemingly less pedestrian than spoken English. It could flow in a confident river, then growl with throaty rapid-fire flame. My beginning steps toward speaking it proved tolerable in the face of a few amused encounters.

Deeper in the shadows saloon girls keeping a rendezvous knew there was another side to their customers' black jackets, longhorn mustaches, silver manners and sermonizing pronouncements. Many a straight laced Taos patriarch though constantly alert to ensuring his own progeny remained strictly virtuous, habitually enjoyed the services of these available señoritas.

On our only drink together at the hotel, Mister Owens described how on an occasional Sunday he'd pass the local church and hear the padre loudly assailing his congregation's fall from grace. Glancing toward one of the more enticing ladies of the Saint Vrain we concluded that the Taos priest must have failed to sufficiently grease the rusting gates of hell.

Noting how these town fathers snapped their fingers to order either another mescal or another woman, made it easy to guess these macho guardians might react violently toward an interloper's interest in one of their lovely daughters. Lifting a toast to my transfigured miracle in a white dress, I would offer the firelight a secret grin. At that moment damn few of Taos's paternalistic regulations affected me a lick. They should have, but in that hard-watered country, where for so long women had endured a masculine silence, only Dahlia's grace spoke to me.

From our first encounter as she walked away I imagined three foxes playing at the hem of her dress, a throw back to being awakened from mescal beans forced upon me by that Apache medicine man. I heard Shash, too, his appreciative *klook klook klook* somersaulting over giggling Navajo girls.

Later, in my bunk back at the Dobe T, the flavor of our encounter tasted sweet as water from the moon. Had it seemed obvious that I was looking at her or, more obvious, that I was hiding from her looking at me?

Dahlia's satin hair gathered in a bun had loosened a fold as she'd handed over a tea that smelled vaguely of buttery steam rising off fresh-picked corn. She'd only offered me a glance. Her father's hired men had taken instant notice. Nervous as sheep dogs, those two old vaqueros had barely disguised a feigned interest in my saddle's rig.

After thanking my hosts, I'd ridden on, hustling the stock over ruts of remnant ice. Half way to the Dobe T I ran into Joey Lomitas, who was stringing a pack mule. I promised him a pint of Taos Lightning if he'd herd in my strays. It was a simple chore; the steers three-quarter knew the way home, as did the mule. Although Joey was habitually wary, he wasn't shy about accepting a generous offer.

I rode back and hitched my horse inside a copse of willows, deciding to scribble a message on the torn counting sheet I carried as a stock tally. What if the girl spoke only Spanish? Feverish speculation made me feel dangerously visible to a clan of suspicious men. Right now only winter's sparkling darkness was on my side. Trying to withhold its frosty exhalations, I crouched by her garden wall until she came out of the hacienda to shake out a tablecloth.

My hasty whisper startled her. She looked toward the wall separating her home from the Little Rio Grande, then hurried toward me. Announcing her name in response to my own she simply said *Dahlia* and began to turn back toward the house, but I stayed her enough to slip the message into her hands.

Every evening I'd wait below the garden hoping to spot her shadow, sometimes having to flatten in the weeds when men came out of the house, at other times failing to see her at all.

Occasionally men would come out onto the porch to smoke and speak quietly. Once I saw a retainer deliver saddle horses, which two smartly dressed younger men mounted and kicked laughing into the night. I was glad for winter's chill. When the weather turned warm the men would be sitting out in the sundown light and our rendezvous chances would be cooked.

When we did meet we spoke as quickly as we could. Even in these brief exchanges her spoken English contained a curious mix of *Almanac* facts and Biblical phrases from the Song of Solomon. The first writing Dahlia slipped into my hand was copied exactly from the *Almanac:* "A strong mind always hopes and has cause to hope because it knows how slight a circumstance may change the course of human events." The letters were inked with an elegant flourish and I folded them into a tiny square to keep in my hat.

Another exchange that played in my ears was Dahlia's admission that *I am oft waiting for my beloved to be stolen into my garden among the beds of spices.* She also declared after a farewell embrace that I should return and *be of haste that I see your yellow hair once more shining in the dark.* Dahlia's inflected speech vacillated between broken Spanish and fluid statements in an English lilted by fragments of Biblical poetry. The dance of her words began to follow me and I'd find myself repeating them at odd moments, sometimes with a flourish of my reins or tip of the hat to a passing bird.

When I first queried the source of what I delicately described as Dahlia's *sweet language,* she explained that she and her cousin Alicia had derived their English from three books left by Alicia's deceased father. The works were a King James Bible, a *Farmer's Almanac,* and Samuel Worcester's *Third Book for Reading and Spelling,* which had eventually disintegrated from overuse. These texts, combined with everything Alicia had retained from her parent and passed on to Dahlia, composed Dahlia's entire exposure to English.

As my insight into Dahlia's narrative grew it was evident that despite her cloistered life she had been disciplined about creating her own version of an education. Eagerly literate, she disguised her intelligence at home but was overflowing with curiosity.

It soon became apparent how dangerously she was transgressing her father's rule. Wanting to build trust, I'd write her notes containing lines of a song or a poem and eventually sketched a small map. I recall one message:

> Each dusk I ride our secret,
> Through a country of no forgiveness.
> Like you, afraid,
> Like you, unafraid,
> and only our eyes for what is said.

After two months of murmured encounters, several more a sighting than a visit, I arranged a meeting in an abandoned granary, a place suspicious to locals as harboring skeletons of incestuous land deals.

I quickly discovered that Dahlia risked even more than I suspected. There were other intrusions upon her life that aroused suspicion besides a stray bachelor like myself. Ever since General Kearney had led his columns up from Santa Fe and laid claim to the whole territory Taos had been divided. Some families made no secret of their allegiance to a culture higher than the one this garrison of uncultivated *long noses* brought with it. Dahlia's father would have rejected me even if I'd hit town wearing epaulets and gold medals big as wheels.

Seduced more than offended by what they perceived as a Taos aristocracy, some newly-arrived Yankees adopted stylish pretensions themselves. It was not uncommon to spot prominent Americans sporting short-cut button-crowded vaquero jackets, ruffled shirts and scarlet sashes, though most of them usually drew the line at umbrella-brimmed sombreros.

Taos's *fandangos* offered entertaining opportunities for would-be socialites to try on more than just the outward dressings of Spanish elegance. From a cowboy's dusty distance I saw how ambition slips through opportune social cracks to see its face reflected in fancy silverware. I was cool to the idea that elegance demanded such a formal and exclusive parade of old world etiquette. It had pleased me that the frontier freed pilgrims to attempt entry through any door that beckoned. It was in Taos that I first encountered a social hierarchy and observed the manipulations of men anxious to climb its mountain.

Several willing United States representatives, both military and civilian, were eager to attend grandiose "calaveras," roundup barbecues designed to show off vaquero roping skills during feasts embellished by parades of fine horses carrying side-saddle mounted señoritas waving elaborate lace fans.

I was usually directed to attend fiestas as a handler either to herd stock toward its butchering or to assist in skinning those animal presented as a token gift to an established rancher my boss sought to impress.

Admittedly I was always impressed. Local vaqueros were artistic in their creation of braided horse hair "mecates," meaning lead ropes, rawhide "bosals, meaning headstalls, and silver-worked saddle conchos.

The rancher and his sons invariably showed up a little late strutting fine horses. Sporting spurs with rowels big enough to plow dirt, these *caballeros* also flourished sombreros a kid could row.

If there was any impolite deference shown toward what some Americans termed "Spanish corruption" it was usually exhibited by an inflated officer seeking any opportunity to remind everyone that New Mexico Territory was part of *these United States.* Such bluster tended to harden local resistance. To my ear and watching eyes the "New" in "New Mexico" had a long way to go before "cowboy" replaced "vaquero" and local "señoritas" quit wafting fans from their high-stepping horses.

My primary curiosity was about Dahlia's own reaction toward us newcomers. An irritation to her family was that Dahlia had a mind of her own. She'd furtively learned English and refused to ride any way other than astride. It was assumed that as the only and therefor permanently unwed daughter, Dahlia was honor bound to nurture her remaining parent until his death. I gathered from Dahlia that had her father provided a shovel she would have dug him a grave. She was and had been a virtual prisoner enslaved to her father's every whim, and she had emotional as well as visible scars to show for it.

I'd found our meeting place when I helped a Mexican drover wrestle his two wheeled *carretas* out of a ditch. The man, who covertly stored oat bales in the abandoned granary, had nailed a milagro over its doorway. He assured me that this tin image of the Virgin of Guadalupe protected his stored hay from thieves and offered me use of the granary anytime.

The granary's beams, chalky with age, sagged over a hewn floor. A stoop-height entry framed by a timbered door cut into thick adobe walls testified to the early residents' need for protection. The windowless one room granary, originally intended as a storehouse, had later been provided with a stone chimney and fireplace. Covered in layers of flour dust, oat seeds, cobwebs and mice droppings, the interior smelled of aged adobe. Set back from a nearby wagon trail and hidden in the trees, it seemed discreet enough to cover our rendezvous.

I had steadily worked to tidy the interior, sweeping its floor, stacking aside the mule skinner's oats, and gathering pinon and mesquite to start a fire. I hoped a fire might give the room a lived-in character further sweetened by white sage smoke. I viewed my task as purifying a ruin. I also hung a purloined Dobe T oil lantern from a rafter and laid out blankets that I alternatively rolled and unrolled, confused as to which might seem inviting without being inappropriate.

I struggled with unfamiliar feelings. What is it about desire that drives men to become a meal for the gods? Was I of one mind or mindless altogether? With senses so enhanced, which one was seizing me? Dahlia had inspired a reverence assailed by longing. My tumultuous conscience engaged in trials over the ethics of feverish attraction. I'd wordlessly beseech the stars, my horse's mane and the doughy walls of the granary hoping to ease a growing hopelessness that nagged at my belief.

Saloons and passing wagon trains had offered women before. My usually drunken sidekicks would disappear upstairs. One night, after bedding his herd on the outskirts of Bernalillo, Jim Kennedy urged me to join his waiting rambunctious crew. *Son, you are past caught 'tween hay an grass. Quit shaking the feather duster, goddamn it. Show a dollar an buy your life a town. Walk right on up to one of those sassy cat-wagon gals, and she'll ... aw Jesus, boys, take this green kid along and git his lily haunches spurred.*

By the grace of Jim Kennedy's encouragement among the wilderness of saloon decorums I first appreciated solicitations from solicitous women.

Most flourishing saloon establishments employed wares referred to as "upstairs girls," "crib heifers" and "fallen doves." Several of these "joyous sisters," to my eye, begged more of my compassion than passion allowed.

There was one notable example: a languid high-styled beauty whose appeal caused a fellow cowhand to elbow my rude stare although both of us were riveting lizard eyes on her. Celebrated as the "Calico Queen of Las Vegas," this courtesan was close-herded by Silent Joe McKlusky, a notorious gunslinger with dull absent eyes and a restless right hand.

In all the ways that woman moved, which were numerous, some part of me moved along. No wonder McKlusky was so silent except for his six guns. The woman's charms had evidently robbed him of speech in exchange for the honor of being her sole protector.

I was convinced at first sight that the Calico Queen could teach me everything I suddenly wanted to know, and I determined I'd enjoy every instant of it if necessary, to the point of making Silent Joe McClusky's last living moment the loudest he'd ever hear. Thankfully I'd checked my gun at the door along with my brains, so had to watch my Queen flounce upstairs accompanied by three cowboys, not one of them me.

I had developed ease enough to listen to bar girls while they drank, smoked, and teasingly rode herd all over me. Occasionally if business was slow we managed to discover it was our wounds that were truly speaking to one another. By the benefit of these gentle conversations I began to consider myself as fair a judge of a woman as she seemed judge of me. I grew to find warmth and familiarity more seductive than more obvious displays.

My mother, modest as besuited her Quaker upbringing, had left family initiations to be delivered by a husband who'd vanished on the prairie before his son's masculine instincts sprouted. When I did come of an age to be curious, watching giggling Navajo girls aroused powerful feelings in me. Farther along my trail, dancing girls kicking frilly garters had provoked a sensory revolution.

Many a hard-earned cowboy mile leads upstairs courtesy of enough cash to speed the trip. So far I had only once managed to match price and opportunity to my tastes. Constantly short on funds I also lacked the finesse and interest in executing what my fellow cowboys called the "two back dance. "

○

I was hunkering by the hearth, its embers simmering enough to illuminate the walls, when Dahlia de Belardes entered the deserted adobe granary I'd arranged holy as a church.

Dahlia and I had spoken little across her guardian walls, usually in whispers impossibly close to the hacienda, and always after sundown. Afterward, I'd drift home through the brushy gloom seduced by shortcuts even my horse refused. I'd neck-rein my mount onward straight into ditch willows, near foundering us in the crazy dark.

Once I cut it so wrong only a lucky screech turned me back. Under a full moon I looked up toward that familiar cry. The landscape was enough silver lit to sight things unseen in the daytime. I glimpsed the crow folding wings into pinon branches above a coyote looking over his shoulder toward a frozen jackrabbit whose big ears listened hard how not to become coyote. Fortunately my horse insisting her neck against my foolish rein turned us around. Wandering a mile across the sagebrush, I'd forgot where I was going.

Returned in darkness I'd Indian-walk past mounds of sleeping ranch hands. Wrestling ropy blankets I'd smile at truth and innocence, hunt for sleep's unmarked trail and, wandering a wilderness of unknown feelings, conclude that my only destination was toward Dahlia, where upon arrival I'd know them all.

Some mornings I had to scurry to the table bootless and unbuttoned just to grab left overs of a flapjack breakfast. That crew of grins at the table was subtle as a full moon. One morning forking eggs Luke the ranch cook dumped leftover grits onto my plate and snickered *extree grub for extree work*. In the habit of accepting food as given, I ate it all.

No matter what sunrise delivered, those days came for me with the promise they'd always kept. I'd swing into the saddle so spryly the rancher's wife once winked at me from her buggy. I scarce remember doing my Dobe T chores, though there must have been plenty. I was stricken enough to spin yarns but, knowing none, tended to laugh the whiskers off jokes that made even the cook groan.

An enthusiastic presence in a bunk house can irritate some folks. After dinner, whenever I was around, Joey Lomitas would jerk the cards closer to his chest and grimace at my kicking up my heels. Even Tobe Miller, a quiet type from Denver, let his curiosity show its itch. One morning he cornered me checking my mare's feet in the corral and hinted, *It ain't usually account of some need to see the stars a feller wakes up of a night an quits his blankets.*

To which intrusion I answered, *Nor either to meet an asshole being that there's usually one close at hand.* Tobe fell back on being quiet. I had to reassure him later, though I should have done so in plainer bunkhouse terms, that my brusqueness was only in response to unsolicited opinions. Tobe puzzled over "brusqueness" but was pleased to hear my apology.

My compadres weren't the only ones sawing their bits. Kept saddled long after quitting time, even my horse's impatient tail cut a swathe through my secret.

Any news is tricky to keep from a small leaky town. Dahlia could usually leave the hacienda only to shake crumbs from a table cloth, gather sprigs of herbs, or brush out her hair. I told her I'd wished her *brush was a snail* and her *braid long as a river* because we scarce had time to hold hands. But my impatience was merely a prisoner of table crumbs, whereas Dahlia endured boot-lick hell. A prevailing fear of her father since childhood had banished her life to its innermost senses. I'd watch her disappear and imagine her tiptoeing wary as a deer inside her own house. As she turned hastily away I'd catch her eye reflecting sparks from the glistening frost. I admired the courage she wore as our noble secret. Later along the cattle trail, squinting through dust, I'd savor Dahlia's bravery like a mountain spring. Whatever kept her spirit alive was welcome to my heart.

Growing up a son of the wilderness, I rarely saw an animal hesitate to follow its instincts. Each creature held to its own unfaltering way. Over the short-grass prairie, through hardwood forest and across rivers and mountains, each trip had conditioned me to track desire to its source. Now that longing lead me somewhere I'd never traveled, it made Dahlia's arrival seem luminous as a dream.

She'd had to wait until her brothers, gone on a cattle deal, had left her and her cousin, Alicia to care take the old man.

I was hunkering by the hearth, its embers simmering enough to illuminate the granary, when Dahlia stepped inside.

Free, and perhaps only now realizing the weight of her actions, she paused inside the granary door. Together for the first time although strangers to so much of one another, we felt protected by a cloak of intimacy. Impressively, Dahlia wasn't hesitant, and there was a calming essence to her ease.

Our first touch was a fingertip dance. *At last my beloved,* she said.

I almost lost my feet.

Careful, Dahlia whispered.

Recovering, in an accidental waltz, feeling the brushed moment of our lips, I took both her wrists. Dahlia's cheekbones, white shift, and long braid seemed authentic to the granary as its hewn *vigas,* thick adobe walls, and peeling *lattias.*

Challenging a ferocity of mistrust, Dahlia had stepped outside her culture irretrievably as a stone thrown through its church's stained glass. With so many boundaries pressing upon us we stood a long moment, silenced by fear and exultant tenderness.

When we drew close, intertwined in an arc of desire, I guided us toward the blankets. Casting its silhouette upon the seed-dusted walls, our embrace seemed fleetingly giant, but instinct assured me ours was a dance of sweet shadows.

Dahlia exuded perfumes of combed wool, cumin, and winter frost. Her hair was so long I could fold its braid in my hand and draw it gently to my lips. In my embrace Dahlia was wildly transported. It was her passion that held us, insisting, insisting, until we lay quieted in the lamp's flickering. In that old granary's half light I felt alive in a faith that whatever Adam once lost had been found and it was bounty enough.

In the calm afterglow where eyes make a lover's treaty, once we found our voices, it was to address Señor de Belardes' rule of daughterly obedience. Despite her efforts with English, a study she'd embraced as a rebellious demarcation between herself and her father's restraints, Dahlia had despaired of escaping her sequestered life.

Every night, she avowed, *like the sister of Solomon I sleep but my heart waketh to hear your voice. I am afraid that my father an my brothers will know and become very bad to us.*

Then we must leave, I said. There are places where we can be free.

Free. Like this. Dahlia lifted the blankets to smile at our nakedness, then her face grew somber. *If my father find about us my brothers will kill thee an sent me to a place far away. My father swear if he hear me speak English any more he will cut off my tongue.*

Dahlia you've always been in Ranchos. Beyond the mountains, there is plenty more country. Do you ride?

Always. Some horses are my frens more than peoples.

Good. We can travel. In time your father will give up looking and maybe then we can return and show we have been honorably sworn to one another.

You no comprendo what is in English compr—

Understand.

Gracias. You no understan. My father's wishes go everywhere. If peoples no respect him his sons do what he want. For my brothers to kill you is nada. A stranger who look like you make fire in my brother's eyes. They will say you are a no good man an just come into my chambers to feast among the lilies.

Feed among lilies?

Yes, this in the Bible how to say a man is kissing the woman in her secret places.

And "chambers?"

Chambers is where King Solomon bed is green and cedar and fir are the walls like in this granero and where his beloved waits for her man whose hair is like gold to tell her she is his vineyard an her breasts are white towers where dove birds fly to him an—

Okay I see, yes chambers but your father is not in the Bible; he is here in Ranchos and I should go to him and ask permission.

No. No. Quicker you take a pistola here, Dahlia pressed her hand to my breast. *My father's sister, when I tell her, advise me to say to you go away. My father tole the priest after my mother died his daughter was sent by God to be always marry to his house.*

Could your aunt tell your father?

No. No. It is in her adobe behind the Ranchos church that Alicia an myself read our books an speak in English. Alicia's father was not Spanish but my father always think my aunt's husban is speaking only Spanish. All these years my father think I visit my aunt to learn woman things. My aunt told me her brother threaten to kill her husban. One day her husban say he going to Santa Fe but never come home. Alicia learn her father's English an we always played speaking it because it make us happy being bad.

Listening to Dahlia I felt the wingbeat of my lost crow Shash and the voices of those Bosque Redondo nuns who had banished me, images from my past that now had returned in the form of Dahlia's family to exile me again. Noting an absence in my expression, Dahlia rolled onto an elbow and kissed my eyes. *Don't fly away, my beloved,* she said.

I'm here, I murmured, nibbling her ear.

You like tasting my ears?

Yes.

I know.

You know what I like?

Love knoweth everything.

Nobody knows everything.

I do after you have done with me all what I wanted and what you wanted and my mind feels quiet like when the sun touch my face like thou lips on my ears.

Thou lips? Or, "your" lips I asked.

Both, she replied, and this response made an end to my correcting Dahlia about using *thou, thee,* and other phrases from the Song of Solomon. I learned to quell my irritation to appreciate their poetry.

Before sunrise I gave Dahlia a gift of silver conchos and walked her to the river road where I swore I'd figure out a way for us to leave Taos. As I watched her willowy figure fade away down the rutted trace, an emerging dawn seemed to explain everything I needed to know. I had a sense of possessing answers to questions I'd never need ask again, an ownership uncannily close to an awareness of death. Barely twenty, I shivered with trepidation that my years were too few to understand a completion growing within me.

After that night we shared only one ominous day in the hills when Dahlia risked following me up the mountain above Taos. Neither of us dismounted. We were both subdued as though the Indian pueblo, its cotton trees, and ponies counting their feet in the pastures knew our union was exposed. As we steadied our horses, I pressed Dahlia to run away with me. *I have money and a good horse for you. Gather your things and I will wait by the granary.*

Dahlia rose in her stirrups and shook her head. *I listen behind the door. My brother say my father has made for me a confession time with the priest at the Ranchos church. He say they must punish me for making the people murmur bad things about our family. It is you must go, Devon, go before my brothers find where you are.*

All the more reason to leave now, I insisted, and tried to take her reins. Dahlia's response was to spin her horse around and plead with a tear stained face. *I cannot my beloved, I cannot. If I leave they will hurt Alicia an maybe her mother and the Pueblo will laugh behind my father and then my brothers must make a big revengeance for their honor. No. Devon, for now it is you who must go. We must say goodbye until another time, maybe after my father is gone.*

Dahlia was sobbing as I followed her between the pinon toward the flats and the wagon route that wound through Taos. When we hit the wider road Dahlia kicked her horse into a gallop and made a lot of dust. Aware that passing locals were watching, Dahlia turned her horse and desperately waved me off. Grasping the consequences for her I turned my horse and walked in the opposite direction toward the Dobe T. On my way back I tried to figure out why neither of us knew how our secret got out. My best guess was that one of Dahlia's aunt's circle had read the signs. In any village wise women, noting how another's fingers pause between woven strands, often suspect a secret is holding the yarn.

Back among the gloom of cowboy sleepers I lay staring into the dark, imagining Dahlia appearing to me, a specter risen from hope.

In the hard swept confines of her father's house Dahlia's solitude was more cramp than reverie. Since her mother's passing she'd had the needs of a demanding family on her hands. Her father was known in Ranchos as a *cabellero* of irreversible morality. He sat close to the fire, on the edge of his high-backed rawhide chair, both hands clasping his hickory cane.

Dahlia's father was all commands to her willful brothers who, in turn, commanded her. Kindling morning's sticks, only lately did Dahlia dare imagine her figure dancing in their flames. She'd shape the ashes upon the hearth as if painting secret images before sweeping them away, and told me in tearful surrender *now I only sweep away your name.*

Dahlia suspected her father and brothers had detected a growing distance. This only made them urge her more coldly to their plates, to their woven shirts, vaquero jackets, and tall boots she polished into sentries of ready obedience. In Ranchos where old families were clusters of grapes bound for one cask, Dahlia's secret life was shared only with ashes, ice-bent trees, and winter birds gathering her crumbs. She sang back to the flock, seeding their songs with messages banished humans deliver to air.

A day and a night after we'd parted on the mountain I had risked a visit to her and discovered my gift of silver conchos wrapped in a cloth beneath the hacienda garden wall. Suspicious and alarmed, I left the returned gift where it lay. The next morning I rode out to the plaza, where the townspeople gather every Sunday, and hid in a collapsed adobe that stood alongside the Ranchos church.

Too clearly her family had not come for something other than regular mass. As I watched, Dahlia's brothers dragged their sister out of the confessional and held her in the wagon before whipping it down the road toward Santa Fe. I almost leaped from that niche with a drawn pistol but the armed men around Dahlia were as steady in the way they controlled her as they were in checking their horses. Dahlia slumped on the wagon seat, her cropped hair testament to a priest who stood on the steps with his hands clasped more by mutilation than contrition.

I watched Dahlia's figure sink into the distance and, hurrying to my horse, rode out above Taos figuring to track the spring wagon. Soon spotting one of her brothers, rifle at the ready, I reined into cover.

Deciding to return to the Dobe T and grab my rifle, my pursuit was slowed by the winding return route through the foothills. I decided to turn back and risk riding to

Alicia's house, hoping she knew where her cousin was being taken.

I cantered down the narrow dirt road behind Alicia's hacienda, dismounted, climbed the garden's adobe wall, and tapped on a back door.

Although we had never met, Alicia immediately knew who I was. She paled as she stepped onto the garden path, a forefinger pressed to her lips.

I'm—

Si, si. I know, she whispered. *Shshsh, Dahlia's father is in there.*

Where is— I began, but from within the house a man's voice frightened her. I tried to grab Alicia's wrist before she slipped away after whispering to me: *Mission Santa Ines, in California.* Hearing steps behind the door I climbed back over the wall to my horse and made my way back to the Dobe T repeating *Mission Santa Ines, California. Mission Santa Ines, California.*

Kneeling by my bunk for the rifle, I was pulled to a nasty halt by a reata that had been neatly arranged on my blankets. The coiled noose had a long braid of shining hair tied to it by a rawhide string.

I hunted through the deserted bunkhouse. The cowboys were likely in town. Perhaps it had saved my life to have missed the delivery, but I was too heart sick to care. Untying Dahlia's braid from the rope I vowed: "one day I will see long hair flowing down your shoulders again."

I might have been better served if I'd picked up and started down the trail after Dahlia right there and then. But, discreetly asking the cook about the trip to California, I was told, *Hell son, that's far side of the country. Feller'd need considerable of a stake to venture it. When Kit Carson's company done it back in 1829 he claimed they had to cross a thousand mile of hot sand. Some men wuz driven to drink their own leakage. Trip'd likely kill any man crazy enough to attempt it on his own.*

Fatefully I made the decision to briefly stay on at the Dobe T to fatten my stake, and this decision had led to me shooting Rusty Cuellar. Hounded by the consequences of his death and pulled by my determination to find Dahlia de Belardes, my choices had narrowed to the point that right now I was looking over my shoulder a lot more than I was looking toward California.

○

Past halfway to Wagon Mound under a crescent moon my mare snorted as she picked her way along a fence line. We'd spooked three antelope whose haunches flared white as they tried to skid under the wire: funny, antelope sure hate to jump a fence. Even in the dark some try to skid under.

A pair of nighthawks fluttered ahead and a chorus of coyotes bragged from their separate outposts before quitting with a collective howl. The country was beginning to flatten, silhouettes of mountain ranges faded to the south. A pine needle scent off the high country was morphing to the dry musk of treeless plain. I dismounted at a stick-gate marker, untwisted its three strands of wire, led my mount through, braided the wire back in, propped back the stick, and walked on.

I rode the rest of the night numb to distance, dreaming myself aboard a giant animal tossing its neck toward the edge of the world. I'd lost Dahlia and maybe killed a man from the ache of it and felt hunted no matter how much I revisited the odds. My situation appeared fixed as walls of any cell that always add up four.

In gray dawn I spotted peaks of the big Wagon Mound, a landmark outcropping that gave the town its name. I recalled the last time I saw it was with my mother when we quit the Mormon wagon train and went on to Bosque Redondo.

This far down slope the frost had quit and dewy gramma grass and yellow and blue flowers poked through sparse hoof-beaten soil. Cattle were beginning to add up in scattered herds and a few quail hustled back from granary cradles where they'd scratched a living. Smoke braided into the early air above the string of buildings perched beneath the landmark cathedral of rock where wagon trains bucking west made the big swing south to Santa Fe.

I could skirt town or take a chance and ride in. Spring meant gathering herds so maybe I'd get lucky and pick up a job moving cattle. A few hard scrabble ranchers in Wagon Mound ran a herd of mixed stock, some of it gleaned one or two at a time from penniless wagon-train immigrants.

I'd already spotted a mix of *Corrientes* and *Brahmas* crossed with original stock from the old *cimmarones*—longhorn remnants of Spanish herds. If winter feed had held maybe these fattening cows would need to be trailed some place. I clucked my horse but she'd caught the lazy musk of settlement and broke into a canter. We bypassed a fence line and continued uphill into the town, passing outlying sod cabins that marked where earlier settlers had tried to make a stand.

Wagon Mound had been fancy in its time. Newcomers sensing profit from passing wagon trains and boomers, prospectors and trappers had dug in. Then the war came and soon prospecting and trapping played out. Now there was only one livery, a reputable dry goods store, and a saloon and hotel that bragged a painted facade above twisted porch supports whose gilt faded into a red-and-turquoise peel. Between these original fronts sat a blacksmith, a saddlery, a bathhouse, and a window under a blue-and-white sign that announced Western Union Telegraph and Cable Office.

A few hitched ponies drooped outside the hotel alongside a spring wagon that rocked behind its mule munching a feed sack. The rutted front street had only one side built up. Maybe no prospective builder had the heart to spoil the view toward the mountains. This gave the place a lopsided setting as though, looking hard east, the town anticipated unwelcome arrivals, drought, blizzards or, worse, nothing at all.

Barely a decade before Wagon Mound had bustled with buffalo skinners, mountain men, teamsters, and curious Indians, a mixed trade that brought shining times and rough pleasures. Nowadays, paused on a western edge of the prairie, Wagon Mound's faded elegance, smaller and quieter, only served to heighten the arrival of a solitary stranger.

I bypassed the livery, tied my horse at the saloon rail, and walked up the street past a dry goods store. At the telegraph office I nodded at a nervous clerk who turned down my greeting with an abrupt stare, sign that I was maybe going to have to seek quick employment. Realizing my haste must be nerves because, no rider could have arrived ahead of me, I turned and walked back toward the ponies, all under working rigs, hitched in front of the saloon.

Forking stand-up breakfasts, five cowboys leaned on the long bar of The Success saloon. A barkeep was pouring coffee and a deep-eyed woman in a floozy hat swept suet across a floor ivoried more by over eager care than age.

The bar, tables, and stiff-backed Spanish chairs were waxed to a luster. The establishment reeked of cordovan wax, treated leather, and sweet trade-whisky beneath fresher hints of coffee, stogie smoke, and bacon grease.

Despite its strict and almost formal tidiness, the Success seemed a cozy saloon. I pushed up to the bar and tapped a spur against its footrail. Hearing me, the barkeep slid a mug down the line and poured me coffee, adding, *Stranger's first mud comes free.*

Could use it, I replied, startled by my own voice. I cat-lipped the hot coffee and discreetly attempted to spot who was who.

The cowboys appeared to be of one brand. Gathered with an easy enthusiasm, scooping breakfast, they elbowed one another, joking over a twisted cheroot they passed around. An older hook-nosed man in a short-brimmed hat looked to be foreman. The hands squinted easily to this boss and to one another, feeling cavalier as cowmen do when common work offers them a corral.

Breakfast? The barkeep refilled my mug.

Like to find a way to it.

Don't have to feel permanent about being broke. The saloon keeper walked down the bar and thumbed the older man in my direction. *Hey Jack, another cowboy looking for the ready.*

By the way he jumped to fix a break in any moment's general spin the barkeep was likely the hub of Wagon Mound's wheel. His town was an island both on the prairie and among surrounding Spanish settlements, many still cool to the "Norte Americanos."

The man in the short brim lifted his mug and walked toward me. The rancher's ease spoke of familiarity with hiring men at the rail. Stub spurs heeled to his boots, he thumb dived a canvas four-pocket vest and balanced saddle-stained chaps over one shoulder. He paused to measure me before stepping in. *Jack Rice. Welcome to Wagon Mound. Guess the barkeep has been here long enough to direct strangers. He claims one day he's gonna run for mayor. God forbid.*

When we shook Rice gripped my hand long enough to study my eyes, a style I appreciate when measuring a man.

You got a rig solid enough to trail cows?

Yes sir.

You scarce appear old enough to scrape your face.

I've got a good mount hitched out front.

Aw righty. Let's take a look.

We pushed through the saloon doors. Outside the man walked one hand around my horse bending once to check a fore foot. When he was done he patted Saloon's neck, slid my rifle back into its scabbard and gave the forward cinch a quick pull. *Yellow Boy repeater.*

Yup. Long barrel. I half-lifted the rifle up to the trigger guard so he could see how its action was shiny clean.

Should do it. Got shells?

Dozen's about all.

Where'd you git that Mex saddle horn? It'd take a week to dally that frying pan. He paused, leaned a shoulder into the horse, and bent its left fore leg with one hand. *You always ride a bare hoof?*

Indians don't use shoes was my offered excuse.

Don't use money neither. Soft prairie is liable to grow a horse a nasty toenail. Got a rasp?

Nope. I used the ranch tack working down in Taos. As we walked back into the saloon his queries continued, in a less dubious tone.

Ever trail cows?

With the Jim Kennedy outfit. Pushed a gather of over two thousand head.

Kennedy huh. How long?

About four weeks.

Guess that's a shade longer than breakfast, he muttered just quietly enough to be heard. Rice had prairie sky-eyes that had seen enough but seldom missed a thing.

As Jack Rice turned toward the rail the chaps slipped off his shoulder. When he straightened up from their retrieval the trail boss was stern. *Got a heavy dew on you, mister, and that pony looked hard pushed. You in a special hurry?*

Not anymore I ain't.

Making up his mind Rice measured me again. *We're fixing to head up the Santa Fe Trail then skirt the Cross Timbers along the*

Arkansas toward Ellsworth. Army is half-assed chasin Indians back onto reserves. Some bands got other ideas. I've cumshawed my way past the Kiowa but dealin with Comanche on the prod is another thing altogether. If you're still interested I pay a drop off price equal to four beeves delivered. Could be more than eighty dollars. This trip is a one-way ride for me. I got a daughter near your age getting married back in St. Louis.

What about water out there?

A few Buffalo wallows and late-spring cricks should get us between rivers. How are you with that rifle? He asked.

Got accurate barking squirrels with my daddy's .32 Lancaster.

Squirrels don't shoot back.

Sure eat good though.

A hint of a smile crossed Jack Rice's face. *Devon, is it? Head on down to the dry goods store. Tell him it's on my ticket. Get a hoof rasp. A box of shells. Grain that played-out pony of yours. I'll deduct it.*

Rice turned to the barkeep. *Shady, feed this feller. Hope you don't smoke, son. We ran this place out of tobacco.*

The barman's four eggs, steak, and corn dodger tasted as fine a meal as was ever vanished. Rice's trail crew stomped out nodding *howdy* as they passed. Two of the younger men seemed brothers, sporting similar new scarves and boots. Lacking pistols and chaps they acted nervously polite. By their black missionary coats, basin hats, and homespun, collarless shirts, I figured them for Mormon boys.

Another was a tall, rawboned Texan under a big brim and clinking a set of wagon wheel spurs. With hands hard as oak knots, tight-fit chaps, a grip-stained Navy Colt, well-knuckled nose, and creased unshaven face, he looked plenty broke in.

The fourth, named Socorro, was a man Jack Rice later described as a genuine throwback Californio. I'd never seen the like. His long hair cinched back by a rawhide knot, the fellow wore a *poblano* hat over a silk head kerchief and tooled buckskin gaiters wrapped over high boots. He also sported a fringed woolen poncho slung blanket style and giant set of jingle bobs. The vaquero's baggy-sleeved shirt and piercing eyes reflected a deal more than style. He also carried a bowie knife in his sash. I concluded anyone attached to breathing might pause twice before judging this character just some greenhorn in a fancy rig.

The men stumped out eager to be in the saddle, which was just fine by me. I counted five cowboys, six of us all told. Not much of a crew given the odds of running into trouble. That spring pushing cows through Indian country was altogether in the wrong direction. Wagon trains were stacking up outside Independence as a rush of settlers long held up by the war were halted by threats of renegade Indians.

Even on the fringes of Taos it wasn't uncommon to find cows skinned along the trail, critters that belonged to you only a short day before. Indians were good at what they did, whether crawling up on buffalo under a wolf skin or stealing cattle under the nose of a night rider.

The Comanches were dedicated warriors who ruled the Gran Comancheria, a vast reach of plains where, raiding from their mountain fastness, they'd earned a ferocious reputation. The Comanche had pushed other tribes as well as most cattlemen out of their territory. There were attempted exceptions to this rule primarily because it was a determination of some drives never to turn back. A cowboy seldom had anywhere to return to. A cowboy was contracted to momentum. His future lay over the next ridge, across the next river, and hopefully arrived, intact and paid, at the next corral. My newly acquired cowboy destiny, risky as it might prove, troubled me less than the posse at my back.

I slung down my coffee and glanced in the bar mirror. It was early, but another night would come quickly enough. Before sleep I'd recalled whooping with joy under those Ranchos cottonwoods after another meeting with Dahlia. Too soon after I had faced the darker side of joy when Dahlia was taken away from me.

On our last day together Dahlia had lied her way free and ridden a borrowed horse up where the mountain overlooked Taos Valley. The bottoms had been flooding and there were melting snow patches under pinon on the slopes. We'd passed a line of Taos pueblo men on a medicine walk down from Blue Lake who had made us feel invisible like Indians do when they want to let someone know who really belongs.

I'd lit us a small pinon fire. Listening, to Dahlia, I tried to catch a few hopeful words but they were as sad as her eyes. I sensed that she was holding something back. I tried to lever it out of her but she shrugged off my query. I was reminded sorrow had been with her a long time before I had. Very soon afterward she was taken away to California.

Much of what I'd heard about California was more story than fact. Certainly the possibility of gold always cropped up. Before the war, men took ship around the Horn to snipe a pound of nuggets a day from Sierra creeks. It was said first-come prospectors had gotten rich for life. I'd heard there were fish in the Pacific sea bigger than an ox team and wagon, golden-haired women running naked on the sand, hills teeming with wild cattle, and giant trees that took a week to cut down. In addition there were the usual yarns of milk and honey: water clear as air, sun all year long, grass high as a man's head, ships of the distant world off-loading goods nobody had seen before. Shining times all around.

California had a glow. I'd never seen an ocean, much less a tribe of blonde women who don't wear clothes. It was a long trick to travel that far west. There was the old Spanish Trail, much of it desert and much of it unmarked. Until I hooked up with Socorro, the Californio working for Jack Rice's outfit, I'd never met anyone who'd actually seen the Pacific Ocean. I had a heart full of reasons to see it now.

I finished my coffee, said thanks to Shady, and nodded a polite *adios* to his back bar mirror. Reflections make me nervous. Living outside month after month and then suddenly spotting my own face following me was a reminder of somebody on my trail. Small wonder Indians don't trust mirrors.

○

My father considered *rest an honest measure of a decent life*. Mine was becoming increasingly haunted. I'd thrown down against the back wall behind the Wagon Mound livery, listening to my restless horse kick its planks. Before sleep I recited *Santa Ines, California*, a place and name that had become a bedtime prayer.

The previous evening I'd climbed the big mound and loafed above town figuring to stay out of sight in case the Taos pueblo trackers had traced my destination. At dawn I saddled my rested pony and plodded out toward the gathering point. When I hit the flattened grass a few jackrabbits sampling wild turnips took off. It was a cloudless blue day, and the air tasted like silver.

Jack Rice's outfit, except the Texan and the Californio, had been collected from the Wagon Mound saloon. There were post Civil War assurances of wealth and commerce pushing toward New Mexico Territory but old man Rice wasn't heeding the call. Tired of wasting time wrangling local beef prices, Rice was bucking the tide and heading back East. It was easy to see the independence in him. My new boss, sure in his movements and with penetrating blue eyes, likely seldom turned back from decisions he lived by.

The cagey herd, lowering and wall-eyed, was spread out untidily. They were prime critters with dewlaps flabby as retired bankers. A good longhorn steer worth fifteen to twenty dollars brought four times that to Kansas speculators eager to promote a growing market for anything that hung sinew in Eastern teeth. The Comanche tended to sell cattle they stole and enjoyed horsemeat over beef.

As I approached Jack raised a swamp-barreled .52 Sharps and waved me from the saddle. *Devon. Tib. Socorro?* The rancher lifted the piece toward any taker. The two Rim Rock boys stayed back. I dismounted and eyed the others. The rancher shook the piece to drum up interest in three cowboys all too polite to step up and shoot first.

I aim to keep my herd, so one of you boys is gonna have to take down game on this drive. Way I have it the best shot gets to hunt and earn choice cut too.

Rice caressed the heavy Sharps and wet its sight. *This looks like history and it's slow to load but shoots reasonably flat. There's three Remington rolling blocks in the chuck wagon if, God forbid, we need em.*

Hunting ahead of the herd seemed an opportunity to skip eating dust. I figured myself a decent enough shot.

The rancher unhooked a mochila off his saddle horn, stepped off a hundred paces, and hung the gnawed leather pouch on a mesquite bush. *Make sure there's nothing moving in your line of sight,* Jack directed. *Everybody shoots off hand. None of this prone business, else we'll be here all day.*

The rancher handed Tib the Sharps and dropped a rawhide pouch dimpled with slugs. The Texan loaded the breech, sighted with one eye closed, inhaled, and squeezed. The rifle offered its deep-throated report. We all squinted hard toward the mochila. Tib had missed.

Jack Rice looked to the Californio then to me.

As a boy I'd first shot an antiquated Kentucky squirrel gun longer but lighter at .36 caliber. Later I'd appreciated the power, speed, and accuracy that arrived with cartridges. The windage of the Sharps was notched on its second step. The butt pad was worn and the buckhorn sights rust-tipped. The piece had a long hammer pull. I shouldered the stock, took aim with both eyes, exhaled slowly, and eased the trigger. The mochila flipped off the bush and flew back several feet.

Looks like we got a turkey shoot on our hands, Jack said, and we watched him walk out to the mochila where he stopped to finger a hole in the pouch before hanging it again. He lifted his hat and moved out of Socorro's line of sight.

Socorro's arms rose quickly in a fluid movement and his shot knocked the mochila off the branch.

When the Californio handed me the rifle I caught the wince of a smile on his lips.

My second try missed. I knew it even as I squeezed the shot off. A good sight requires you hold steady all the way through. I had let go thinking I was on target instead of just staying on it and not thinking about being on it. My father claimed *a clear shot comes from getting yourself out of the way,* advice I suspected had more applications than to just a steady aim.

Socorro swung up and sighted. This time I saw him slightly drop the barrel as he triggered the gun. The mochila didn't budge.

You dropped that shot, I blurted.

Si. As you say, Socorro admitted, handing over the Sharps.

I slipped another slug into the breech and while sighting quietly asked. *Why?*

Somethin in my eyes.

The sun?

A memory was all he said, evading my glance.

I took my shot and watched that mochilla flip over the sagebrush. Jack Rice came toward us making plans every step of his walk.

As for hunting I'd need to be alert for watering holes, thickets, and gullies that offer cover. Antelope were common but stringy. Buffalo was more popular.

I was beginning to imagine the possibilities of an enemy. I'd seen wagons rumble into Taos carrying dead and wounded cavalry. Bloodied, those troopers looked as though they'd visited hell and returned humbled, chastened, and grateful just to spit.

Socorro approached me to shake hands. *Socorro Alvaro Diego Requelme.* The vaquero pointed at the Sharps. *Si. Memories. One is how a heavy piece slow my horse. Also if a man is pick to hunt, he work for the cook. I cannot understand our cook. He speak like he got hay in his mouth.*

At least the man was honest about not wanting to carry the Sharps. *Thanks for missing.* I grinned. *Next time we shoot for a job, I might have a memory too. My name is Devon Young.*

Encantado, a pleasure, Deevong.

Socorro, Old-World formal, attempted to speak with such care that I hadn't the heart to correct my name.

Our start continued to get better. It proved impressive to watch the Californio do just about anything. A practiced ease gave him a quick and alert eye. He certainly looked smooth in the saddle and avoided dismounting as though it was a failure of manners. I saw him reach down and grab a buffalo chip off the ground at a full gallop and throw it just to startle a rider who was dozing off. Anytime something startled the herd Socorro was first to announce, *Is nada amigos. It is nothing.*

We shooters caught up with the herd, let the cows string out, and sorted ourselves into place. A few of the cows had lain down and it was time to consider them fed and ready to go. The Mormon boys took both flanks. Socorro roamed forward and kept an eye on our small remuda.

The Californio's liver stallion sported a tooled Spanish saddle. The Texan was less considered; worn to many a herd he was molded into a double rigged mother hubbard saddle. Under his wind-bent brim, wearing wrist guards and big-heeled boots, he appeared pure southern plains. In contrast, wearing homespun shirts and black hats, both mormons, eighteen or nineteen at most, were new to the trail and tended to hang back and keep their own peace.

Socorro had his own mounts. His big stallion and a long-tailed flourish of a mare that lifted her feet as if escaping hot coals. Riding Saloon I once tried racing his stallion for fun, but Socorro reined in after he took a big lead before circling back and slyly tipping his hat.

The Texan and the old man had taken swing by the time I took my place in the drag to begin shaping up our slow complaining herd that had walked along all morning.

Following the cattle's languid behinds, I was also assigned to keep our back-trail covered. The Taos posse had already conditioned me for the task. Hell, if an ant from my past had shown up I'd have spotted it. I'd been paying such close attention I'd developed a swivel neck.

Keeping rear-guard my horses and I worked out a rhythm. We'd amble along at herd speed. Every mile or so as I guessed the distance I'd give Saloon a kick, circle around to scan our back trail, then return to the drag. I'd worked only three days at this habit before Saloon learned to break off on her own impulse. After the break for noon chuck I tried other horses. I found one smart enough to keep time. She was a paint mare with a piebald left eye that told me she might be jumpy which proved true, but when she did spook the horse was a good runner and could sense distance as well as Saloon.

Before buying Saloon I'd had plans about acquiring a better horse. Top of my list would be any one of the three Apaloosas I'd seen. I was told the breed is a rare presence so far east of the rainy mountains in the Palouse River country. Possessed of great stamina, Apaloosas are also called "iron horses." To get one requires a big trade, likely in exchange for a plenty sparkling woman, a stack of prime buffalo robes and a year's supply of everything it takes to be human. I was fortunate to see examples of these spectacular spotted Indian steeds.

The three Apaloosas I encountered had probably been stolen from another tribe who in turn had probably raided them from the Nez Perce. They were ridden by three bonneted Brule Sioux chiefs sporting eagle feather bonnets. As a sign of their peaceful intentions, approaching our wagons the chiefs zig-zagged or "snake walked" their horses. Although willing to accept our offer of tobacco those Indians wouldn't even dismount, never mind consider trading an Apaloosa for the barrel of whisky, two repeater rifles, and the mountain of frew-fraw our wagon master piled on the grass.

The entire contents of my saddle bag were well shy of the price of a fancy Apaloosa. Back in Santa Fe, I'd swapped for my mare the two remuda ponies

Kennedy's trail boss had given me. She was a fair cutting horse, responsive to the rein with a nice soft walk and willingness to be bridled on a chilly morning. I tried out several names for her and settled on "Saloon." I guessed it was a name to her liking by the prick of her carved ears. When I wasn't riding Saloon I saddled the piebald mare and simply called her "Horse," as in, *Horse, you have a heart like a mountain, Horse, you sure are a good listener, Horse, it's good you have a mind when mine is on holiday.* There was nobody else to talk to back there eating dust until my tongue became an old shoe.

After awhile, even though the "Horse" belonged to Jack Rice, I determined to name her Agate, because of a swirl in her eye. The other remuda stock, dominantly late-cut geldings, would nip if they smelled she'd been around Socorro's stallion. When a mare came into season we had to string her behind the chuck wagon. Socorro was forced to double-hobble and picket his randy stallion more than once.

We'd make ten or fifteen miles a day, more if it was over a worn trail where a buffalo herd had opened the ground between swathes of sagebrush. Hitting such bare spots late in the day the herd drifted off course to seek better grass. There were few signs of buffalo and consequently the graze was mostly untouched wherever we stopped. I noted how a cattle herd's progress left a scarred and compacted trail, courtesy of cloven feet and close cropping much more damaging to the prairie than a buffalo's spongy hoof imprint and grazing habits.

I hoped to see another big herd. So far I'd only spotted a lone bull dusting his hide and a stray trio of bachelor bulls roiling a water hole. Such buffalo wallows are a prairie saloon for many animals, many of them predators who benefit from critters attracted to water.

An hour or so into our second morning the trail boss dropped back. We rode and walked, following yearlings and anxious mothers bunched in the drag.

Best way to move cattle fast is slow, Jack Rice observed.

I sure heard that before, I said.

Ever been up to Kansas?

No sir. Came close well east of here with the Lazy D outfit.

Rode that way a time or two myself. Seven years back, in the Texas coast country. We made a herd that took half a drought winter to corral. Must have been a million wild longhorns multiplied in those thorny breaks after Texans went off to fight. You could gather all the ridgebacks you wanted. We started north with around two thousand head. Those vacas was quick to smell you and run for the nearest thicket or charge dipping them big nasty horns. We lost horses to those wicked boogers. Drop two or three loops on a big bull and he'd still try to kill us. Thorn brush, cactus and plenty rattlesnakes. We were up the trail scarcely a week when Comanches scattered the herd and killed three men. Five of us rode back to Texas dead broke and started all over. Rice picked up a buffalo chip and bounced it off a yearling trying to duck out from the drive. *You read, son?*

My mother taught me and anybody else nearby who wanted to learn.

Way you move when you speak tells me you been around hand-talking Indians enough to acquire the habit.

My mother was a school teacher to the Indians in Fort Sumner. Maybe I grew up part Navajo.

Read this. Rice reached into his vest and unfolded a wad of paper. *This came down the wire the morning I hired you. According to Sheriff Guitterez, some cowboy shot his man over in Taos. I was sending a message myself. This was posted on the territorial board. Telegraph clerk claimed he saw a young stranger with yeller hair come into Wagon Mound yesterday. My guess is, he saw you.*

Scanning the telegram, I saw no point in denying my identity. *It was a bad end to a contentious card game.*

A duel?

Hardly organized enough to be called that.

Who's the feller?

His name is, um, was, Rusty Cuellar.

You plugged Rusty Cuellar?

I did.

Then was it at least a fair fight?

Rusty halfway offered to shake hands then drew on me.

Rice nodded as though justice was done. *Sounds like that feller's style.*

You knew him?

Knew of him. Started an argument with one of my men and was about to back shoot the feller but Socorro laid him low. When Cuellar came around, we had to listen to his whining. It boiled down to me buying the sheriff off.

We remounted and walked our horses on. The country flattened and rolled as last peaks of the Sangre de Cristos mountains dipped far out of sight and eroded ground forced us to skirt another run-off gully.

You're two ways unlucky, Jack Rice continued. *It ain't as easy to outrun law like the old days. Telegraph line been run up from Santa Fe though it was cut some of the year. Indians roping down the poles. Second, Guitterez is someway a relative to Rusty. Half of Taos spreads their cards on the same blanket. I'd take a hot iron and burn that town off your map. If Guitterez's boys caught you they'd string you up in that plaza where Kit Carson raised the flag back in '61.*

It's a good thing Taos ain't on the way to California, I interjected.

California?

It's where I aim to go after we finish your herd.

You plugged Rusty Cuellar fair an square? I'm tempted to forget it, specially now you're riding my brand. He's the only one, by God, is he?

Never come close to shooting anyone else.

I wouldn't drown in sweat about it. That gutbucket sheriff won't trouble to haul his ass east of Cimmaron. The flour mill there's about his limit. Hell, if he left Taos overnight, it'd take him a year to get his own chickens back. Between water rights, land boundaries, politics, and nail-driving religion, that town might never sort itself out.

I don't want to raise a fuss. If you think it best, I can break off now and make my own way. I offered to do this although it was a very bad idea.

Hell you will. We're single-handed on both wings already. Damned if I'm going to eat dirt after my own herd. Between you and Socorro over there, we'd likely have to make a list for all the men on the wrong side of your triggers.

Around noon we heard the wagon bell and rode up to the two-wheeled *carretas* set up beside a tidy fire warming coffee, fry bread and beans. Our cook, a grizzled Englishman, had a bent left leg, diamond-blue eyes, and a shock of wiry gray hair. Soon the whole outfit cantered in to eat.

So far June had been dry but windless. We loosed our cinches, dismounted, and hunkered on the seedy ground, dipping beans with fry bread between gulps of silty coffee. Maternal as a prairie chicken, the cook watched us wolf down his makings.

Passable, Arch, Jack Rice knuckled his lips, *for a stove-up limey raised on cold taters and smoked fish. Next time,* Jack looked at me, *maybe we'll get fresh meat.*

Smoked fish? Arch Chapin retorted. *Kippers. A kipper is wot you are tryin to descroibe, Jack. Luverly. Yew wouldn't know tasty*

138

grub if you was served it on a silver spoon. As for meat, someone shoot it an oi'l bloody well cook it.

Arch watched us skim our plates. This cattle drive was another of his and Jack Rice's *considered investments*. The men had shared fortune good and bad and now intended one final venture. Arch enjoyed the way his humor unnerved trail hands, who bowed to an unwritten law never to abuse the cook.

Arch told me that he didn't set out to be a trail cook. He'd signed on to a packet steamer from Liverpool to Canada at fourteen. As a cabin boy, after two crossings he jumped ship on the St. Lawrence. Over several years he'd drifted south and been hired to unload stock from Texas cattle boats on the Louisiana coast, finally taking a crack as a working cowboy.

Between the Rio Grande and the Nueces River with Paint Caldwell, Arch chased Mexican raiders out of the prickly pear country when he was barely seventeen. In 1864, already in his late fifties, he'd hired on with three outfits teamed up to make a big drive north. Below the Kaw River lightning stampeded the cattle, and two cowboys were killed attempting to wheel the herd. Arch lay trapped under his horse, where Jack Rice found him two days later. His hip broken and one leg badly fractured, Arch would never work from a saddle horse again.

The cook's Cockney English sounded as if he were trying to bed lizards on his tongue. Unable to follow the gist of Arch's tortured dialect, Socorro usually feigned understanding with wan smiles and polite nods.

Okay, boys. Let's tighten em. Jack Rice hung his mug on its hook and went for his horse. We all fanned out along the herd. Arch urged his wagon ahead, negotiating an occasional gully but most of the time grateful for the tedium of flat country. We trailed cows until the sun dipped low enough to mesa the sky, then stopped where the chuck wagon was set up, dismounted, and stretched our aching backs. Arch Chapin had dropped his kitchen tailgate and was starting another fire.

I lifted the Sharps from the chuck wagon and rode out. I spotted a falcon making a stoop on a prairie dog and three wolves flattening their bellies before slinking away into thin air, but saw no game.

Taking first watch, Tib rode out among the herd stamping in the near darkness. The rest of us watched the cook fire's embers and one by one drifted away to blankets unrolled on the seedy ground.

The night was littered with stars. A half moon suspended before a swathe of the Milky Way glowed with rust-tinged light. In the western horizon's clouds I imagined I saw the furl of a long dress, the curve of a neck and bobbed amputation of a woman's hair. Rolling toward sleep I felt comforted by ancient companions among dreamers young and old. After her brothers' wagon had carried Dahlia off toward Santa Fe, I'd cantered my horse across the church plaza, between a knot of local grandmothers. Several nodded kindly at me. The lined faces of those matriarchs recognized my sorrow as a familiar price of their own merciless history.

At rotation the Utah Mormon named Ezekiel who'd recently hailed from what he called *Rim Rock Country* whistled me awake. I slung the saddle on my picket horse and headed out for another night ride, usually a contemplative chore I much enjoyed.

Jumpy longhorns tend to stampede at the crack of a stick. It was a cowboy task to sing em down, and if you couldn't sing, sweet talk em. Ezekiel and his brother Luke had a repertoire of Mormon hymns. My style of cajoling a restless herd was to recite poetry in a musical whisper. A nightrider was tasked to keep things so quiet you could hear daylight coming.

At sunup I rode up on the cook wagon. Arch Chapin was kneading his bum leg to life. *G'mawnin*, he said. *Scrounge me a few barstard sticks, theres a bloke.*

Recognizing the word stick, among his strangled lingo. I began foraging. It was difficult to catch the drift of the cook's Old Country dialect. Only after my ear adapted to his linguistic trot did I begin to understand him, and listening became infectious. The man possessed a dry though ready sense of humor and enjoyed spinning yarns. Equally appreciated was Arch's strong coffee: *jitter juice*, Jack Rice boasted, *brewed mean enough to run a one-legged man into hell.*

o

The brand moved east and crossed the Canadian River's heavily silted waters. We pushed the herd through a wide stretch running only belly high yet still lost a yearling. Four days later we hunted along Ute Creek for another safe crossing. The herd wheeled about in indecision until our bellwether steer charged into the current.

Our next crossing would be Corrizo Creek southeast of Round Mound. So far we'd lost four head to turbulent rivers. About mid-morning we ran into an army squadron heading back to Fort Union. The listless column of buffalo soldiers wore insignia of the Tenth Cavalry. Two supply wagons drawn by hollow-backed mules conveyed sick and wounded men. Their white officer negotiated with Jack Rice for coffee and sacks of sugar in exchange for two pouches of tobacco and a letter of credit to Fort Nichols. Jack gave away the coffee and sugar and refused to accept payment.

The entire troop of forty-six had been reduced to twenty-eight. Dysentery had disabled two troopers. Five more had either been killed or taken captive and slowly tortured to death. More sick and wounded lay in the wagons. Only a week before the Comanches along with a few allied Kiowas and Arapahoes, had attacked Fort Larned on Pawnee Fork, killing fourteen and wounding twenty-four.

The Comanches were the dominant warrior force. Despite their numbers having been reduced more by smallpox and cholera than warfare, they remained formidable opponents.

The Comanche, identified by other tribes as "people who fight us all the time" called themselves *Nermenuh*, which means "people." Texans considered Comanches to be the finest mounted fighters in the world. They defeated the Mexican army in 1759 and had resisted every attempt since to drive them from the plains. Sam Houston had naively declared the tribe *subjugated* in 1840, while-thirty two years later the tribe continued to ravage much of Texas and eastern New Mexico. Jack Rice's decision to drive his herd north was a calculated risk. He'd gambled that our route would take us enough west and north to avoid trouble. The sorry appearance of the approaching cavalry train suggested that Jack Rice had miscalculated the Comanches' ability to strike far and wide.

We watched the soldiers dismount as one rider came forward to meet with Jack Rice. Rangy and disheveled, with thick sideburns, anxious reddened eyes, and prematurely sunken cheeks, the officer declined to dismount. Picket duty along the Santa Fe Trail dictated thirty-day patrols. The unpredictable predations and tactical skill of the Comanches, a stubborn prairie wind, tedium, and tainted rations made chasing Indians an exhausting and often fruitless trial. Hit-and-run attacks had deprived the troopers of sleep, and the hostiles had burned one of his supply wagons.

Cap'n Charles Hitchcock, United States Tenth Cavalry, the man announced, barely saluting Jack Rice as he eyed our cows ambling through. The captain appeared cold and officious. A regular, hollowed by tedious barracks duty, he returned an undisguised contempt to Rice's studied indifference to his rank. *Mister, I assume this is your outfit.*

You are contravening military policy against settlers negotiating this territory in protected trains of less than thirty wagons.

We ain't settlers. We are cattlemen, armed and capable.

What's your destination?

Ellsworth.

You realize you will veer hard east straight across the Comancheria?

That's the only way up from here but we're pretty far west.

I suggest you turn about. Scouts have reported attacks clear to Lower Spring.

Last I heard you army boys had taken care of things.

You understand the army cannot offer you protection.

Never counted on it.

Even if you do make it alive through to Fort Nichols the command there will not allow you to continue.

We aim to keep our eyes open.

Jack had every intention of skirting Fort Nichols.

Evidently the only functioning officer, Hitchcock directed his sergeant to collect our offered supplies. Continuing to glare impatiently at what he assumed to be a ragtag outfit of ex-Confederates, he was eager to return to the tedium of the stockade. Indian fighting exasperated veteran officers used to conducting battles in neat formations. Prairie vastness, stealth, and hit-and-run raids erased any tactical advantage acquired through conventional warfare.

The officer repeated his warning, allowing that if Jack Rice *chose to seek trouble his own way, so be it.* As a survivor of the war between the States, Hitchcock felt obliged to declare *the devil with it. No use offering good intelligence that you Confederates don't respect. These Indian renegades intend to drive whites from this country. If the Comanche capture any of your cowboys they will torture them to death. This skimpy outfit tempts a night attack, and a strung-out herd is easy pickings.*

Rice stood square in our defense. *I've fought my share of rustlers. As for a night attack, an Indian who dies in the dark can't find the happy hunting ground.*

Hitchcock scratched a sideburn triumphantly. *That so? They must have found a new religion. Comanches always take advantage of a full moon. They attacked us three nights in a row. My men had to man rifle pits at every bivouac above the North Canadian River.*

Rice wasn't about to turn back. *Day or night, if they want my herd, they'll have to ride through us to get it.*

The captain was already turning his horse. *You won't be the first cowman ended up selling life instead of beef.*

As the soldiers stooped their horses forward I caught a familiar whiff of saddle leather and stale sweat, a musk reminiscent of Bosque Redondo, where among the unchastened Navajo I'd witnessed the boredom and corruptions of garrison routine. These black cavalry men represented a new breed. Many were ex-slaves recruited to fight in the Indian wars: "buffalo soldiers," so named by warriors who honored them as brave and stubborn adversaries. We watched the column trickle into the distance. Everyone held his reins, knowing we'd carry on despite the risk.

Jack quickly divided the army tobacco. A cavalry recruit was allotted a two pound monthly ration of navy plug worth eighty-four cents. Tobacco was a common currency in barracks card games. Most cowboys chose to chew but Tib had recruited the Mormon boys as fellow smokers. We watched the Texan pull out his "bible" of papers and adroitly roll several quirleys to pass around.

Jack Rice exhaled. *Well, boys, you saw it. Those brunet blue-bellies got shot up good. Least we got some tobacco from the deal.*

Jack Rice lipped his cigarette and, drawing alongside Arch's wagon, pulled down a side board exposing the rifles. *Time for these Remingtons. If they come at us on the run fall back in the drag. If the herd stampedes follow its dust and shoot from there. Arch, keep your wagon near the back. If Satan had rowdy children they'd be Comanches. Back in Texas they could shoot six arrows to one of our bullets. Now they tote rifles and, if that surly officer was telling the truth, don't care about dying at night.*

Rice was about to turn away but after a heavy pause added, *Comanches take pleasure prolonging torture. Don't let them take you alive.*

Tib and the Mormon boys selected Remingtons and checked their actions. They looked scared having already heard tales of Comanche savagery. For those braves too proud to accept reservation life vengeance had become a feast born of desperation. Overrun by immigrant tides and buffalo hunters, the Indian had little hope of sustaining a traditional life. Long-held tribal animosities were forgotten; a gathering of bands had united on the warpath.

The hostiles, persisting just north and east of our small herd, had not recklessly thrown themselves against the bluecoats. The casualties excised from Hitchcock's detachment had been strategically picked off. The Indians could shoot bullets from ambush or steal close with their bows, silently strike, and melt back into cover.

We continued our push toward the Trampas River. As if the soldiers' misfortune had invited a devil wind, ever since the cavalry ghosted through our journey was twisted. The ground grew parched, forcing us to lift our bandanas against its pale talcum, a fitting mask since Indians perceived white skin as "too little cooked" in the Great Spirit's first people-making fire. At breaks we checked the breeches of our rifles and poked grit from eyes dried to almond squints. The land was beginning to sprout brushy sections. We were pushed to guide the herd around these thickets, wary of possibilities for concealment.

The drive developed a solemn quietness. We bent into the afternoon dust, forked our beans more deliberately, shook out our bandanas, and rubbed fatback into cracked lips. Our horses were starting to lean down.

The country took on a relentless glare that played tricks with distance. It became an escape to stand in the stirrups and squint ahead in a bone-weary hope the sun might speed its descent.

Time on the trail might have made us more alert, but in fact contact between riders became more strung out. Alone in the drag I'd catch hazy glimpses of another rider or our cook wagon, and at times someone would ride up to seek help cross-hauling Arch's rig over a gully. We kept the cattle stretched in a string to discourage strays, a style that makes being short-handed an even tougher challenge in stretches of broken country.

o

Scarcely an hour into morning I was trailing the herd as usual. To avoid a ravine the lead cows had swung east through scattered brush. Somewhere ahead Tib and the two Mormon boys had dropped from sight. At the first rifle shots, seeing no sign of anyone, I hoped it was Tib who'd shot something to eat.

A low sun narrowed my eyes. Squinting ahead I saw the first horses racing out of cover appeared riderless, then I heard a falsetto scream and three ponies magically sprouted Indians. These trick riders fanning out alongside our milling cattle began discharging rifles that quickly set off a thunderous stampede.

The turned steers charging toward me presented a widening river of horns, their hoof drum broken by rifle shots and war cries. I jumped my horse hard right and, between a few skidding steers dodging us and my horse fast-footing a couple more, managed to race clear. From somewhere close Socorro and Jack Rice had pulled alongside the running cows. We fired pistol shots to turn the stampede but the Indians had the jump on this tactic. Our entire herd was rushing past on a heads-down race to anywhere else.

As they passed through at full tilt the Indians took potshots from the saddle and from under their horse's necks. Each Indian we sighted presented a fleeting target at best, especially if hidden on the far side of a half crazed horse. On the fringe of the billowing dust, noise, and rampaging herd I caught a glimpse of Jack Rice. Spurring my horse toward him I felt Agate shudder. The mare pitched forward, throwing me into a running stagger that carried me several yards before I fell.

Jumping to my feet I saw I was only yards from where Socorro had pulled his horse down to sight across the animal's belly at any passing target. As I stood and swung off hand seeking a clear aim, I saw one rider flip sideways and tumble into the stampede.

In the time it took the Indians and the cattle to pass I hadn't triggered a single rifle shot. Stunned by the speed and pounding hysteria of stampeding cows, at the edge of my vision I glimpsed a rider swinging a rifle toward me. I'd barely felt his bullet graze past my left knee before it plunged into my horse.

Vainly struggling to regain her feet, my mount buckled, first at the forelegs then at the back, until, rolling over, she fell heavily on her side. Speedily evaluating her, Socorro pressed his .44 to my horse's forehead and fired. Kneeling by Agate as she went instantly limp, I saw in her fixed eye the end of our shared destiny and murmured my thanks. Agate had served me well during our many miles together.

Socorro managed one telling shot. The herd and our remuda were scattered. The raiders had disappeared; the one Socorro hit lay grotesquely twisted by the cutting weight of cloven hooves.

A horse with its reins dangling trotted toward us. The older Mormon boy rocked puppet like in his saddle, then dangled awkwardly over his horse's neck. As we slithered the lad from his saddle we barely held his weight from a hard fall. He was blood-soaked, with two leaky holes in his back where rifle bullets had penetrated. We slung him across the saddle; leading his horse, I followed Socorro in search of Tib and the dead youth's kin.

A half mile or so east the Indians had jumped Tib and the other Mormon youth. Two arrows had pierced the Texan, one in the back and another in front. It appeared the cowboys had been stalked from a gully. Socorro traced the prints of three sets of moccasins to a spot where someone had held Indian ponies. The Mormon brother lay on his back, eyes wide to the last surprise. An arrow had passed clear through and broken his neck. The shaft and point emerged from his throat, its undisturbed falcon fletch barely arrested in flight by the spine.

Socorro and I hooked our hands under each man's armpits and dragged our friends alongside one another. Socorro gently covered each face with its owner's hat. The youths, in their dark cloth and collarless homespun shirts appeared the more fragile, their motionless stares erasing the fleeting illusion that in a miraculous instant they'd awaken.

Tib's shape sprawled heavily in leather chaps, his head fixed into a backward toss as though attempting to release a final warning cry. His fringed tobacco sack was still looped around his thumb. It appeared that the two men had gathered for a smoke and just as the other youth rode up had been immediately ambushed. The mounted brother had tried to run for it, and the shots that took him down had started the attack.

Turning back, we spotted the cook wagon. Alive, Jack and Arch lay prone under it, rifles in hand. Arch's rig was pierced with bullet holes. Unfazed by the entire commotion, his mule stood calmly in its traces.

Jack rose and waved his Remington toward our departed herd. *Comanches. They ran clear through us. Likely still running my stock. Any sign of Tib? The other two?*

Momentarily frozen by this question, I let my face convey the answer.

Arch struggled to his feet. *Got all of em is it?*

I nodded.

That right, Socorro? Jack pursued.

Socorro looked toward me.

I bent my head, barely able to share facts with the prairie grass. *Looked like they bunched up for a quick smoke and got dry gulched. Tib took two arrows, front and back. They shot one of the boys standing, then the other one in his saddle, and right away must have charged us.*

Jack Rice looked at the sky. Arch nodded and limped past the wagon to unconvincingly check his mule.

Where'd you find them? Jack asked.

Yonder, I replied, *on the other side below that line of brush.*

Arch clambered onto his wagon seat and his mule followed us across the swathe of churned-up ground. Halfway to our own dead the Indian that Socorro shot lay mangled by trampling hooves, revealing a bloody socket where Socorro's slug had exited the right shoulder. The lower half of his face was painted solid black. He wore a rawhide skull cap with three eagle feathers sewn into its crown and a blue cavalry coat that hung down over a long breechclout to his high top moccasins. He looked no more than twenty. The Indian's mud-daubed pony stood nearby, its rein trailing the ground.

What about him? I half whispered.

In response to my question, working with considerable effort, Jack Rice leveraged the dead Indian's knees to his chest and folded the stiffening body into a crouched position. *This one ain't Kiowa or Arapahoe, he's Comanche, an*

Comanches fold their dead like this, Jack explained. *More than they'd likely do for us. Bring his horse over here.*

I led the pony to Jack, who hitched its single braided rein around the dead Indian's wrist. *If we manage to snag some extra mounts we can come back and finish this,* he said.

I had no idea what Jack meant by that. We left the pony standing above its owner, continued toward the line of brush, and waited for Arch to get down from his wagon bench. Jack untied a shovel and a mattock from under the wagon. It took some hours to hew a respectfully adequate resting place. Socorro and I took turns steadily digging until we'd opened a common grave.

Superstitious of removing anything of value from them we arranged each man side by side and gently shuttered their eyes and crossed their arms. In final rest Tib seemed fit company for the other two. It was a helpless feeling to lay out friends fallen in such a desolate spot. Our sorrow, transfixed by a prairie grave, was stirred by Arch's half-swallowed cough.

We lowered our hats as Jack Rice's wellspring of steadfast respect spoke an epitaph to touch all corners, which I believe it did. *Lord, only sorrow can speak to what we feel about men taken so young. They didn't offer up much of a story. The older one claimed they'd planned to run off. He said they'd heard that out west after a day's work men rode home taller in the saddle.*

Jack Rice looked around as if for permission to speak We all nodded for him to him to continue.

153

Lord, they rode toward sunset and it guided them to where we now lie them down in these green pastures and pray they will find comfort closer to you. Amen.

He threw a handful of dirt into the grave and we took our turns doing the same.

Jack started to speak over Tib.

Lord. I have talked to you several such times before and still don't figure on understanding your ways. Tib was steady a cowboy as any I met. After getting some Yankee canister shot in him he calculated he'd given his fair share to the war. He was Texas born and raised to give his best to whatever outfit he took up with. That counts my brand too. God forgive me I hired him and it appears he has given up a great deal more than expected for it. So be it.

There were no large rocks for a grave marker. After filling the hole we dragged mesquite into a pyre. When we were through holding vigil the embers kicked about the burial left a scattering of ash to discourage wolves. We rigged a crooked cross from a splintered hackberry trunk and lay it over the grave, deciding an upright one might attract plundering.

I walked back to where Agate lay and worked to free my saddle and rifle scabbard from beneath my fallen mount. It was coming daylight when Socorro came back running six horses including, to my relief, Saloon. Socorro's own mare was not among them. Eyeballing what Socorro brought in, Jack picked up a Remington, walked over to the spot where the Comanche lay with his pony hitched to his wrist, quickly dispatched the animal, lifted his hat over both corpses, and walked away.

Back among us, Jack explained *Comanche kill a pony for a fallen warrior, I heard sometimes several ponies for a brave who ain't afraid to die standing up. I guess that Indian Socorro dropped rates at least his own pony. No matter what strange Maker these Indians lift their arms to you can't fault them for guts. Besides, seeing us grace one of their dead, maybe they'll leave ours be. Never know what good deed might raise things up.*

An early wind was sifting ashes into our eyes and remnants of the scattered herd bawled at an absence of riders to move them. Jack eased his shortbrim back onto his head. *It appears to me hell an high water is here. Can't see us wrappin cows clear to a railhead with three men and a lame cook.*

Arch snorted and shook his head. *We got orses ain't we? Gawd an Crise, Jack. Skin this lot back ter Wagon bloody Mound? Then wot? No ruddy market even if we ad enough stock. We push on, that's wot. Got caught nappin by those feather eaded barstards is all.*

We should get moving, coming or going, I urged. My frozen response to the Indian attack had left me feeling exposed toward all four directions.

Jack gazed across the cinders toward Ellsworth. *Arch, you hold fast here. Devon and Socorro, round up whatever cows you can. We can bunch ride em. Hold the leftovers tight. Forget about chasin strays back in. Hell, if we make it home alive I'd call it even.*

Socorro slapped his leathery knee. *Our trail leff by this cattles is plain as a river. Them Comanche make camp an eat them selfs greasy then sneak back an get us. Comanche mostly want scalps.*

I knew of a poor bloke who died after having the soles of his feet cut off an made to dance for this lot, Arch chimed in. *You fellers better get crackin.*

We spent a long following day chasing cows. We tried to avoid silhouetting ourselves on a rim in case any hostiles spotted us. The only sign of company were tracks heading southwest and ash and of a roasting fire, remnant of where the Indians had cooked one of our horses, whose meat they reputedly relished more than beef.

The stampede had spooked our already scattered cattle. It was tricky rounding up a dozen widely dispersed cows and herding them toward a gather. We'd started out with over five hundred head and by dark had counted a nervous bunch of just over a hundred.

The moon was waxing three quarters, illuminating the prairie with sharp-shadowed pools of light. I cradled the .52 and dozed before taking my turn outriding. Arch snored under his wagon tongue. Jack was wrestling his blankets close by. I admired the rough kinship of these partners. Restless in sleep, by day Arch Chapin and Jack Rice rolled along like dice smoothed by frequent use. It was once again apparent that Jack was fortunate to have hired Socorro, a seasoned vaquero whose five acute senses were harmonized to a canny sixth. Socorro calculated every new horizon, lay down to sleep like sunset sinks over the edge of time, and rose quickest to any hint of trouble.

It was clear after the attack made it known that he wasn't keen on keeping the herd. Suspecting the Californio's instincts were good ones I determined to stay close on his tracks. Throwing down for another sleep, I murmured, *Santa Ines. California. Buenos noches, Dahlia.* This was the first night I wrestled with the idea that *buenos noches* might foretell not only an *adios* to her but to everything else.

o

Arch was our prairie pilot and nightly set his wagon facing the direction we intended to go. Always the sailor, he had a ship's compass. I seldom saw him look at it. He'd provide incoherent directions such as: *haul to, a quarter circle right of sunrise an hold course to me wagon.*

Some days the prairie offered a featureless ocean of short grass but the sun, curving its steady path overhead, regularly set almost at our backs. We were drifting northeast, three riders and a wagon bumping along behind a diminished herd.

For protection we stayed close and seldom pursued any wide straying steers. Halfway across the swathe known as the The Indian Strip, even a few strays greatly thinned our stock. So far we'd sighted two scouts surveying us before dropping over the rim. Taking turns sighting through Arch's brass navy telescope, we agreed both riders appeared to be Comanche.

The landscape was showing signs of a wetter country. Grass stems were thicker and longer, with occasional oak galleries and hackberry stands offering cover along the traces. We had made an early stop after managing to shoot three fat geese flapping low over our heads after our cows scared the flock up from a grassy slough. Arch was getting together a fire and had set us all to plucking goose feathers when the Indians tried us again.

The braves had picketed their horses below the brow of a rise and flattened themselves among the hackberry brush, probably surprised to spot us doing exactly what we were doing sitting on our butts and pulling feathers off dead geese.

Luckily I was alerted by a crow's warning call. The medicine bird croaking low overhead caused me to drop the half-plucked goose and grab my .44.

The Indians had neither counted on a crow's warning nor on Socorro dropping two of the four braves who made a rush. This time I was also quicker to my pistol and shot one. A fourth turned and ran.

Neither Socorro nor I knew how the fight had fully transpired because, ducking low from separate sides, we'd rushed to out-flank the remaining Comanches. But before we could do this they scrambled from the brush and ran for their horses. One, after struggling to get himself onto his mount, galloped downhill after the others. By the time we had pushed through the thick brush the Indians were well out of pistol range.

Returning at a run we stepped over the dead and dying we'd dropped. One had collapsed only yards from where I'd hunkered. The other two were both heart shot. The first, lying in a pool of blood that ebbed from his upper thigh, had bled out. Feathers and goose down drifted everywhere. Brandishing rawhide covered war clubs, these young bucks had mounted an uncharacteristically brazen charge on foot straight into our guns.

Socorro figured this madness out. Beckoning toward one brave who lay face up with his eyes wide open, Socorro declared *these Injuns was all loco drunk.*

Turning to seek Jack, anticipating that he and Arch had again dived under the cook wagon, we found our boss on his knees beside Arch and the chuck wagon mule dead in the traces. The cook was propped against a wheel. As we bent toward him Arch slowly lifted a hand, whether to turn aside our aid or wave a last goodbye I cannot say, and gave a long sigh and slipped sideways to the ground.

Jack Rice's reaching fingers clutched at his best friend's arm. Murmuring *Arch, Arch,* Jack held fast to the bloody sleeve as Socorro and I eased Jack against the wagon as wheel.

Jack groaned and fell back. *I'm hit in the belly. Got no legs neither.* A dark bloom expanded where Jack had awkwardly tried to heave his shirt upward. He drew a bloody palm from his wounds and held it toward us. Getting gut shot was a slow but certain way to die, often after days or even weeks of drawn-out agony.

Jack's winced smile spoke past our faces. *Good old Arch. More guts than you could hang on a fence. After I pulled him out from under the horse that crushed his hip he lay in a wagon for months then got up and declared he'd just have to stump around like a gammy pirate and learn to rustle beans like a Mexican grandmother. Never looked back. Liked to brag he was "miles ahead of me."* Jack strained to reach over and gently shutter the cook's lifeless eyes. *Bless it all Arch. Seems like we played it to an even draw.* Jack's blood-drained features possessed the bright eyes of a young man and the age lines of an old one. Brushing away stray goose down that clung to the dying man, I riveted my eyes upon his. Jack's return look was unflinching, a deep and open invitation to examine a brave man's momentary and likely life-long truth.

After scrounging in the wagon for cloth Socorro ripped a shirt into strips. We folded the coarse homespun into a pad and used these bandages to cinch the belly wound. We next covered Jack's legs under a sheath of blankets. Claiming himself *enough comfortable* Jack directed me to a leather doctor bag beneath the wagon seat.

The bag contained a flask that Jack tilted empty. The case also contained a folding pouch, which he directed me to open. I removed five wads of greenbacks and a thick envelope containing letters. Jack's directions were given in a labored whisper punctuated by painful gritted spasms, yet his eyes remained steady. *That's seven hundred dollars in paper money. Burn all the letters except the one addressed to Molly. Arch's compass is in there too. Everything in that little sack is his. Arch has no kin, you and Socorro go ahead and divvy* it. *Either one of you can forward my daughter's letter and money if you get through. I suggest you kick hard toward Ellsworth. I'd quit this jinxed herd and leave it as a distraction. It's up to you. Possibly pushing our beeves on might spite those murderous sons-a-bitches.* Jack nodded toward Socorro, then to me. *Mebbe help this kid get to California too.*

As darkness closed in around our fire the two figures before me, one appearing to lean and the other to stretch in sleep, were illuminated against the wagon wheel. Jack had remained still except for an occasional pained shift of his shoulders when suddenly he asked, *Devon. There's a red tally book with a pencil loop in my saddle bag.*

I sorted through the satchel and handed over the little book.

Push a few big embers closer so I can see to write. Yes, that's good enough. Now leave me be.

Socorro and I remained hunkered. Jack looked steadfastly at us, challenging our disbelief in his request. Jack's next words were quieter. *There's nothing to be done. All I'm asking is for what's required.*

Neither of us moved a muscle. Jack's dry lips formed a wounded command: *For God's sake, boys, I'm asking for you to go mind your horses.*

We obediently rose, took up our rifles, and walked blankly to our horses, all the while knowing they would be grazing as usual and didn't need tending. I walked up on Saloon, untied her hobbles, and led her toward Socorro's shadowy outline. We were standing quietly while our mounts nibbled the short grass when a pistol shot cracked the darkness.

In the abrupt silence of Jack Rice's final gesture Socorro turned and grabbed my shoulders, and we stood immobilized by the gravity of that single shot. After a while Socorro, his voice thickening, turned toward his horse. *Madre Dios, I had plenty of this country. Tomorrow we take care of this thing. I don want to do it now, not in the dark.* It was the only time I heard Socorro break. Riding in silent homage, we left it up to our horses to find their own circuit. The cows were quiet and the sky so black its clustered brilliance radiated clouds of stars. Through the night hours Socorro and I rocking numbly in our saddles, barely gripped the reins. Finally toward the glimmer edge of dawn we plotted details of what had to be done. Morning would require a task we wanted to arrange well before sunrise led us toward sorrow.

○

Buzzards were already circling and a red wolf slunk into cover as we dismounted alongside Arch's mule where it had collapsed. It was a hard moment trying not to look at Jack Rice's mutilated head where he'd slumped across his longtime partner. It was as though I dared myself to witness the aftermath of a man savaged by a ravenous beast.

Jack had left a neat blood-stained message by his feet weighted with his clasp knife. Composed on the narrow tally book page, it read

No need to dig boys
Arch always wanted
burial at sea or set adrift
in is own smoke.
Fine with me.
Burn the wagon too.
Amen.

I read this out loud to Socorro. Seized by its request we rode off to catch the only two remaining horses we could see then scrounged through Arch's wagon, gathering his cook tripod and iron pot and dry beans and other possibles enough to get us to Ellsworth. After retrieving Arch's telescope, monies, Jack's letter to his daughter, extra ammunition, two Remingtons and bridle gear for two pack horses we hitched dally ropes to Arch's mule and dragged the dead animal a good way from its wagon shafts.

We did the same for the dead Comanches. The three braves in beaded moccasins and breech clout chaps looked like they had no business being laid out so young. They surely did smell powerfully of a concoction I'd seen transform Navajo braves into drunks liable to do violence to anyone at hand. Indians named the white man's poison "firewater" because its potency was tested by being thrown on a fire. Spittle dried on the dead Comanche's lips bore the stain of burnt molasses and chewing tobacco used to disguise the black powder, turpentine, and other foul ingredients passed off as "trade whisky."

After laying out the Indians' bodies side by side we left them for their tribe to take care of. Of no mind to act polite, we shot no ponies to honor the Comanches though I did feel a touch of hesitation. Violent as our introduction had been, I had to respect the Indians' courage. I recalled my mother's opinion that *the red man had been cheated of his way of life.* Now even as an act of self-defense I'd had a hand in that cheating process, and was beginning to feel like a trespasser on the Great Plains.

Lifting in turn Arch Chapin and then Jack Rice into the wagon bed, we crossed their arms and set Arch's compass at their feet. Gathering branches and uprooting dead wood, we worked fast tying half hitches and urging our horses to haul sheaves of dry brush.

After numerous trips we heaped the fuel inside and over Arch's wagon. Next we leaned a stockade of thicker limbs around the pile. This last effort took longer but we suspected cremation required substantial fuel. Casting around camp we tossed excess supplies onto the mountain of brush, saddled up, loaded the pack horses and with our trail outfit set returned to the final task.

I hollowed a tiny cave beneath the pile and packed it with kindling. Hesitant to light the match we both stepped back as if anticipating an arrival of another presence that might excuse us of this small final act. Our silence and the prairie seemed entwined. The great patience of surrounding wilderness offered its reminder of how all things reside with both the living and the dead. Momentarily, Socorro seemed separate from where I paused, burdened by a hesitation to think, act or even breathe.

Jack Rice, true to his instinct, had hired me and given me his faith with small concern for its details. Having to arrange his body alongside the cook's in his own chuck wagon filled me with tenderness and sorrow. I recall little of their kinship other than rough banter around the fire: clearly their silence had said more.

Other than my parents I'd possessed few accompanying souls but now I felt the haunting presence of many more. Waking to the immediate task before me, I was beginning to understand why trail-hardened men often hesitate before they smile.

We held our hats and knelt in silent prayer then Socorro set light to the kindling. As the flames caught, a breeze quickly growing into a wind, forced us back and tongues of flame began billowing plumes of white smoke.

The wagon crackled and crumpled as heavier branches collapsed inward across its spokes. I watched the wheels tipping into the coals and caught a glimpse of two charred shadows. We kept tossing on fuel until it was all gone. The acrid smoke provoked a memory of Dahlia's reata that I had burned in the Dobe T's bunkhouse stove.

We stood vigil over the pyre until after several hours it had burned down to an ashen swathe of shimmering coals. Walking to our horses and taking heed of Jack's advice, we rode through the scattered cattle and abandoned them. The longhorns had started out wild along the Texas coast, now they were free to be wild again.

With the sun dipping we spurred our horses into a steady lope. If the Comanche spotted the burial smoke they'd quickly pick up our trail. We had little of value except four good horses, our rifles, and our hair: likely scalps and vengeance were attraction enough. Jack Rice had once reminded me, *Son, a Commanche'd take a particular delight weaving that yeller hair of yours to his war lance.*

We pushed our mounts and the pack horse alternately walking, remounting, and kicking ahead again. By nightfall now in rolling country, we'd made it to what I guessed was the western bank of the Arkansas.

Arch Chapin had enjoyed demonstrating *land lubber* navigation. He'd scratch a dust map for me tracing the Arkansas River up to Fort Larned. I still had the gist of his directions but had no way of recognizing which river was which. Knowing a river's possible name isn't worth a lick if you don't know which damn river is in front of you.

Before dusk, we watered the horses from a feeder creek, dropped their packs, and picketed them in a grove of trees. Though we then untied our bedrolls, neither of us moved toward rustling up some grub. We stood measuring one another expectantly.

Socorro beat me to the punch. *You can have the cooking.*

My solution was immediate retirement. *Uh uh. Gracias for giving me the job, but you can have it back.*

Amigo. I am the old one. ¿Sabe?

Yup. Age. Wisdom and experience qualify you best.

Kwolleefeye?

It means, er, you have earned the savvy to do important and highly respected chores, especially cook chores.

Socorro laughed. *It means, Devong is full of shit.*

You trying to make me out a liar?

Yes.

Tell you what, Socorro. You show me how to cook, then I take my turn.

Okay pendejo, you make the fire and you go for water.

Socorro scrounged in the grub packs, dug out Arch's dried figs, a tin of sugar, Arch's blackened coffee pot, and our mugs. I noticed it took me longer to gather fuel and kindle it up than it took Socorro to fetch supper.

Socorro then handed me the coffee pot grinning as he if were handing me the entire state of Kansas. I grabbed it and skidded down a brushy trail to the spot where we'd earlier scouted a spring and slowed its flow with a well-placed rock.

At first sip that prairie water tasted only faintly mossy. The little creek had a swift song and its passage down a dusty throat healed more than my thirst.

I lingered over that spring a long time, pondering how many migrant centuries of layered buffalo chips filtered my drink. Its trickle reminded me of a melody, made up during a tipi bone game back in Bosque Redondo against five visiting Tewa elders. Along with a team of other stockade outcasts, I'd chanced a challenge to the old Indian men. Collectively we bet two decent skinning knives, a cavalry hat, several banknotes of dubious specie and a book, which the Indians found an odd way to store kindling.

After prolonged discussion our opponents tossed down a mothy buffalo hide, an unstrung osage wood bow, a decent clay pot, and a tortoise shell rattle that had lost its handle. These contemptuous offers signaled the Tewa had only condescended to accept our challenge.

Spring Water Creek Water Spring Water Creek Water Spring Water Creek Water Spring Water Creek Water and *chun ay chun ay way o chun ay, chun ay chun ay way-utah* ran the words to our two hopefully hypnotic power chants. In the tipi bone game each team has to sustain a refrain until a player on the opposite side of the fire signals his hunch about which opposing player is holding the power. The "power" consists of four segments of deer leg bone, two marked by a black band and two without. Two players each hide two bones. The guessing team must indicate by hand signals how the bones are distributed in an opponent's grip.

If they are "guessed" the holding team has to throw their opponents a small stick until all seven of these tipi poles are surrendered. Almost all the tribes play a version of this bone game, also called "stick game," "grass game, "or "moccasin game." Contests can last days and have been known to settle the outcome of tribal wars. Stakes consist of wives, slaves, pony herds, prime hides, weapons, beadwork, even scalps. Great players are esteemed as seers possessing magical insight.

Our team's monotonous water refrain proved to be a thirsty one and worked like the charming song it was intended to be. By a secret signal we'd shift to the second chant just for an instant then charge back to the water song. Our determination, being the stockade outcasts we were, was to prove ourselves by hurling power across the fire and create lapses of focus that allowed us to read our opponents. Most human beings, probably more out of boredom than focus, would have fallen prey to singers as repetitious and captivating as we were.

My team included a half-blood horse breaker, known to the cavalry soldiers as Toothless Jim; plus a disquieting bassoon-voiced Kiowa squaw named Talks Walking, who regularly begged whisky at the fort gate, and Kiernan Murphy, a lanky Irish sergeant's son who normally stuttered but somehow fell to reciting *spring water creek water* steady as a clock. In fact Kiernan appeared willing to carry a refrain nonstop for a year if necessary. Talks Walking also led the assault in a vigorous falsetto. We dismantled the opposition in seven straight passes.

When their turn came to make the final guess the Tewa fell to bickering amongst themselves. We presented such a phalanx of unintelligible oddballs that the elders couldn't read us at all. The speed of our win was tantamount to a massacre.

After the disgusted Tewa had surrendered their tipi poles my teammates drifted off to boast. I was immediately accosted by Joe Cheval, a French metis who served as army mule skinner and sometime scout. He'd watched our gambling from just inside the tipi. At the time the Bosque Redondo Navajos were avoiding me. They also steered clear of Cheval because of his disfigured face, dark temper, and startling habit of breaking into war dance steps.

By his furtive manner I gathered the Metis sought to impart some stealthy confidence. In the shadows his scarred right eye, crooked nose, and twisted upper lip appeared more mask than living face. I thought it wise to humor him.

In his usual erratic half whisper, half shout, Cheval grinned: *Them Tewa, you sure see troo 'um plenty good, oui? Injuns tres unhappy losin plenty stick because you nevair quit song. Them ole injun seen troo plenty human being. Cept not see troo you. Per'aps them deer bone like you too much, oui? You beaucoup lucky damn white boy. Iroquois people say you got kiche spirit, can talk to animal like old time, eh?*

Cheval whirled another unnerving spin, turned to walk away, then jumped back into my face. *Ze black medsann bird sit on you shoulder. What appen to im?*

My crow? I replied *Oh, Shash, he, he's gone.*

Cheval became more agitated. *Tink you fool Cheval? Cheval know what never fly away. You tink my talk jus whisky talk?*

Unable to sustain polite confusion and unnerved by his ferocity I stood transfixed by the Metis's twisted face.

You an Joe Cheval, we see. Joe took another compulsive step and tapped his forehead. *Mon ami, you skookum long seein to other place.* After a final conspiratorial poke in the ribs Cheval, asserted, *sure damn see plenty evyting* as he stumbled away.

"Skookum" was used to signify plenty of whatever power or talent a human had. Joe Cheval's insistence on my capacity for "seeing" and the shiver it had provoked faded from my thoughts, and the memory of his jagged scar was replaced by the sound of trickling water. Thrust back into the shadow reality of surrounding brush, I jumped to my chore filling our coffee pot and hurried uphill.

Socorro, who was feeding sticks to the fire, sounded more tired than gruff. *You get loss?*

Yes, in a memory.

Socorro accepted this reminder of his own favorite excuse and watched as I dumped coffee and an equal quantity of sugar into the pot before balancing it on the intersection of three stones.

After it boiled Socorro tested my brew. *Chinga hombre. A sugar woman teached you to cook.*

And all you "teached" me is how to divvy dry figs.

Devon, you too smart a coyote.

Yep. A starvin coyote.

Socorro emptied his grounds on the fire. *Tomorrow I make us tortillas. Arch make biscuits, not too much tortillas.*

And sneaky beans, I said.

Beans who talk behind your back. We both kicked out the fire and walked to our bedrolls. Sleepy attempts at banter quickly dissipated into the quieting imprint of our vanquished friends. Much had been wrenched from my expectations since hooking up with Jack Rice's outfit. Now, overwhelmed by recent events, I simply slid under cover, rolled the trigger guard of my rifle toward my chest, and set my pistol within reach.

o

We entered Ellsworth close on the heels of a milling herd of longhorns urged into a sweeping turn by whooping Texas cowboys. The place was bustling with raw energy; much of the fanfare derived from mobs of animals herded straight through town. Our first glimpse of what made so much fuss possible was of a steel-wheeled locomotive spouting smoke as it shunted down the tracks. Neither of us had ever seen an "iron horse." The screeching chimney-headed monster spooked our mounts into trying to run.

Wrangling my horse and catching my first acrid railroad stink of crushed rock, creosote, and sun burnt iron,

I sensed that we'd crossed some divide into another country.

The stretch of summer landscape we'd recently crossed was newly marked by a serpentine swathe of human progress. I was subdued by this evidence of human ambition, having thus far lived on the fringes of its onrushing tide. Squinting west down iron tracks narrowing in the distance, I felt my life invaded. Irreversibly, prairies and mountains were being settled, just as foreseen by an Ogalala medicine chief who predicted that *more white men than falling leaves will take our country and make little islands for us and many big islands for their four leggeds and their big tipis that never move.*

The traditional strongholds of the redman and his best hunting grounds had already been given new "American" names, even those places held sacred by the native bands who first hunted them long ago. Meanwhile I watched newcomers arriving from the East, some descending from railway cars capable of transporting what took fifty prairie schooners and many harsh months overland to accomplish.

Witnessing the efficiency of a transcontinental railroad filled me with wonder and also trepidation. Confused about how I'd fit into such an emerging new world I felt torn between entering town or spurring my horse and riding away.

Working to quiet my fidgety horse, I watched more men disembark an arriving train. Several jumped off and hit the ground running. I quickly learned where these men were hurrying to. Ellsworth attracted a mixed crowd besides just cowboys eager to hand over their money to others bent on taking it. The local paper reported: "hell never sleeps in Ellsworth." Just about every Texas drover was heeled with two guns. The main street bustled with frontiersmen, gamblers, buffalo skinners, speculators, loose women, and a mix of pickpockets, horse thieves, beggars, staggering Indians, and scores of either drunken, or about to be drunken cowboys.

There was such a variety of card cheating that hucksters openly sold marked decks and an assortment of illicit equipment designed to shorten the odds. Among the strolling easy-going cowboys a wolf-eyed parade of crooks drifted from one saloon to another, either seeking to bump into someone or avoid bumping into someone. Darkness magnified Ellsworth's saloon tinkle punctuated by gunshot invitations to a party where anything goes.

Nauchville, the town's woolliest section, presented a tent city of brothels and gambling joints. As of yet there was no jail. The most omnipresent evidence of jurisdiction was a noose dangling from an infamous cottonwood tree. A short list of hired marshals had consistently quit town or quit breathing. Local businessmen hoping a taste of higher culture might quiet things down imported a saloon opera appreciated by citizens and rowdy cowboys alike.

The front page of the *Ellsworth Reporter* boasted the town was soon to have a theater. I detected little need for more drama, stocked as Ellsworth was with crime, rotgut liquor, gunslingers, demi-mondes, and random violence.

After briefly surveying the town, our first duty was to mail Jack Rice's money and letter. Our second priority was a bath and our third priority a bath.

A passerby directed us to the Kansas & Pacific station office directly opposite Beebe's Dry Goods Mercantile. We hitched our horses and paid a clerk seventy-five cents, which included ten cents to seal and another fifteen cents to certify delivery of Jack Rice's bequest. An animated clerk assured us that *though a shade costly, your envelopes' conveyance could might possibly require less than a week or so to St. Louis where final delivery depends upon the time it takes to find said address.*

It is an abrupt aspect of civilization to remind a cowboy of civilization's existence. The rail clerk's grimacing nostrils were eager to provide a map to help us navigate the distance between ourselves and hygiene. After walking us outside the man thumb-dived his waistcoat where he stored authoritative advice. *As I see it you boys require some hot water in addition to a variety of refreshment so to speak, along with livery for these here horses?*

We nodded in captive response.

There's several barns around town less'n you want to run your horses in with loose stock and throw a hay slice or two at em yourselves. By the day, that costs ten cents a head, more if you tip one of them breed loaders to feed whatever passes for hay down there in them corrals. Lookin at your rigs, 'specially that nice liver stallion, you might end up roping nothing but daylight when you go to collect them horses, not to mention their saddles.

A stubby fellow with longhorn whiskers twisted to cheroot thickness by daily applications of mustache wax, the clerk continued his monotone of assistance. Apart from an excessive attachment to advice his only appointment to railroad formality was a black cap with silver letters advertising "Kansas & Pacific." Beneath a three-quarter split tail coat, his long johns appeared gray more by neglect than design, and his laces trailed from their eyelets as though his boots held mice.

The Dusty Trail is the closest livery. I seldom direct folk to it. I hear his feed can be sour and there's a tendency for Texans to sleep it off in there. Course it's only thirty cents a head. Now, Shanghai Pierce and his top hands drop their rigs at Mabry's. He charges forty cents. His livery is tidy, his feed clean, and his boys keep a good watch. He's right around the corner. Two buffalo skulls nailed above his stable doors. Bill likes to buy an sell a horse or two. Tell him Benjamin sent you—

What about the bath? I interrupted.

The clerk paused to scratch over this question. *Well, there's the Grand Central Hotel has beds but its baths ain't completed yet. Er. You see. It's there's a complicated selection in regard to a feller soaking his hide. Some of the, um, opportunities is set up to sorta liven up the experience, if you catch my drift.*

We just want a hot bath, I said.

Hot you say?

Hot enough to drown tics. Clean too.

The necessity of equating *"hot"* and *"clean,"* appeared to represent a local challenge. The clerk restored his whiskers to a perky imitation of steer horns then concluded: *Hop Sing's.*

Hop Sing's? I was about to query further but the clerk stepped back, satisfied every solution had been achieved.

We led our horses in the approved direction. En route Socorro and I reckoned up our cash. Arch Chapin's contribution amounted to four twenty-dollar gold pieces. Socorro had twenty-four dollars. I had thirty-two. Plenty Texas cowboys would end up with less than our hundred and thirty-six dollars after pushing a herd north clear across the Staked Plains.

Mabry, a genial, barrel-chested man in a shoeing apron, seeing our approach, whistled two ferrety boys to take our reins. We untied our saddlebags and rifles and, carrying these, followed into the barn where saddles were hung and both stable boys started dry-brushing the horses.

We watched this process for a few minutes, then followed Mabry into an entry crib where he conducted business from a dryrotted banker's desk, its wood held together by termites holding hands. A chalkboard sign listed various livery charges. Basic keep was forty cents a day or three dollars a week. The latter, beside the usual crib of mixed prairie and Timothy hay, included two scoops of grain.

In Taos I'd seen bed prices for humans at six cents a night and eaten a steak dinner for as low as fifteen cents.

Noting my eyeballing his prices, Mabry explained, *Evything this far west is close to double. Timothy hay goes for ten dollars a ton if you can git it. Grain is a dollar a bushel. Some of the shipments get dry gulched. The town is looking to collect a tax to bring in a lawman for a hundred a month. Bill Hickock wuz paid a hundred and fifty plus what he could skim off a faro table. So far I never lost a customer's horse or his saddle. How long you fellers figuring to stay?*

Socorro looked at me and shrugged.

The prairie sun and whatever the next horizon presented had shaped our days long enough to make decisions concerning time challenging.

Time to wash off the dust, I said.

Mucho dust, Socorro grinned.

Three days then, huh? I suggested.

Okay, Mabry chimed in. At a dollar sixty, three days is four dollars eighty. How about I throw in the grain and we make it five dollars even?

I handed over one of Arch's double eagles. After hefting the twenty-dollar gold piece Mabry inquired if we'd be willing to accept change in specie, *reglar National Bank notes,* and disappeared behind the barn before returning with our paper change. *You boys headed back up the trail from here?*

Riding to California, I replied, watching Socorro shake his head as though anticipating what we were getting into.

Riding? Hell, Sacramento is over fifteen hundred mile. A sight more given the territory, plenty of it rattlesnake desert, not to mention Indians an outlaws and with only four horses. Might get lucky and take you three months if things goes smooth which they won't. Why not take the train? You can put your mounts on it too.

I thought the tracks only went a ways out from town, I replied.

More or less extended them sixty miles out, Mabry said. *But the track bed is surveyed clear through to Ogden. It would be easy to follow the survey markers an catch a train in Utah clear on through to California. I hear a feller can board a fancy carriage just ahead of the caboose, smoke cigars, and eat an drink with his feet up all the way to San Francisco. Or best you ferget about having to ride all that way to Utah, head due north an pick up a train at Grand Isle clear through to California.*

Although "feet up" sounded expensive, I felt a surge of interest in the possibility of eliminating months in the saddle, especially after hearing a reference to "desert." I'd crossed stretches of high desert sagebrush but had heard a true desert was a sandy vastness of bleached skeletons, hollow-eyed skulls, and raving settlers lost miles from water.

Socorro's primary concern, especially since the loss of his fine mare, was for the welfare of his liver stallion. *What about our horses?*

Take em along, Mabry suggested. *Trains are rigged for cattle but a horse or two is just another paying customer to the Kansas & Pacific.*

How much? I was calculating if a letter to St. Louis cost seventy-five cents by weight a horse to Sacramento might cost hundreds.

Got me there son, Mabry furrowed his brow. *Benjamin down at the depot is likely to know.*

Where is the agua caliente? Socorro interjected.

He means the bathhouse, I explained.

Mabry lowered his backside onto the creaky desk. *Hop Sing's is what you want. It's further down past the dry goods. You can spot the steam a mile off. Won't be pestered by chippies wantin to climb in the tub an soap your balls. Hop Sing's wife's towels is white as a nun's butt. You can get a haircut an shave. Laundry too. If'n you need fresh duds the mercantile's right on your way.*

Shouldering our saddle bags and rifles, we walked down the street directly to Arthur Larkin's Mercantile. The store was plentifully stocked with more dry goods than I'd ever seen in one place. The proprietor's brother boasted he'd *sold many a cowboy his first set of store-bought clothes.*

After wandering between the aisles of piled-up clothing I began to acquire an interest in "store bought" myself. Three pairs of wool socks cost a dollar and three pairs of cotton socks cost a dollar. Having never owned three pairs of socks at one time, I picked up three pairs of each.

My moccasins were shot and my only boot soles were fixing to make conversation. The store offered footwear in five styles. Larkin's most comfortable and priciest style, commonly referred to as "preacher boots," had a stove-pipe cut with stitched and pleated higher grade leather at the top to soften their rub. The cheapest footwear, used Army boots with square toes, were a dollar a pair. Preacher boots were five dollars. Trying a few pairs on, I found a fit.

I also picked up a "New York Mills" white shirt for two dollars, two undershirts for a dollar fifty, two pair of denim pants for six dollars, two sets of drawers at two dollars fifty and selected a "scout" style hat with a flat brim and round low crown at four-dollars fifty. The clerk, who by now was eagerly carrying my selections, toted up my bill. It came to twenty four dollars, three dollars more than the local rate for a three-year-old steer and quadruple what I'd ever invested at one time in new clothes.

I caught up with Socorro at the counter. His six dollars worth of purchases consisted of socks, a calico shirt, one red bandana and a box of ten-cent rather than five-cent cigars. Given the unique cut of his Californio rig, it didn't look like Socorro was going to replenish his particular style of gear anytime soon. Fortunately his tooled leather leggings were made to last as were his vest and poblano hat. Every inch a vaquero, Socorro stood out along the Ellsworth boardwalks in a way that provoked curiosity in some cowboys and plainly irritated a few others.

Our purchased gear smelled new and enhanced how we did not. We paid up, had our goods bundled in twine, and made a beeline for the bathhouse.

Hop Sing was an industrious chinaman working hard at being three places at once. The street facade of Hop Sing's bathhouse was a thirty-by-ten-foot-high canvas gaudily advertising three steaming tubs, each occupied by a grinning cowboy with his hat on. Inside, if inside might be considered a skyroof and six foot canvas back wall, three large wooden tubs stood in descending order of height, heat, bathing quality and water clarity. Hot water derived from a wood-stoked locomotive boiler salvaged from a train wreck was pumped by hand first into Number One Bath, whose overflow was in turn drained into Number Two Bath, until arriving in Number Three Bath, after which the much-cooled and grayish water was allowed to drain off into the moldy rear of Hop Sing's steamy premises where it was used for the first wash of laundry.

He pointed at his list of charges, also priced in descending order: Number One Bath was thirty cents, Number Two Bath was twenty cents, and Number Three Bath, ten cents. Hop Sing endeavored to maintain Number One as hot as possible so dispensation of its used contents could be marginally satisfying to occupants of the lower tubs.

Hop Sing's wife dispensed towels and soap. A long-haired buck skinner with a double-barrel shotgun watched from a high stool at one end of the bathhouse.

Previously there'd been bath fights triggered by arrivals of dirty cowboys unwilling to pay the price to soak in Number One Bath. Hop Sing pointedly waved at his shotgun handler, assuring me *Don't be scare cowboy. Hop Sing have Number One Bath no trouble.*

Hop Sing tried to enforce a maximum of six men per tub or a six-man minimum, depending upon demand. There were only three of us, ourselves and a bloated cattle buyer who was drifting cadaverously on the surface almost comatose with alcohol.

Socorro and I set our new duds on one of the benches, stripped off, and climbed aboard Number One Tub, which proved so steamy it drew the saddle ache right out of us. Our timing was fortunate. When we finished our soak we climbed into our new duds minutes ahead of another arriving outfit.

It is metaphysical how hot water washes off more than sweat and dirt. Hop Sing's tub washed away our fiduciary sense too, because, after donning the fresh duds we'd paid for, we paid for a shave, paid for laundry, paid for Fire Fly ginger ales, paid for the fancy Grand Central Hotel's tablecloth dinner, and paid for a six-dollar room with a ceiling ten feet high and a view of the tracks. For the first time in my life I slept between white sheets on a mattressed bed two feet off the floor. To say we had started living "high on the hog" would assume hogs survive at higher elevations than our funds. I for one was blindly willing to pay for comforts so new to my experience.

We signed into the Grand Central and watched the bell boy carry our possibles upstairs. Then we sat down to a dinner of prairie greens, kidneys with wine sauce, and added a roast Mallard duck, finishing up with Prairie plum cobbler and at Socorros's suggestion glasses of western brandy. The bill amounted to seven dollars. Attempting one of Socorro's ten-cent cigars and feeling jaunty in my new clothes, I didn't miss campfire beans one bit.

Maybe it was the brandy started him, but from his usual midden in my skull Gaajii started whispering to me again. Socorro noticed. He leaned through a puff of sweet cigar smoke and squinted into my face as though studying something recently arrived. *Devong. Devong.* Socorro was tapping my chin with his finger. *Where you go, hombre?*

I stared passively back knowing he'd caught me engrossed by the voice of my secret host. Socorro tapped his cigar ash and leaned forward over the tablecloth. *Doan fool me amigo. Back there on the prairie, I watch you. Is poco de brujo in you, hombre. Me, I doan worry what you can do. I see you my fren.*

Reaching across our fancy tablecloth I took Socorro's hand, a solid grip I held to his gaze, and in this meeting felt honored to know that all along he had seen more of me than I'd thought. I suspected the somber Californio was a man of some power himself who rode the surface of his own mystery. I realized he suspected the crows that followed me were a sign of an alliance the vaquero respected but did not seek to have explained.

Socorro, between us everything is always okay? I attempted to reinforce my assurances in broken Spanish. *Entra nos otros, todos est siempre tranquilo, tambien, siempre poco incensato. ¿Bueno?*

Socorro grinned his tooth-glinting Californio grin and lifted his glass. *I doan need to be explain any bullshit you do, amigo.*

It was near midnight before we stepped out. We inquired of the desk man if he could offer a guess regarding train fare and routes to California, inclusive of two horses. Given current expenditures and forthcoming obligations we figured our immediate worth to be around fifty dollars.

The clerk sent the bell hop down the street to inquire at the railroad office, insisting we attend his return. The bell hop came back accompanied by Benjamin, who scuffed around several seconds drumming up the possibility of a tip. The two cigars Socorro offered him more than satisfied his expectations because even if he'd just been rousted from sleep, which apparently he had been the Kansas & Pacific clerk was happy to deliver more advice. First the man lit up one of Socorro's ten-centers and wafted it in the general direction of California. *There ain't no track laid from Ellsworth yet. Won't be for quite a spell. It's up there in Nebraska the transcontinental goes west. Central Pacific goes via Cheyenne, Wyoming, to Ogden, Utah, then clear on through. Only other choice you fellers have following the overland route is to* rough it. You'd be crossing the Rocky Mountains to pick up a train in Ogden if you survived. My advice is don't risk it without more folks an without somebody who already has done it an that ain't anyone I know of. There's more bones along that route than there is graves. I'd say the Jupiter is by far your best way.

The Jupiter? I asked.

It's a train, son. Say you were to ride direct north of Ellsworth to Grand Isle. It's around a hundred and sixty mile. I know folks done it in a slow wagon in fourteen days. It's good goin this time a year, you might do 'er in less than half that. Grand Isle is a big depot. Price on immigrant class to Sacramento runs forty-four dollars. Second class runs sixty, first is eighty.

What about our horses?

Depends. If you go lower'n first class with horses, you'd might have to wait days for a train coupling stock cars. First class is every other day and usually pulls a gussied-up caboose for the eastern money and a livery car for their fancy blood stock. There's likely seats if you have the ready. Rates is higher for horses than for a seed bull because owners tend to want to stop and have someone walk their horses at least twice between Omaha and Truckee. Then there's feed, water, and the livery fee. That's included though.

How much?

Only charges I found said, "same charge per horse as per first class passage."

Eighty dollars! Multiplied by four that came to three hundred and twenty.

It's pricey but a hell of a fine deal. Crossing this whole country on rails is the flat out wonder of the age, son. Right now if the track ain't somehow blocked an the weather holds up a passenger can make the trip from clear back East all the way to San Francisco in five days for a hundred and twenty-five dollars immigrant class. California takes around two days from Grand Isle. Though you might have to wait to get on as our trains are real popular. When folks started figuring the usual crossin might take six months plus cost of a wagon team, supplies, and maybe risk gettin sick or even kilt, they began lining right up. Out of Ellsworth here it's all stock shipments after bringing in gamblers, speculators, and dubious wimmen. You might could head up to Grand Isle, wait a few days, an pay immigrant for half what first class costs.

I felt winded hearing these prices. A working cowpoke pushing cows would need to save half a year's pay to get to California with one horse.

The railroad man finished calculating accounts to our faces and concluded we needed three hundred and twenty dollars plus grub money.

Guess you are right on that figure, I admitted. California and Dahlia were drifting further and further away from hope and from my available cash.

Benjamin was about to turn on his heel when more advice occurred to him. *You two been lucky this far. Why not try bucking the tiger?*

Say what?

That's what we call betting on faro games. Hell, last week a greenhorn from Abilene walked out of Brennan's with over three thousand dollars.

Where's this place? Socorro became animated.

Brennan's is right on the plaza. Jest follow the noise. They run a passel of games in there. Never know, someone lucky has to buck the bank. Brennan's is reckoned honest as they get. Right now anyways. Least it's no wolf trap as I see it. Oh, once in a while they get a bunco artist risks a shenanigan, but anyone caught sanding cards is liable to end up staring over his toes.

You know this game? I asked Socorro, but my query was already addressed to his back. The station clerk looked pleased to see Socorro following his advice. He stabbed his cigar on his boot and pocketed its stub. *Looks like your sidekick's in a rush to git lucky.*

Me too, I replied, hurrying after Socorro. It didn't matter how I got where I was going; I was going.

○

As I pushed through its swinging doors Brennan's saloon felt bigger than my life. The place was crowded with cowboys, tail-coated merchants, wide-eyed immigrants, dance girls, and so damn much money in greenbacks, silver, and gold coin. Money chasing luck, bettors chasing aces, kings and queens flipped from decks by swivel-necked dealers with cinched-up shirt sleeves, fast hands, and flinty eyes on the scout for cheaters.

Socorro made a beeline to a nearby table and stood waiting for a player to back out and open up a chair. At his side I studied the game. Faro is played out of a "case" that holds a standard deck. Each card is dealt face down upon a suit of cards painted on a board: aces through kings, usually in spades. A player bets on the card that is dealt, betting that a turned card will either match the card it has been placed upon or not. The odds can mount up to twenty-to-one on a single game if a player chooses to "parlay" which is a way of rolling one win onto another then onto another, up to four times. The odds against doing this four successive times are usually set at twenty-to-one on the last card.

Remembering my last poker game back in the Dobe T with Rusty Cuellar, I considered skipping the whole idea of playing cards in favor of taking another road to fortune that might present itself, but second thoughts told me that might mean a year or more punching cows.

A skint cowboy quit, slowly stood up, balanced his sombrero crazily upside down on his head, and waddled from the table before diving to grab his hat. Before taking over the cowboy's chair Socorro dug his knuckles into my chest. *You doan know cards an they doan know you. Talk to them polite, Devong. Talk you secret talk an,* he clucked his tongue, *the cards mebbe show me their faces.* Socorro slid my split of our fifty dollars into my vest pocket and took the empty seat at the table.

Wherever cards were floated onto green felt faro was the favored game. Having suffered the consequences of bunk house cards, I'd lost the urge to gamble. I expected faro offered the same horseshoe toss carpetbaggers hurried west to play along with their desire to plough virgin soil, cheat on the turns, and profit from weeds. In the near riot of cow town saloons the faro table was always quiet. Perhaps in light of its simplicity of pure chance, silence around a faro table reflected more belief than concentration.

Since hitting town Socorro and I had been seduced by an impulse to harvest the comforts of charmed lives. There were times across the plains when I was sure we wouldn't live to kick the sky. Others had travelled and fought with me, and died. As a bearer of their inherited voices I momentarily felt obliged to venerate my lost trail companions by living well.

Whispering to an overhanging chandelier I lifted my hat reverently with both hands. *Kings and queens of fortune's saloon,* I whispered, bowing to the saw-dusted floorboards, *you are so full of light, come bring us brightness.*

I was lively, lively enough to see my way through hard days, though admittedly I often sensed something was coming but couldn't venture a guess as to what it might be. Certainly I was meant to follow any road that opened toward Dahlia. There was no harm in me when I felt her healing joy, her luminous image that I carried so lightly.

I drifted toward one of the saloon's side bars whose blackboard advertised TWO BEERS TWO BITS. I chugged down my first glass. Beer was more quenching than water until I finished one and felt thirstier. Recalling

Socorro's advice I was more *polite* with the second glass and leaned on the bar to watch the scene.

Brennan's wafted the kinship of whisky, dust, sweat, and musks of busy courtesans, one of whom brushed toward me through the crowd. The woman must have returned from outside and I detected a lingering coolness of night as she sallied by, though even waving a thin cigar she exuded perfumes of her own parade. Studying the woman's black hair, dark eyes, and abundance of silver jewelry, I momentarily thought she might be Dineh and tried greeting her in Navajo: *Ya ta hay.*

Hearing me the woman flounced her skirts and pirouetted to face me at the bar. *No idea what you're trying to say, son.*

It's Dineh, I said.

What's that?

"Dineh" is what the Navajo call themselves, an explanation that elicited no interest.

How's about buying a lady a champagne flip? We got a fine chemist at this rail.

The woman had a husky voice and a creased smile. She smoked restlessly and did not appear old enough to call me "son." I shook off the invitation to buy her the flip, a pricey concoction of champagne, brandy, egg, syrup, nutmeg, and cream.

Got a name, cowboy?

Gaagii Hasleen. Offering her this Indian name out of distrust, I detected a rush of summoned wings and a familiar voice thicken my throat. *It means Crow Man,* I explained.

The woman clasped my left hand in hers and did a dip as she fluttered her saloon eyelashes. *Like the pretty black bird,* she said, tilting backward under my chin and pouting her reddened lips.

I was uncertain if her stage-acting was in play or in mockery. *Yes ... like a black bird,* I said.

Are you superstitious? she asked, holding me steady with her gaze. Her Spanish eyes contained an impatient fire from long ago, she was Spanish too in the way she scuffed her heels and head movements accompanied each phrase. Consequently everything she spoke exposed a translucency of feeling.

Superstitious? I responded. *I guess folks need be careful about sorting what we see from what we want to see.*

Well, someone wanted my name to be Blackbird too.

Who might that have been?

My mother named me Merle, she said, *Merle Gibbs. In old country lingo Merle means blackbird.*

There's several kinds, I replied.

I'm black Irish, the kind that likes to collect things, she said. *Like a raven.* I felt a familiar tingle of the fate that follows me.

Ravens scavenge the dead, I said. *It's crows are attracted to shiny things.*

Merle rattled silver bracelets festooning both her wrists and her woman's smile seduced the crow inside me. I could feel Gaagii lift his wings as he reacted to the predatory glint of darkening eyes.

You must have just hit town, she said. *I smell a hint of Hop Sing's bath soap an can see it made your yeller hair shine.*

I had plenty to wash off.

Where'd you come in from?

New Mexico. Comanches killed five of our outfit and run off the herd.

Whoa. Lucky you made it through.

I had been too sorrowful to feel lucky until we crossed the tracks into town, where all at once everything was slipping by so fast we felt obliged to run and catch up. *My partner an me got a little carried away, picked out some storebought duds and splurged on a room upstairs at the Grand Central.*

One of their high-toned rooms with the big windows?

Yup, windows, big staircase, white tablecloths an all, but now we're too broke for train tickets.

Could get lucky at one of our tables, she said.

I stifled a grimace. *Yep, lucky. Lucky as dirt huh? Losing all of my twenty-four dollars would get me bust and afoot.*

The sun don't shine on that attitude, she said. *Where's your sidekick?*

I lifted my beer toward Socorro's table. *He's the one in the poblano hat.*

Tall Mexican-looking feller?

He's not Mexican, he's a Californio.

What's the difference?

I shrugged. *You need to ask him about that.*

Merle waved toward the man dealing Socorro's table who slightly lifted his head in return. *Give me your twenty four dollars.*

Are you serious? I laughed. *If you were standing next to Adam, I wouldn't know you from him.*

Merle stepped close as if to nuzzle my ear. *See the redhead feller dealing your partner? Folks get lucky at his table if I take a notion to bring them around.*

You know that dealer?

Can't say I know him. Besides ten cents a dance, she winked, *I keep whatever else comes extra. If you don't get lucky I'll give your twenty-four dollars back.*

Sounds a little bent to me, I said.

Maybe you need to see luck happen before you pass judgement. I've seen lots of cowboys blocking the trail to their own success. Sounds like things been riding downhill for you lately but things can change.

The way Merle Gibbs glanced at me exposed a vulnerability in her that seemed to me all she had to gamble with. Impulsively deciding to brave the risk, I handed over my money and followed her as she sashayed between the tables and bent close over Socorro's shoulder. Socorro sat up stiffly when he felt the rim of a woman's blouse graze the nape of his neck as Merle straightened up to watch the game.

My sidekick's chip pile appeared slightly ahead. Watching the redheaded dealer pull another card out of the case, I detected a glow around one of them and guessed it to be a jack of spades. When it was turned, I realized I would have won. Merle exchanged pleasantries with the dealer standing directly behind Socorro, who'd just lost his bet on another turned card.

Play resumed. Right off Socorro hit a winning streak. He'd been betting a dollar a turn but upped his ante to five. If he let it ride, after winning two turns he'd have won eighty dollars and after that three hundred and twenty and then four times that. In Brennan's saloon twelve hundred and eighty dollars was a large though not unusually majestic win, but one seldom achieved, as the odds were steeply against it. The excitement of high-stake wins attracted onlookers who reacted boisterously whenever our dealer flipped another winning card.

After several short good and bad runs Socorro ran out of the house money that had put him ahead. Starting out again from his original twenty-five dollars, he resumed his five-dollar hands but began to hang back doubling his bet, "calling the turn," and parlaying only the last three cards. Sticking to this bet he doubled up, and rapidly eighty dollars became three hundred and twenty and then, yes, twelve hundred and eighty!

Socorro quit and stood up like he'd been kicked. Our dealer, appearing sheepish about the house losses, was pulled off the table and replaced by another of Brennan's minions. Socorro calmly waited to collect his winnings.

Flush with excitement, I was far from cool. Kings and queens were doing cartwheels in my belly.

Socorro threw the dealer ten dollars, scooped up a thick wad of cash, and passed a sheaf of it to me as we headed for the door. I had turned to introduce him to Merle Gibbs and thank her for our good luck, but she'd slipped away.

It was early morning when we exited the saloon. The front street tinkled with faint music under dimming lights. The dirt underfoot had a fresh tobacco smell. Farther down the street where light was less in evidence we heard gun shots and a passing cowboy declared, *another cowboy jus won a free trip to hell.*

When I told Socorro about my encounter with Merle and her twenty-four dollar tip Socorro halted in mid-stride.

You tell that señorita where we stay?

Yes, I admitted.

Feel to me I smell a problem. Some steerer bring you to her house dealer. He lets us win then follow us.

Steerer?

Cappers is the ones work a table. Steerers is the ones brings you there.

What now? I asked, but Socorro was glancing at two men stepping off the boardwalk to cross the street. We crossed too and ducked down a gap between buildings. Thinking to drop our pursuers we headed toward our hotel but spotted the two men lounging in the shadows directly across from the Grand Central.

Looks like they know where to go, I said.

So do we, Socorro replied.

We acted unconcerned as we passed the two men and entered the hotel. In the lobby we pushed our winnings toward a surprised desk clerk and told him to lock the money away. Taking our room key we climbed upstairs, lit the lamps, and took a ready stance on either side of the door. After a reasonable wait Socorro signaled me to turn down the lamps.

Returning to my post after a good wait and hearing nothing, I stage-whispered to Socorro, *What makes you so sure they're coming? Maybe they were just looking to bushwhack an easy target.*

Lessee. Some faro dealer start throwin good cards after big bets jus when his lady fren come stand on my back. I think, why this pinchi redhead sudden losin to me? He work for the house so is

*not his money. Then you tell that señorita where we stay, then she
take twenty-four dollars an take you to my table. A steer is no
assident. An that redhead dealer throwin mucho dinero away? I
think somebody plan to pick it up someplace down the trail.*

Minutes later we detected a creaky attempt to muffle
boot steps coming up the stairs. In the instant the key
we'd deliberately left in the lock turned I heaved the door
open and Socorro hauled a man inside with one hand
and simultaneously dropped his partner with a pistol
butt to the head. I was covering the first man with my
Colt as he was attempting to scramble from one knee
when Socorro knocked him cold enough to skate on.

Socorro glanced around and directed me to take
down the room's braided window sashes. Both crooks
remained stunned, one bleeding from the temple and
the other sprawled on his back, eyes wide open.

After disarming the men of a shoddy pocket Colt and
a percussion pistol we hogtied them with the satin
rope I took off the curtain rods. Both disheveled buffalo
skinners smelled of sour whisky. One had a big patch of
hair missing from his scalp and wore two grimy shirts
one over the other. His pants were greasy black and
his boots flap-soled. The one we'd dropped first was
a skinny youth dressed in a filthy buckskin coat over
knee-high cavalry boots. His shoulder-length hair was
oily and several broken teeth grimaced between scabby
lips and a scraggly beard. Both hide men smelled rank
as bad luck buffalo skinners.

Socorro assisted the older man's revival by heeling him in the ribs and hurling questions at him. *Who pay you? How you get here?*

His partner, who'd come around, lay staring balefully at the ceiling. Socorro heeled him in the ribs too just to keep things even, then cocked his pistol at the man's crotch.

Mebbe I make him a steer, huh Devon?

No. No. Please mister, the skinny one pleaded, *we wasn't plannin on making no holes in nobody. We just come to git back the money took off Red Tyler.*

Sure. Thas why your guns was loaded, Socorro said coldly.

Red? The faro dealer in Brennan's? I nodded to Socorro.

That's him paid us, Skinny admitted.

Socorro uncocked the hammer on his .44. *How much?*

Forty dollars.

He tell you where we were? I asked.

Yessir. At the Grand. Like I said, we just come to take it back to Red is all.

Where is he? Where he be? Socorro's tone unnerved me. I was uncertain whether he was intending to shoot the man.

He got a place upstairs back of the Pie Emporium.

Which place? I asked.

There's only one. Hey mister, Red can git hot. He, he won't take kindly after payin me an Elmo here for nothin.

Socorro dangled the man's pocket Colt from his little finger, flipped open the cylinder, and let its cartridges cascade onto the man's chest. *For nothin? You was'n goin to do nothin.*

Socorro took ankles. I took armpits. After lifting the men onto separate beds I held a gun while Socorro did a rodeo job of cinching wrists and ankles to bed posts.

When both men lay helpless and spread-eagled Socorro removed their boots. The skinny one's boots each had a coin pocket containing two twenty-dollar gold pieces, which Socorro took. *Gracias*, he smiled. *This pay you got for doin nothin to nobody will pay for these nice bunks.*

It was grey dawn by the time we packed our gear and left both men splayed on hotel beds with mouths stuffed with their own socks. We retrieved our money, paid the hotel bill with the gold pieces, pocketed the difference, left the sleepy clerk a dollar tip, and instructed him to leave our upstairs room untouched until the afternoon.

Carrying our rifles and gear we headed straight to Mabry's livery, rousted his stable boys, and had them grain and saddle up our horses for a long trip. Directed to a nearby mercantile, we purchased two double-pannier rigs for the pack horses and enough coffee and supplies to see us through fourteen days. We balanced our possibles on either side of the canvas bags and lugged them to the livery where the stable boys rigged them to our pack horses. Even after all this preparation it was still early, and we were set to go.

Molly's Pie Emporium was down the street from Mabry's, close to the spot where the boardwalk ran out and gave way to hastily thrown-up shacks and tents sporting painted signs, some scrawled across canvas flaps.

We walked our mounts and pack horses to the back of the pie establishment and tied all four alongside a big buckskin and a pretty calico mare hitched to the foot of a stair that led up to an unpainted door.

When we pushed quietly inside, Red and Merle were both asleep. Socorro took off his hat, unholstered his pistol and brushing it gently across the dealer's nose, whispered, *five dollars on the black king, five dollars, amigo, por favor jus one more card.*

At *card* the redhead shot bolt upright in bed and stared crease-eyed into the tunnel of Socorro's long-barrel Colt, which several times in the past had offered no guarantee of a tomorrow to troublesome men wearing a lot more clothes than Red Tyler was now.

Merle, also stirred to wakefulness, sat alongside her bed mate clutching a blanket and did her prim best to portray innocence forsaken more times than angels might count. One of her eyes was closed black and both lips were swollen and crusted with dried blood.

I leveled my own pistol, and announced *Morning, blackbird, we came to take you folks to breakfast.*

Prodded down the stairs in his long johns with hands tied behind his back, Red gingerly lifted a bootless left foot into the stirrup of the big buckskin so Socorro could boost him over. The dealer sat woodenly in his saddle. When the man commanded Socorro to *Keep your greaser hands off me* Socorro flashed his knife and replied *Okay next time I not to use my hands.*

The lady protested that she was still in her nighty, a frilly long skirted outfit altogether amusing to Socorro. He bundled Merle unceremoniously onto the calico pony and used a latigo strap to secure her wrists to the pommel. For good measure I hobbled our guests' horses side by side, satisfied there was no chance to try a run. *What about some pie?* I suggested with a new moon grin.

Red Tyler spat pointedly but Socorro, noting my enthusiastic appetite for apple pie, nodded, *Como no.*

What's your favorite? I pressed, but Socorro only shrugged as I abandoned our guests to his care, soon to return from a just-opened Molly's bakery with a crusty cobbler still warm on its tin plate. Wolfing that pie, I came close to buying another one. Even Merle had to stifle a smile over Socorro's offered bite from a wedge he held up to her lips.

Everyone this side of our law was feeling exceptionally fine. The horses because they wanted to go and we because we were rigged-up, well-supplied, and had fulfilled the duties of Wild Bill Hickock, the ghosts of

Ellsworth's assassinated marshals, and were both sticky with apple pie.

Merle, cold and unhappy, directed the cat's claws of a tirade toward Red. The dealer remained sullen. Aside from the discomfort of tied wrists, both were unnerved by Socorro's steely determination. They had no idea what was next. Neither did I.

o

It is a testament to the cowboy convention to mind one's own business that no one challenged two riders leading a man and a woman in their underwear out of Ellsworth, Kansas in broad daylight. Once clear of town we tied each of our captive's lead ropes to the pack horses and continued alongside them at a leisurely pace. We headed west on a traveled wagon road for perhaps an hour before turning north and following traces of a much dimmer trail. We crossed several shallow streams and rode through rolling grass land before stopping under a copse of choke cherry trees.

How far you think we come? Socorro asked.

Mebbe fifteen mile, I estimated, figuring our party had maintained a steady walk for over two hours.

Socorro helped the woman down from her saddle, undid her latigo ties, and watched as she rubbed her wrists.

You gonna shoot me ain't you? Merle declared as if stating the time of day.

Socorro remained expressionless. *Same as your fren was gonna to shoot us.*

Mister there's plenty others in line he woulda paid to do it. Came close to being me a time or two, she sobbed. *Don't know why a body can be so forsaken.* She fell to her knees, stared abjectly into the grass, then clasped her hands together and began to pray out loud: *Lord, Jesus was lost an he was found, please bring whatever I lost around. Amen.* Straightening and wiping at her tear-streaked face, Merle Gibbs lifted her chin defiantly. *If you cowboys is looking for me to beg for my life you're gonna have a long wait. You pricks is no goddamn different from other men who done me wrong all my days.* She turned her back. *Might as well get this over with. The next sleep I get is gonna be the best I ever had.*

I'd never seen Socorro's face so shadowed by sadness. As for myself I was stricken by the sight of hope drained from a beaten woman's life.

Socorro turned to me and asked *What you think Devong ... Devon?* He politely corrected my name for the first time.

Shaking our heads at one another, we knew our bluff was called. I rode over, handed Merle a canteen, and took the reins of her calico mare.

We left her standing in the grass. She watched us awhile before turning back toward Ellsworth. I hoped my guess of around fifteen miles proved accurate and a measure not too risky for a barefoot woman.

Feeling apprehensive that we'd come close to punishing someone already too long banished from hope, I rode close to Red Tyler's mount, lead his horse out of earshot, dropped its reins, and returned to Socorro.

What say we give her a horse. Her life is all wore out and Ellsworth is no decent place for a barefoot woman tied to a string of bad luck.

She steer herself into this, Socorro replied. *She know her fren paid those rateros to rob an kill other men an it was gonna be you an me.*

Did you see what he did to her face? That's Red Tyler's work too.

Socorro glanced back at Tyler. *Mebbe you right about the woman but the dealer is no good too many ways to fix.*

Relieved to hear this, I turned my horse, took the calico's rein, and led it after Merle Gibbs. When I handed over the reins she swung wordlessly into the saddle. She turned to canter off then swung back and reined her horse alongside mine. *I seen Red Tyler gouge Missy Jensen's eye out one night on the front street of Abilene just for holdin back two dollars. I met some lowdown crooks in my time an he stands first on the list. He's had at least three men killed in the same deal you got caught up in. I'd as soon be shot by you fellers as have Red catch up with me knowing I seen him hogtied an carried off in nothing but his skivvies.*

You say Red done for three men?

That's jus three that I know of. If things had gone the other way between you an those buffalo lappers he sent there'd a been two more.

I looked over my shoulder toward Socorro awaiting my return. *Things seem set to go sour between me and red heads, I* said, thinking of Rusty Cuellar. *I suggest you head back to Ellsworth and jump on the fastest train with the longest ride. We'll make sure you get a head start.*

Make it a long one, she said. *Forever would be about long enough. Offhand, you might check Red's saddle bags. He always carried his take in them an hung it on the bedrail, but he come upstairs foul drunk the night you cottoned to his game. I think he forgot to bring his money cache upstairs.* She gathered the reins and spun her horse into a gallop. I watched the woman making distance and felt comforted that if she nursed her horse a little more than she kicked it they'd make town in a few hours. As for her entering the town in her nightie, I suspected Merle Gibbs was undeterred by a necessary display of scanty clothing. I couldn't help but smile at a vision of her on a train chugging east from Ellsworth, Kansas.

Once we'd started our own horses, Red's demeanor shifted from sullen to talkative. He'd scarcely looked to his companion at all before she left. Now it was clear Merle's release would not be his, Red tried to cajole us into revealing his fate: *I can see you fellers act gentleman even to a painted cat like Merle. Doubt she'd appreciate you though. I helped her out of a bad deal. Bought her off a joy wagon outside Fort Arbuckle. That drip-nosed gal was thin enough to fit a shotgun barrel. Cost me three jugs of rotgut whisky an a pound of twist. After a month's vertical holiday from those fort boys she turned out right pretty, for a whore anyhow. Caught on quick too. Hell, that woman is so slick she will likely turn a dollar on the way back to town.*

In reply we nudged our horses to a quicker walk, which only served to encourage the dealer's tongue. He continued making appeals in respect to why we had kept him and abandoned Merle Gibbs. The more he pleaded the more we urged our horses until he finally recognized silence as his only hope. Meanwhile when I told Socorro what Merle told me, his response was: *We keep this ladron long as we can then walk him straight to hell.*

We made camp twice more and kept Red Tyler tied. We threw him a few of our leftovers and as much water as he wanted. Well into the fifth day Socorro stopped, released the man's hands, and ordered him to dismount.

Once the dealer was on his feet, the careless way Socorro stepped close and waved his Colt toward him was a calculated enticement. Sure enough, Red Tyler made a grab for Socorro's .44. After a few seconds of wrestling, Socorro kicked Red's feet from under him. Even as the dealer fell backward in the grass Socorro held his iron close on him. *You fall easy, cabrón. Maybe it's time you doan get up.*

As Red struggled to his feet Socorro cocked his pistol. When he felt insulted, Socorro's disposition camped where pity turned cold. Never having faced his temper myself, so far I'd been unsure what Socorro was liable to do.

How far you think it is back? Socorro asked over his shoulder.

I was relieved to hear this question and, knowing one of us reckoned distance just as well as the other, took it as a hint to add a little weight to Red's conscience. *I'd guess an eight-day walk. Course that's not accounting for time gettin lost, not to forget a feller traveling bare ass might attract a variety of predatory interests.*

Bareass? Socorro responded. *Ah si, good idea.* The Californio returned his attention to Red Tyler. *Bueno, pinchazo. We leave it to the wolves to see your ass. Take them off.*

Red's face turned to chalk but he refused to budge a prairie inch. Socorro continued staring straight through the man: *I tell your best deal. Drop your stinkin clothes.* Stripping down to his longies was all there was left in the talking department for Red Tyler.

Socorro walked to his horse for his canteen pointedly emptied its contents then handed it to the naked man. *Out here water is scarcer than bird shit in a cuckoo clock. Looks like we rigged you up the same as you was when God make a mistake an let you in. Mebbe this is the last time you get to show how much is left of what He made.* This curt sermon, punctuated by a boot in the rear and a pistol shot that whistled past his right ear, compelled Red Tyler to turn and run for his life.

Run! I shouted, lifting my hat. *Run, you cowardly, woman beatin, no good, dry-gulching skunk!*

Enthusiastically urging Red Tyler on, we emptied our cylinders over the pink-skinned fugitive. Watching Tyler almost out of sight I figured his barefoot trip foretold at least eight nights in the wilderness. Many a frontiersman had faced much worse and come through kicking. Still, it would be a rough trip with little to scrounge except prairie turnips, soap weed, and watercress, although I knew he could survive hunger for weeks as long as he found water. I wondered if wolves or bears sensed a naked human on foot was easy prey. Neither of us had feelings whether Tyler had enough sand to make it back dead or alive. Most outfits would have left him swinging from a cottonwood with nary a backward glance.

We considered justice had been lightly served and in turn had adopted some of Red Tyler's bad habits ourselves, as we'd taken his horse and been fortuitously enriched, thanks to his crookedness, by over twelve hundred crooked dollars.

After riding another mile down the trail I recalled Merle's suggestion to look to the dealer's saddle bags. The left satchel contained some silver change, three decks of playing cards, and a box-like cheating contraption employing a hidden bottom and spring to eject an "extra card" whenever a discrete sleight of hand released its mechanism. The other satchel held eight hundred and sixty-eight dollars in greenbacks, a buckskin folder containing three cigars, a set of silver cufflinks, and a gold ring that Socorro declared *precioso*. We now had over two thousand dollars in our kick.

Watching Socorro light up a cigar as we rode on, I recalled another of Claire Young's handy quotations and pondered if its advice supplied legitimacy to the acquisition of fortune and purpose of our deeds: *If you can't find a door, make one.* My mother, however, never mentioned what was waiting on the other side.

Below the Platte River an untouched wilderness broken by expanses of open country provided a rich variety of game. In the lower lying sections numerous flocks of geese, assorted duck species, and other long-legged migrants rose steadily before us before circling back into the reeds. The deer seemed more curious than wary, and we spotted several bears excavating camas roots from the soft ground.

At one point topping a rise we ducked into cover when we spotted a distant figure standing by his horse. From such distance it was hard to determine if the man was a hostile or not because he was wearing a jacket. Socorro watched him mount the horse. *He's an Indian, mebbe a scout.*

How can you tell from this far out? I asked.

Indians mount from the right side, Socorro explained.

We watched the rider canter off to the west and remained out of sight for several minutes before walking on, seeing no further sign of anyone.

Around noon on our sixth day we reached a grassy ridge that offered us a grand view of the river valley. We knew that somewhere parallel to it ran the Kansas & Pacific railroad that would lead us directly to Grand Isle.

As we held our horses on this overlook my eyes wandered with thoughts of Dahlia. I wondered how she was enduring our separation. It was not a failure of belief that challenged my hopes so much as a vastness of the landscape. Below our hilltop stretched only a fragment of a country not yet fully identified as "America," an immensity that dwarfed the affections of two untried youths. As a reflex response to any fear that Dahlia was lost to me, whispering *Mission Santa Ines* continued to be my benediction.

Socorro broke my reverie with a vaquero whoop and kicked his horse into a sliding descent. Following, I allowed our pack mounts to find their own way down into the spongy thickets and brushy flood plains of the Platte River. We shortly made a crossing at a very wide spot and were briefly swept downstream, clinging to our saddle horns until we hit the shallows and staggered soggily ashore.

Drying off, we spotted a flatboat floating downriver and hailed it, but the crew were unwilling to lose way or possibly risk an encounter. However, in answer to our shout as to the direction of Grand Isle, a rudder man pointed upriver away from the Platte hollering, *Jes foller the railroad!*

After navigating more swampy riverbank we pushed uphill through willow thickets. Emerging onto a grassy bench beneath the bluffs we immediately spotted railroad tracks. We dried out and followed the rails until in less than an hour we entered the outskirts of a town.

Grand Isle's depot, located just opposite the original settlement, originally began with a water tank, an agent's office a boarding house, and a railroad eating house. Heavy immigration had transformed the depot into a bustling town with prospering businesses, a post office, three banks, and command of trade throughout that whole northern country.

A standing train was disgorging passengers, many of them German-speaking settlers bound north to settle the Loup Valley. Any doubts we'd had regarding available transport were erased when the station agent explained seats on the just arrived train were plentiful but it lacked a stock car.

When I expressed that back in Ellsworth we'd been told to board the Jupiter, the agent surveyed our dusty state and rolled his eyes. *Every mother's son wants to ride the Jupiter. Next through-train after this one is due this afternoon.*

How soon till we can catch one that will take our horses?

It's a Diamond Stocker pulling first class livery.

How much to get on that train? I asked.

Don't know if they'll let anyone on her. First time a Diamonds' come through here.

Socorro fished in his vest and lifted out a double eagle. *Mebbe they like to let a feller on with this, uh?*

I barely glimpsed the man's arm as he retrieved Socorro's bribe. *Two tickets first class to Sacramento with how many of horses?*

Two, I said.

Let's see. Reckon that would amount to, about two hundred and seventy-two dollars.

Before providing him payment I inquired *Where can we sell three extra mounts?*

They decent?

Cut above that, saddle broke too. See for yourself.

Where they be?

Hitched back of the depot.

The agent removed his cap, reached under his desk, placed another on his head, and stood up. This new cap's tin badge read STATION MASTER.

We walked out to where our five horses stood; a knot of settlers were already discussing their finer points.

The agent made a quick study of the three horses we pointed out and abruptly pulled us aside. *I ain't about to wrangle. Fact is there's so many folks coming in decent saddle stocks getting scarce as hen's teeth. You might drum up a better price for those mounts, but it might take you some time and …*

What you leading up to mister?

Swappin these horses and tack in exchange for two tickets with transfer options for the Jupiter out of Ogden on through to Sacramento. That would include first class livery aboard both legs clear through to California, even San Francisco if you want. Plus I buck the rules to get you on.

Even though this deal greatly favored the railroad man, Socorro and I exchanged accepting nods.

I'll have two men ready with the ramp so you can load your mounts. Keep quiet as a horse trough about our arrangement. Some passengers is company men.

How long is the trip? I asked.

A shade under three days if the train don't get stopped by sunk sleepers, Indians, avalanches, brake trouble, or a fireman trying to push time. Luck to you both. The man shook hands and hurried off.

Socorro and I transferred gear to our saddle horses and gave each remaining animal a final ear scratch of appreciation. Then we accepted our tickets from the station master and lined up as directed. Neither one of us had ever been on a train. Clutching our tickets and gripping our rifles we waited alongside the horses.

When the beast pulled in it skidded to a screeching halt, billowing pillars of steam pistons hissing fierce as a cornered puma. The locomotive's brake momentum groaned as though straining to extract death itself from the grip of damnation. The engine was painted gold and green with diamond-shaped embellishments and a furious red stack above a menacing bucktooth cow catcher.

The fancy new train awaited service like a termite queen. The worker bee duties of its hectic opera sparked an importance in everyone involved, from coal-covered bunker men to uniformed porters, luggage mashers, yard crewmen, water tenders, and an engineer who lazed through his port as though charged with hauling important cargo, come hell or high water, with nary a concern for man or beast. Our station master ranged alongside the platform ostentatiously thumbing his watch chain's vest pocket.

I scarce recall urging our reluctant horses up the ramp into the stock car and helping a colored groom cinch them into their own stall complete with water trough, grain bucket, and better hay than they'd seen in months. The only other animal was a racing stallion, blinkered, padded, and cinched-down like a storm tent. *If this is how they ship blooded horses*, I asked myself, *what's to be expected of how they ship their owners?*

The compartment Socorro and I secured smelled of varnish and newly upholstered seats. We slid its door shut, stacked our possibles and rifles on overhead racks, put our heels up, and exhaled with relief as though we'd just outrun a bank posse.

In minutes the train was grunting slowly out of the depot, and soon we were watching the Platte River slipping past our windows. We were settling in when our carriage door skidded open and a tall bony fellow in a railroad uniform entered. As though about to reveal some veiled secret, he introduced himself as Orville Wanamaker, *cousin to Dolf Wanamaker, the station agent who jest bought the three horses off you fellers.*

Orville wiggled onto the edge of a seat and began a running commentary that seemed destined to accompany us all the way to Ogden. Orville's voice was compressed to a turkey-necked squeak and his salt-stained uniform emitted rank hints of sweat and stale beer. It also appeared his cousin Dolf's conspiratorial wink ran in the family.

Orville's presence bore a silver lining. He was shortly departing us but, leaning closer than comfort, had to explain: *Ole Dolf is honest as the day and he got kinda windy that you might get extricated off this train. So he come up with the notion that I deadhead up the line carrying this flimsy, that's what we call a paper used for railroad messages. This paper is official as you can tote an certifies you boys is on railroad business clear to Ogden where you switch to the Jupiter to California. Yessiree. Cal-if-or-ni-a where there's wimmin eager fer any prospect with sand enough to throw a gal over one shoulder and a shovel over t'other.*

With this assurance Orville Wanamaker tipped two fingers to his cap and exited our compartment, allowing us to lower a window, take a breath of slightly coal-smoked prairie air, and resume the glories of railroad travel.

Hours passed as the train rocked through one panorama after another. The compelling insistence and rhythm of the rails gradually erased the impression of motion altogether. It was as though scenic beauty had distilled to reverie and made us spellbound witnesses to the West.

We made very few stops to take on water and wood. I recall several Nebraska depots, North Platte, Ogalala, Chappel, and then, in Wyoming, Cheyenne, Laramie, and Rawlins, with a final stop in Bryan before proceeding on to Ogden. The station master back at Grand Isle hadn't been kidding about wood trestles thin as rope. More than once, Socorro and I grimaced when our train descended at a reckless pace onto matchstick trestles tooth picked hundreds of feet across some impossible gorge. But the Diamond Stocker careened on until I became persuaded nothing could stop its hurtling progress over the travails of ten thousand Chinese, Irish, and ex-slave laborers. An army of men had transformed what had only recently required a six month ox-powered crosscountry journey into a six-day transcontinental construction miracle.

But it was the glimpse into the wilder backcountry that most captivated me. We passed numerous herds of antelope, some gathered in the hundreds. We ascended steep snowbound passes at a crawl and at their summits gained an exhilarating momentum alongside whitewater rapids and rocky gorges lined with conifer forests. Then down onto miles of high prairie and up again through aspen forests and stands of big timber on the shoulders of sentinel peaks. The elevations were dotted with bighorn sheep, mountain goats, and below these in the sheltering glades and sedge ponds, wood buffalo, elk, moose, and deer.

The rattle of rails in the night acquired another heartbeat, a strident pulse ominous in its determination to conquer darkness as the train tunneled blindly onward through a shrouded country of starlight and stray sparks. Amid this smoky mechanical progress I'd half dream Gaagii stirring as if alerted by my own sleep-shattering fear that we were speeding toward a chasm, tumbling headlong toward a mangled interlocked embrace of angels, demons, horses, buffalo, prairie schooners, burning tipis, ox wagons and stampeding cattle, with Rusty Cuellar's frozen grimace calling me back to startled wakefulness. Ever since that first rail journey I've known that nights on a train will never be my friend.

Time was swallowed by speed and it seemed only hours before we were approaching Ogden. We'd in fact been on the train for one overnight and well into another day. The pantry steward brought us a tasty lamb stew, thick slices of oat bread, and two high mucky mucks, a sweet drink often laced with whisky or rum. I'd fallen asleep and when I awoke we were well into Wyoming. We turned south toward Ogden, where we were to unload our horses and transfer to another train onward to California.

Arriving in Ogden we hastened to get our horses. They'd been offloaded twice on the way to Ogden and walked only briefly, so they were enough cowed by their circumstances to follow our lead down the ramp without any fuss. I was comforted to see Saloon, stroke her muzzle, watch her ears flick at my voice, and inhale the familiar presence of horse.

Observing so much remote backcountry through windows, I'd begun to feel myself a prisoner of glass. I looked toward wandering again where iron wheels and inner voices gave way to the *scree* cry of a hawk, hollow *clup clup* of a crow, and the trickle of a mountain brook.

I was eager to explore wilderness that for so many miles I'd only observed from the confining *huff huff* of a clacking train.

In Ogden another iron horse was already making steam. After flashing our tickets we were speedily directed toward its first-class carriages, our mounts loaded this time into a livery car carrying three other horses. We were told it was seven hundred and fifty miles to Sacramento. I calculated that on horseback over the terrain we'd just travelled it might have taken months rather than our scheduled twenty-two hours given that I figured I could handle more glass for now.

Our next compartment was similar to the first one but a good deal more worn. Free of Wanamaker's previous constrictions we were now free to wander the train, among its assorted second-class passengers, we encountered a group of migrant Cornishmen known as Cousin Jacks stocky fellows with the broad forearms of hard-rock miners. These men were bound for the Sierra foothills and chatted with us curious in regard to Socorro's line of work and suspected purpose of his Navy Colt.

Observing the tall and colorful figure Socorro cut on board the train, I realized how fiercely this new world was causing his to retreat. At one point in our trip Socorro said *This train ridin make things go by so fast it make a man disremember what he's seen.* Socorro casually allowed the miners' curiosity for his pistol, unloading the Colt for their examination and handing it over for inspection as though it were a hand-worn kitchen tool. To Socorro, fond as he was of its function and feel, a gun was no more than a useful object like a rope or saddle.

In Ellsworth I'd witnessed first hand how the trail-worn uniqueness of Socorro's Californio rig had been its own protection. His wheeled spurs, sash, and serapi appeared odd yet native enough in style to deter quick judgment, and sufficient for cowboys to recognize a true vaquero. Born to the saddle, Socorro had been shaped by its necessity of ease. Unburdened by yesterday or tomorrow, my friend embodied characteristics wilderness had taught him, a life habituated to roll onward like prairie grass and rest in the stillness of the open sky. I liked to think something had rubbed off, that thanks to Socorro Requelme so much of what the prairie had taken from me as a boy had been replenished.

Fifty-six miles west of Ogden our train reached Promontory Point and blasted its whistle past the spot where the golden spike had been driven to mark the joining of the rails from east and west. Informed of this American railroad history, the Cornish miners toasted its accomplishment from jugs of "scrumpy," a potent apple cider which happily shared. We soon passed out of Utah Territory into Nevada, steamed through Toana, took on water in Carlin, and headed for Winnemucca.

My first impression of the Great Basin was of its trackless scope and constant dryness. An alchemy of immensity and aridity combined with a relentless sun warped hours into mirages. As mile after mile staring toward horizons turned distance into reverie, I would be startled by faces abruptly closer to memory, ghostly voices of a multitude murmuring an accompaniment to the mechanical hypnosis of our train.

So much absence makes a beggar of emptiness, but I perceived little else save desert solitude to fill it up. I was equally fascinated by a landscape entirely new to my experience and, by the sculpted varieties of its rock formations strangely reminiscent more of the impact of water than wind. The entire country seemed so conquered by sun that its only movement was the shimmer of heat above worn pinnacles and boulders of sand-blasted rock.

The region sobered me to the possibility that we once might have been foolhardy enough to challenge its unrelenting furnace. Certainly several parties had managed to cross by the further southern route but not here, not at this latitude where no sign of recent habitation existed on the baked, treeless land.

When we stopped at Winnemucca that night to take on water I stepped off the train to stretch my legs. Though it was very warm an occasional hint of wind brought wafts of relief. I relished the scent of desert air, dry but surprisingly free of dust despite the puffs of breeze. The hovering silence, heat, and encompassing desolation conveyed infinite space, overhead a cloudless luminosity glittered with swathes of the Milky Way.

I was overtaken by a relief derived from more than just a respite from my sweltering carriage's claustrophobia and the iron squeal of locomotive wheels. The vastness of the desert crossing had gifted me escape from a fear that I was destined to be forever on the run from past deeds. I strolled past the cars until clear of their locomotive's steamy hiss I then exhaled into the darkness, relieved to realize there was a lot more of my life to remember than to forget.

I recalled a very old Navajo in Bosque Redondo who had sat cross-legged by his hogan often for days at a time. When I'd ask Blue Jay what the elder was doing, my friend responded, *traveling*. Later, still curious, I inquired of an amiable buck skinner how a Navajo could sit so long unperturbed by events around him. He explained that the man was visiting places he had hunted and camped, because an Indian's life was inseparable from the landscape. Taking his cross-legged journeys was as real as travel to the old man; the experience of every place he had known lived inside him.

The buck skinner's explanation had refreshed my understanding of the distinction between loneliness and solitude. Many Indians appear silent because, knowing nature speaks, they attend its "conversation." Most of my days then had been lived outdoors. I'd spent hours entertained by the shenanigans of a prairie dog town, watching the rough and tumble of fox kits outside a den, or face-off with a wolf in mutual acceptance that neither of us intended harm. Tracking taught me not only the language of animal behavior, sign, and scent, but also to gradually realize that the entire surround of wilderness was involved. I considered myself more a participant in this invitation as a receptive guest than as a hunter. I'd sat hours in a forest glade just like that old Navaho man and be approached by wild creatures, catch an instant of myself reflected in a doe's glance, and have chickadees alight on my shoulder. It is difficult to trace the movements and habits of a creature's nature and not develop a kinship.

The backcountry emboldened my senses toward humans the same way I was drawn to everything else, instantly, intuitively, trusting instincts that had always guided me. My first immediate intuition of Dahlia had been more recognition than desire: a lightness of movement, a resonance of voice, an unveiling of eyes, her native grace redolent of wilderness imbued with the innocence of an unassuming presence. My most enduring kinship a glance that united Dahlia de Belardes and me as bold friends. Traveling so far west to track her down I was entering unknown territory alive with anticipation. Eagerly imagined, California was rumored to be another Eldorado, a settler's dream of all things bright and beautiful, a land of mountains and rivers without end, a pilgrim's paradise bounded by a bountiful sea.

Strolling back along creosoted sleepers of the railroad tracks, I smiled at details of fantastic rumors and was reminded to take my journey step by step. Re-boarding I swung myself one-handed from the carriage rail; hinged there a long moment, I felt my life gather freedoms of a journey that had made me immensity's child.

We pulled out of Wadsworth, Nevada, at a crackerjack pace across dry farm sections interspersed with fields of cattle and horses. Shortly after we began a slower ascent into foothills and crossed the state line into California, animating Socorro and me out of our torpor.

My quest for Dahlia which suddenly seemed more imminent than I dared hope, was amplified by our enthusiasm to see California itself. As for Socorro, he made it clear his journey ended here, musing *Amigo, I was thinkin of not makin it home to my country before I got too old to cook my cojones across that stinkin desert. Now this train cross it so quick I get no dust on my boots. I remember this territory pretty good but it looks changed. I see fences, towns, more peoples. I hope some place left for a vaquero like me.*

The train's reliable piston beat had started to labor our chugging slow ascent through the spectacular Donner Pass. Winding up into the Sierras, impressive man-made cuts through granite formations displayed engineering accomplishments on a scale I'd never before seen. Our precarious route followed a river canyon with soaring cliffs rising from one side of the train and breathless drop-offs falling from the other.

All at once we flashed into darkness. We'd entered the snow sheds and the locomotive crawled on through this wooden tunnel for what seemed an eternity. Periodically we had a respite from our car's thudding echo and from the sequestered smoke inside these chilly avalanche shelters. We'd fleetingly glimpse a trace of snow before finally clattering free from what amounted to thirty miles of confining darkness.

When we did break out of the snow sheds into mountain sunlight, our westward descent proved much more gradual. Perhaps ten miles farther down we rolled into Truckee, relieved to have transited the grand gateway into California, one that held a reputation for blizzards, avalanches, derailments, even cannibalism.

Our train paused in Truckee and had to remain awhile because, as a kid peddling hot coffee explained in theatrical jargon for everyone in earshot, *Yup, they need a jerry gang to grease the monkey and freeze a hub after a hotbox or two over the Donner. We'll depot here to cool so the ash cat can bake his cake and make enough fog so the eagle eye can drop a lever and let the big dogs roll.*

The gist of this railroad lingo vanished with the kid and we began our final run into Colfax where the Cornish miners got off. We then continued to Sacramento.

Eager to arrive, we began tidying our saddlebags, slickers, and bedrolls, and brought our rifles to hand. We took stock of our money. Sorting greenbacks and counting our stake, Socorro and I divvied up over nineteen hundred dollars. I felt confident of making a good start, as I'd been told by one of the Cousin Jacks that a relative in Grass Valley had bought foothill land at three dollars an acre. As I watched Socorro fold his share into a pouch, it occurred to me we'd soon be parting ways. I had yet to either query him about his plans or formulate my own.

What happens after we get to Sacramento? I asked.

When Socorro didn't answer immediately I hoped my query wasn't too abrupt. This was the first time I'd considered that Socorro might have a map of his own. Along our back trail we'd never discussed his life much. I guessed that Socorro was around ten years older than I and I'd picked up a few hints of his wanderings. He'd crossed from California into Arizona through the southern desert. Three in his party died on the way. He'd worked cattle down in south Texas and as far north as Montana. He'd dipped back down as far as Mexico a few times and then worked three years along the Texas coast and up into the Panhandle. Jack Rice had mentioned that Socorro had survived his share of dustups and left some bones in his wake.

Socorro was the best horseman I had ever encountered. His tastes were clear: he disliked cold weather, cheaters, walking, sweet coffee, preferred tortillas over biscuits, and seldom used his spurs. He respected Indians; I guessed he was a piece of one himself. He had Old World manners. I saw him cross himself a few times, usually after rather than before trouble, yet sometimes at dawn he'd also pray to the sun and leave little medicine bundles on rock outcroppings. He had an eye for the few women we'd seen. Most of them didn't hesitate to eye him right back. I'd grown to appreciate his cowboy skills and quiet courage. I felt let down at the realization that he had a life that was about to take a road apart from mine.

Socorro knew I saw he was reading me and grinned. *You won't finish nothing here in Sacramento.*

No, I don't guess I will.

You got to find your woman. How you gonna do that?

I have the name of the place they sent her to Mission Santa Ines.

Bueno. Mission Santa Ines. And where is that?

I guess it's not far from here.

No, amigo. That place is a day's ride north from Santa Barbara. I have people down there. It is a long way an they got no trains to it.

I have a good horse, I said.

Your horse doan speak Spanish an you doan know the way. Mission Santa Ines is a small place. Everybody there will be watchin your muchacha. What you think her family tell their hombres to do to you if they catch you sniffin aroun?

Caught short by Socorro's question and by answers I didn't have, *I'm going to find her* was all I could blurt out.

Devon you an me seen a lot of country but no place like California. Not too hot, not too cold. Those gringos breakin their back diggin miss the best gold. You can grow anything here. Fruitas. Maize. Plenty horses, vacas, plenty feed, plenty wood, plenty water. Alta California! La vida sucre, amigo. So we go get your novia an then, maybe, find one for me.

Find a woman. Easy as that?

My frens can find out easy who is in Santa Ines. They got some nice sisters an cousins. Mebbe my frens is old but the gorls is not so old.

I didn't know what to say that might convey my appreciation for Socorro's help. Reaching to shake his hand I was also curious *how come you never mentioned finding yourself a señorita before?*

Socorro's reply typified his ownership of every moment: *There was no before.*

As our train entered the Sacramento depot and wheezed to a final stop, I cornered a porter who stuck his head through the door to announce the end of the line. He hadn't heard of Mission Santa Ines but pointed us toward the ferry dock to catch a river boat toward the coast.

We hurried to offload our horses. The depot showed no indications of places to hitch or corral animals, and when we got to the stock car, which was just ahead of the caboose, a railroad man and a constable were waiting.

Looking for two saddle horses? The railroad man asked then responding to our nods, warned: *We don't allow no stock through the depot. Your mounts an tack is in a holding chute across the tracks. After you pick em up follow the lane on down behind the sheds until you're clear past the buffers.*

A poker faced constable with handlebar mustache and blue uniform stepped forward and pointed to our rifles and sidearms. *Gentlemen, ordinance requires you carry your weapons unloaded within city limits. Saturdays an Sundays you can't be carrying no weapons at all. Lucky today is a Tuesday else I'd have to take your guns an then have the judge set a fine.*

We obediently emptied our gun chambers, pocketed the shells, and levered our rifle actions to show they were unloaded. Satisfied, the constable became quite amiable.

Where you boys coming in from?

Started out after a herd in New Mexico then rode up to Grand Island from Ellsworth, Kansas, I replied.

Ellsworth? Ain't that where Wild Bill Hickock shot two men?

Socorro corrected the story. *That was up in Hayes City. The outfit I was with run into him on the trail after he kill two men an peoples in Hayes did'n want him bein sheriff no more.*

You met Wild Bill Hickock?

I seen him.

The constable stepped forward. *Allow me to shake the hand of a man who met Wild Bill Hickok,* he said, vigorously pumping Socorro's arm. *Looks to me you fellers has seen interestin times an likely handled them jest fine. Liable to find California a mite tame. Easy to keep it that way: keep a smile on your face, steer clear of the gold camps an opium dens, and this whole state's yours for the askin.*

I took an opportunity to inquire as to how we'd get over to the coast.

Just follow the corral fence until you hit the ferry terminal. The "Sonoma" is docked there but she don't carry stock. There's plenty other small operators will take you to Benicia, around a four-hour float down the river through the Carquinez Strait. After that you can ride toward the coast an pick up the Mission Trail. Might follow a stage route, even hire on as protection for some of their fancy passenger coaches.

Much appreciated, I replied.

The constable remained eager to pick our brains. *You reckon there's truth to the claim Wild Bill kilt a hundred men an all of 'em fer good cause?*

Most was Indians an the rest was just slow, Socorro concluded and turned on his heel.

o

The ferry terminal was an expansive wooden dock berthing an enormous paddle boat and a string of smaller side-wheelers. We were assailed by several ticket agents eager to offer passage downriver. We settled on a brightly painted boat named the "Delta Lady." After paying three dollars each to corral the horses on the lower stern deck, we paid two dollars for our tickets and took a place standing along the rail of an upper deck.

A knot of workmen noisily played cards while a number of Chinese men huddled nearby nervously eyeing our rifles.

It was pleasant trip down a river that opened up into a widening delta. The current was strong and aided by our noisy side paddles carried us along at a swift pace. I took note of the mix of brushy islands and swamp along the riverbanks. The river carried plenty of traffic. Smaller boats and barges headed in both directions, which forced our pilot to steer a tricky course sometimes not altogether to the benefit of wake-tossed skiffs seeking to drop fishing nets or simply cross the river. Most fascinating were the myriad flocks of water-birds, geese, ducks, and a variety of wading species. Socorro and I, along with passengers crowding the rail, watched a boatman struggling to haul in a large, odd-looking fish, which one man explained was a sturgeon, and *mighty tasty.*

Close to dusk we made port in Benicia, which was basically a big single-ferry dock at the foot of barren hills. Warehouse buildings and several shacks were all that broke an otherwise featureless riverbank. Apparently the location was a major crossing point, as there was a large ferry about to cross back across the delta. We clattered our horses down the gangplank, saddled them up, and soon were following the only uphill track that lead inland.

It was good to be on a horse again. We had purchased a sack of grain for our mounts and decide to ride over the first range of hills and find a spot to sleep. There was a slight breeze and it was warm, but the immediate landscape seemed devoid of good grass, being mostly brush scattered across dry clay ground with squirrels scurrying from hole to hole and little sign of larger game.

We'd been given rough directions in regard to the trail west and were eager to break free of what we saw so far to be an inhospitable hardpan region. To add to our discomfort, when we bedded down we were attacked by swarms of mosquitoes until Socorro built a smoky brushfire. We attempted sleep and awoke in clothes smoked as buffalo jerky.

We continued through the dry yellow hills and rode all day following a wagon track south along the banks of a delta, passing stands of bullrushes and skirting swampier stretches. Cutting farther inland from the river delta, we began to encounter gangs of Chinese workers excavating drainage ditches and, farther south, digging even larger irrigation works. In established farming sections, fall ploughing was conducted by staggered horse teams involving as many as twelve animals, all of them heaving disk rigs that generated great clouds of dust. These activities were my first glimpses of commercial agriculture and the large-scale efforts required to drain and irrigate extensive croplands.

Deciding to camp outside a pueblo called Alviso we encountered an old man walking a mule cart loaded with cut tule reeds. Hailed in English he simply waved, but when Socorro tried Spanish the old-timer stopped, produced a jug of water, and proceeded to describe our route farther west.

The gist of his information was to continue a few miles to a barge landing, cross the delta, and continue west toward Mission San Jose. The farmer described the road as El Camino Real but also explained it was *muy triste* in that the Mission had been badly damaged in a large *temblor de tierra*. From there he said we should follow the

Camino Real connecting all the other Missions where some *Católicos* would gladly help another Californio.

Curious as to the meaning of *temblor de tierra* I asked Socorro, who explained how the earth shook mightily, opening enormous cracks in the ground and causing buildings to collapse, often with a great loss of life. Alarmed at this description, I wondered how often such catastrophes occurred. Socorro pressed a finger to his lips as if even discussion might provoke one. Meanwhile the old man crossed himself several times.

That night we camped alongside the wagon road in a stand of lemon trees. Next morning, true to the old man's directions, when we veered west again we encountered a muddy lagoon where several flatboats were unloading farm equipment. After a short negotiation we walked our horses onboard and were alternately sailed and poled across half a mile of shallow water to the opposite shore.

Mission San Jose was now just a day's ride ahead of us. The country had changed, as lazy yellow hills now yielding richer grasses were interspersed with verdant valleys with orchards and scattered groups of fenced-in cattle. We followed an easy trace that wound over low hills and across valleys. Settlements were common. We rode up to a ranch house with a shady ramada in front offering berries, nuts, fresh bread, and assorted fruits, some of it entirely new to my taste. The owner's wife was jubilant at our stuffing her offered flour-sacks and seeing our admiration of her fields and orchards. It struck me that this truly was country of green bounty, so far-flung from the sparse prairies and hard climate I had been born to.

That evening we saw San Jose in a broad valley and pushed on through darkness to the mission itself. The building was under repair after earthquake devastation four years prior, but clearly not to the majesty it had once claimed under Spanish rule. We were directed to a low adobe where we could water our horses and sleep. An English-speaking monk appeared and suggested a small offering would suffice. He promised us a brief tour of the Mission grounds come morning, explaining that President Abraham Lincoln had returned Spanish missions to the Catholic Church in 1865 after they had been secularized by the Mexican government in 1833. It was clear this renewal had not enriched the mission's status, as it was run down and the surrounding community equally poor.

Come sunup the cleric briefly guided us around his mission before wishing us a safe journey and setting us on the stage road that was the beginning of our access to the Old Mission Trail. He also explained that all the missions were set roughly a long day's ride apart, and that with luck we'd make Santa Cruz by nightfall unless we encountered blockages over the pass.

As we rode out I looked back over the shattered remnants and collapsed walls of what had once been an imposing architecture. In respect to California's earthquakes, crossing my fingers, I philosophized that there is a fly in every ointment.

The Old Mission Trail was well traveled. We passed numerous single riders and teamsters pushing oxen across the valley toward the foothills where low clouds shrouded the coastal range. We climbed steadily over dry grassy ridges spotting deer, a few elk, and one soaring bird with a greater wingspan than any I'd ever seen. We overcame several stagecoaches, but one marked Pioneer Stage Line Delivery passed us at a furious gallop. At a summit we caught up with its lathered and blowing horses.

The initially dry foothills began to show scattered copses of tall evergreens interspersed with stands of oak and madrone, and what I took to be walnut. I assumed the taller evergreen species to be California redwood. Once we achieved higher reaches of the wetter Coastal Range we continued uphill, progressing under redwood stands in an almost spiritual silence. I suggested to Socorro that we pull off the trail and venture into the forest so I might see a giant tree up close. Socorro raised his palm for me to wait. Several arduous miles later we turned off the wagon road on a flat where a tree sprouting three trunks resembled a giant candelabrum. Socorro tethered his horse and signaled me to follow him.

After shouldering through some brush that fringed the trail I found myself navigating springy duff among deeply shaded fiddle ferns. The forest floor was a litter of decomposing trunks and splintered branches hosting sage-colored moss on fallen limbs thick as the entire trunks of most trees. Scattered shafts of sun anointed a reigning silence with windowed light. I'd never entered a woodland grove as silenced by immobility and timelessness. To say a redwood "soars" would be like ascribing "winged" properties to flying buttresses of a man-made cathedral. Bowed to veneration by the majesty of its creation, I was more inspired by the redwood's rooted grip than by its height. The oldest trees hosted small nations of living things secreted among tree bark gullies, and lightning-scarred trunks towering above exposed boles that had sheltered centuries of creatures great and small. That glade of great trees became earthbound as a mountain in the dominion of my soul.

My reverie was broken by Socorro who, assuming an exaggerated posture of contained impatience, waited for me to return to a world he inhabited. He led me around the largest redwood's trunk and together we stepped under a blackened arch into the nave-like interior of the fire-hollowed tree. Socorro unsheathed his knife and began to scrabble under the mulch and leafy detritus. After considerable effort he stepped into the light and displayed a large flat skull.

Studying the heavy eye sockets and great teeth I was perplexed. *Bear? How'd you know this was in there?*

Socorro's response was an enigmatic grin as he shook the skull, and caught a thumb-sized crystal still partially wrapped in the desiccated scraps of a buckskin sachet.

I come up here long time ago with two Esselen trackers an a Chumash bear doctor lookin for his son. We trace him through every village along the Mission Trail clear up to the coast Miwok who tole us there is a big tribe of bears all up an down these ridges that hunts into the Central Valley where plenty bears eat the Maidu people. The ole man figure his son come up this way an found sign of a ghost bear, an it had kilt him.

What makes a bear a "ghost bear"?

Bears was all naked people a long time ago an got all hairy from not bein particular of what they eat, diggin so much grubs an ants an bulbs an roots their bellies got grouchy. A skinned bear look jus like a people without no clothes. Ghost bears watches human people so they can learn to make fire again but they never can because bears like people meat more than the people who wore it.

What was the Chumash feller after?

A Chumash aimin to be a bear doctor got to find one that wants to be a people and trick it into swallowing some special medicine that kills him. Then he skins that bear and wears it so power comes to his dreams then he is a doctor who can suck out poison. We found the son half-eaten down on the coast side of this trail an the ole man say we had to find that grizzly else it would follow us an eat our people too.

How did you know which bear killed him?

Prints an sign was all around an jus like the ole man claimed, that bear liked watchin. We tracked us up here an I dropped it with one shot close as I am to you right now. The ole man made us burn the hide an bones except this skull, which he give to me after puttin a crystal inside to stop its ghost travelin in the dark.

Socorro ducked back into the tree and re-emerged without the skull. Tucking the crystal into his vest pocket, he lay hands on the redwood for a silent moment. *These big old trees keep us California people small enough to see where we are.*

Back on the wagon trail, it grew rutted and broken by protruding roots that required selective progress over washed-out rock strata and across eroded gullies. Additionally soaked by a fluctuating drizzle, we felt fortunate to be on horseback having come across wagons tipped into ruts or stuck in mud. We stopped to offer aid to two of these foundering teams, which was much appreciated.

Reaching another summit and pausing to water our mounts, we were pleased to note that the pool's runoff flowed west. So far the wagon road had proved challenging to the stage lines and ox teams, but this seemed due to recent rain. Downhill progress proved slippery for several more miles until the redwood forest began to thin onto scattered glades and grassy knolls. When the finishing mile of the road became precariously steep, we passed two wagons using log brakes to slow their downhill skid. Rounding a steep-sided turn I caught my first glimpse of the Pacific sea. Turning triumphantly to Socorro I flourished my hat and whispered to the sky: *hold on Dahlia, I'm on my way.*

o

Santa Cruz was a bustling port. We were both drawn to its pier to watch the great sailing ships unloading and loading cargo. Many of the vessels were taking on lumber, some to carry far afield or ship south along the coast. I was fascinated by the tall-masted schooners and parade of ox wagons bringing enormous saw logs to be laboriously windlassed into waiting holds.

A weedy shoreline smelled of the sea, and its salty ebb wafting from the anchorage compelled my imagining beyond the great masts rocking at anchor toward a rolling distance abruptly razored at its horizon. I'd never viewed the curvature of the world nor sensed how its edge dropped off so cleanly.

I realized that this was where every westward wagon turned around or was forced north or south. Crowds of gulls mewed about us and we watched stubby-winged birds dive with a hearty splash, surfacing with a struggling catch in their baggy craws. Below us among the creosote pilings big-eyed seals barked and frolicked, some chasing fish that two girls tossed, giggling, into the maws of these whiskery acrobatic creatures. Enchanted as children ourselves we stood transfixed by the scene until a molten sun's radiance slipped out of sight.

Heading back to get our tethered mounts, we walked across the nubby planks of the pier toward land. A stocky sailor wearing a gold earring and smoking a cheroot leaned over the rail. He had a seabag at his feet and hailed us in an accent reminiscent of Arch Tobin, our old trail cook.

You blokes lookin for lost cows? he joked.

A whole herd of them, I replied. *Where are you from if I might ask?*

See that square-rigger over there with its hawsers lined to shore anchors? We'll load timber, then up-anchor. Bloody marvelous, redwood is; awful big stuff to move, though. We got gum trees where I hail from. Not much use. Wood dries out harder than a donkey's pecker. We'll flog these California logs for a good profit. Likely load up on oak down the coast then tack back up for more.

You've sailed the seven seas? I asked, a phrase that likely revealed my own seamanship was limited to penny pirate books.

Damn near all of em, mate. Not for everyone, mind you. Looks calm as a virgin's dreams out there right now. Just wait. Seen it kick up twenty-foot seas. Lost a mast or two in me time. Where you blokes hail from?

We travelled across country from New Mexico.

New Mexico? Never heard of it. Must be a long trick from this beach. By the cut of yer jib I'd wager you've seen a thing or two. Ever had to use them horse pistols?

Bypassing this query I inquired if he knew of anywhere we might get a meal and spend the night.

Fair dinkum mate. Keep straight up the hill an there's a row of establishments. Watch it as you pass the local dive. Saucy girls of every stripe. When they flash their knickers an arsks, loik to troi somethin new, sailor? I answers: fair enough sweetheart how about leprosy? Further on past the Sheilas on the game there's the "Rusty Anchor." It's awroit, clean bunks an decent grub. Couple of yankee dollars'l get you a bed. Staying there meself. Might as well show you. I'm Harry Fraser, rigger on the Mary Anne out of Sydney, that's downunder case you ain't heard of it. Captain's a right cracker. Reckons to make his fortune in California. Not my cuppa tea. Oi aim to crew down to Panama, sign articles on a steam packet, an get 'ome. No more ruddy canvas for me.

The sailor offered these details as we walked up the hill together, hitched our horses, and entered the Rusty Anchor, a weathered clapboard lodging where we sampled fresh fish quite savory though a shade slimy on the tongue as well as steamed spuds, a tasty bowl of shellfish stew, thick bread, and sudsy mugs of ale. Having never dined on mussel, clam and crab stew I sampled the soup warily but was soon scraping the bowl. We insisted on hosting a meal for our chatty host who described, among other yarns, naked cannibals, naked women, naked savages with bones in their noses, and painted portraits of nakedly tumultuous seas.

The establishment was blithely nautical with porthole windows and hatch-cover tables. We occupied captain's chairs while a buxom waitress served us on heavy crockery designed to survive the culinary manners of giants. I gathered that Pacific ports are richly-charactered versions of the sea life. Our boots and saddles felt as much in place as oars on a wagon.

Later, as I settled into sleep, my bunk's sideboards and the low-ceilinged cabin were as close to a ship as I'd ever been. I let shafts of oceanic moonlight caress my eyes as I sailed into the sleep of a wanderer always going home.

At sunup we grained our horses and found the old road that began downhill of Mission Santa Cruz. The structure, virtually in ruins, was overlooked by collapsing adobes occupied by a remnant population of Awaswas Indians. This small coastal tribe had been converted by Spanish missionaries a century before. Forced into cheap labor and almost considered slaves, half the Indians perished of white man's diseases. Of what we saw of the surviving Awaswas many appeared dispirited and sickly. A few old women offered to sell us some skillfully woven reed baskets.

We urged our horses into a steady walk behind a stage driver who indicated he'd be happy to have us follow along. The man passed us a worn mission map and pointed out passenger stage layovers at San Juan Bautista, Señora de Soledad, San Miguel Archangel, and San Luis Obispo de Tolosa.

We stayed back from the stagecoach but after a few miles, discomforted by the slow pace and constant dust kicked up by the stage team, moved ahead and allowed our horses to walk or lope as they chose. The foothills to the east were heavily forested with redwoods rising to a broken mist-shrouded skyline. Closer to the sea the land offered a mix of oak-studded hills and grassy meadows, with many brushy arroyos and standing ponds.

In a full day's ride we made San Luis Bautista. The crumbling mission's grounds were extensive with a large grassy plaza surrounded by rolling stock pastures and fruit orchards. There was a good well and a cistern with easy access for our horses, which we hobbled in lush grass behind a partially-collapsed bell tower where we threw down for the night. At sunup before saddling up we lazed in the grass entertained by our horses' foamy mouths as they crunched the windfalls of a nearby crab apple's tart fruit.

When returned to the wagon road, our journey passed quickly as we walked our horses up and down long easy slopes and across rough bridges. We watered the horses and rested at a few stage stops whose operators offered a ready hospitality. In addition to its people's goodwill, California sunshine seemed a permanent fixture. We often rode through a variety of loose stock sheep, goats, cattle, and horses, many of them grazing at will. I'd never enjoyed such an open and pleasing ride through gentle rolling hills.

We continued this steady progress between one Mission and the next and in four days made San Luis Obispo. As we approached Socorro came alive with recognition and began to point out remembered landmarks, including the names of vaqueros he'd ridden with fifteen or more years previous, a time, he claimed, when much of central California was for the taking. Riding downhill toward San Luis Obispo, Socorro turned us off onto a faint trail he said would take us through *easy country.*

A mile or so from the mission road Socorro pointed to an oak grove above a creek that entered a grassy clearing and suggested we let our hungry mounts wander among its flowers to graze. We dismounted and were about to unsaddle when Socorro pointed to fresh tracks that flattened the grass. By their size the prints must have been made by a large bear.

Amigo, it's time you rope a California bear, Socorro grinned. *Is best with four ropes but it can be done with two loco vaqueros. Me an you. The bear always go for the man that don't miss so we both got to make our throw. Which paw you want a fron one or the back one? You got that big Mex saddle horn to wrap your rope. If we keep him on a tight loop we'll stretch this bear.*

Then what?

Mebbe we eat him.

I followed Socorro over a low rise and stopped where he was pointing his hand like a pistol at the very large bear busily excavating a hole in a grassy mound. Catching our scent the grizzly rose onto its haunches and began clawing the air in our direction. We ducked back below the rise and ran to get our horses.

I'd seen plenty of bears, most of them smaller than this one. I'd also seen some nasty scars and heard campfire yarns about the ferocity of a grizzly attack. One cowboy narrated how he'd seen a bear break a cow's neck with one blow. I'd also seen deep claw marks on tree trunks and had come across the body of an Indian that had been mauled.

Socorro was shaking out his reata. *Grab your loop.*

My horse was already fighting the bit and starting to crow hop. *We'd have to be loco to try and get two ropes on a full-grown grizz.*

Verdad, is very big oso. Socorro replied. *But I do this before when I was young.*

Just "you" did it?

Si. With my amigos.

Amigos. How many amigos? I asked this question while standing up in the stirrups and looking toward the knoll where the bear had been digging. I could see its head and shoulders and hear its jaws making bone-chilling clicks that carried uphill toward us. Both of our horses, wall-eyed with fear, were side-stepping and fighting their bits.

It would be a heap of work, I said, *skinning that big old bear.*

Bear grease taste muy saboroso, Socorro began, but the bear had dropped to four legs and, bawling like a mud-sunk cow, was closing on us at a dead run. *Mebbe we do this tomorrow,* Socorro hoarse whispered as we spun our ready horses and hightailed uphill. Grateful for its crest, we paused to look back at the bear now on his hind legs half-heartedly flailing its huge forearms and curling its purple lips toward these interlopers with six legs, four heads, and two tails smelling of fear, smoke, salt, and fresh meat.

Lifting my hat in respect, I was glad I neither had to rope, shoot, or eat him nor feel those nasty bear hooks ploughing my guts. *How many amigos did you say?* I pressed Socorro.

Four, he laughed, *one for each feet.*

How would we have got our ropes off his paws?

Shoot him. Then I show you how a skinned bear look jus like people with no clothes on.

I guess they taste like us, too.

I never eat no people, Socorro shrugged.

Backtracking to the mission road we continued our journey making it to San Luis Obispo by nightfall. The mission was largely deserted, although there were a few scattered goats and cattle; we were greeted by local Indians who lived in and around the ruins.

After traveling two more days and nights we passed La Purissima Concepcion, our last landmark before approaching Mission Santa Ynez. The Santa Ynez Valley lay picturesquely between its surrounding hills. From the near distance we studied the mission, one of the few that was not only intact but well cared for. Horses and mules filled the corrals, and ox carts and people milled about in front of a main church with a tall bell tower. There were a few low adobes, several fronted by tidy gardens where several women were tending flowers. My heart quickened at the possibility that one of the women might be Dahlia, but at this distance the figures appeared too much alike to tell.

Keeping cover under a grove of oak trees, we paused to make a plan. *I go down,* Socorro said, *ask aroun in Spanish, an mebbe make a fren. Fine out if you señorita is here.*

Ask them about Dahlia. Dahlia de Belardes, I said, dismounting and leading Saloon deeper into cover. I hitched her and returned to watch Socorro ride slowly down the hill onto the mission grounds.

It was dark when Socorro returned.

She in there? I asked, trying to conceal my anxiety.

I meet with a nice abuela, give her half a dollar, an she tell me evything I ask.

Well?

You gorl been here since her brothers bring her from a long way away. She been sick. She think Dahlia a nice girl, like to be in the garden, but a man watch her all the time outside an lock her at night. She show me the door, it look easy to open, easy from the outside.

She's sick?

The abuela think is mostly bein sad has made her sick.

Think Dahlia can ride?

The woman say they got no horse.

What do we do?

Socorro looked back toward the Mission. I take you down the valley an see if my cousins still live behind the hills. Is not far from here.

247

Then what?

We come back in the night an take her, hombre. The abuela show me the place. Look, see them adobe with the tile roofs, that one with the big red pot at the door?

Think we can take her without making a ruckus?

Nobody I see got guns.

Then what?

I knew some Chumash people mebbe still got a doctor fix her.

Anybody down there act suspicious?

Sushpishose?

Anybody think you were looking for Dahlia?

The old woman. A monje talk with me an I jus ask him some way to the next mission. He tell a woman to sell me these, Socorro produced a loaf of coarse bread and a small round of goat cheese.

A monje?

A Católico who wear a long dress an big cross on it.

We walked farther uphill toward the road, threw down beside a big split rock, and shared the bread and cheese. It was a long night. I lay in the prickly oak leaves listening to Socorro breathe, and watched the sky through overhanging branches. It was still chilly when daylight arrived under a cloudy sky. I'd gotten up once before dawn and walked back toward the mission, but under a half moon I couldn't see much. Returning, I pressed my forehead against an oak trunk and tried to settle my restless hopes.

○

At daylight we heard the slow tolling of a bell from the mission below. After hurriedly saddling up we headed out. Rejoining the mission road we started at a gallop until the horses began to blow, then alternately walked and loped toward Santa Barbara before turning east onto a dusty track. The surrounding country was sweet to the eye. To the west a range of hills were dotted with rock outcroppings and ancient oaks, many of them with great branches that touched the ground. We spotted numerous deer. Some, heavily antlered and scrounging the acorns, looked up indifferently as we rode by.

We continued east through grassy hills. Fenced sections held horses and shorthorn cattle. Farther on Socorro led us onto a horse trail and we left the fenced land behind, climbing slightly through a narrow cut then descending into a broad valley broken by low hillocks.

Soon the cut narrowed between two pinnacles, opening before us onto a circle of adobe huts and beehive-shaped shelters framed with willow saplings interwoven with cattails and reeds. Several Indian women were occupied pestling flour and stripping willow bark.

We rode past these shelters up to one of the adobes, where a man came out to meet us. His wife, a small Spanish woman, immediately recognized Socorro and they held hands in a warm greeting as the old man looked on approvingly.

This is Librado Kitsepawit an his woman Amada. Amada is my cousin. She got three nice sisters, Socorro lifted his brows. *This Chumash clan is called the Samala. Librado speak no Spanish. I can ask Amada to find out a doctor.*

A Chumash doctor? I replied.

Si, hombre, these Chumash doctor have fix sick peoples for a long time.

I waited outside and observed the activity around me. Two women continued pestling acorn flour in stone mortars; another was weaving a basket into an intricate pattern. Several children played a game with a large brown seed that they took turns tossing into a hole, stepping back, and throwing it again, until the longest toss that hit the target won. They also made a game of touching my pistol and running away. Their fathers wore ragged mission clothes and many displayed shell necklaces and crucifixes. The settlement, nestled far enough in the backcountry to distance it from the mission trail, appeared well kept and felt peaceful.

In a while Amada and her husband emerged with Socorro. *They can get a doctor. He say if we need a horse he sell us one but they got no saddle. I fine out a lot happen since I leff California. These peoples was in the missions had to work too much an get punish all the time so they run away here. Some of these wimmins is born like me, part Californio an part Indian. Amada say they sad the white man pretty soon take all Chumash places.*

Librado directed a man to lead us to a stick corral that held a dozen or so ponies. Most were scrubby except for two. We pointed to a buckskin mare leggier than the rest. The man walked in and threw a rope hackamore on her. The horse reacted well, making no fuss. I rubbed her along her neck and shoulders before we led her back to the village.

Seeing us bring in a horse, Amada let the mare nuzzle her face. *She say is her horse,* Socorro explained, *the best one.* She and Socorro spoke for quite a while, continuing to catch up after a long absence, and Librado tried to intersperse their conversation with comments toward generating a *cousin price* for the buckskin mare.

He say he make good trade for a cousin, Socorro said. *Forty dollars. But he want our iron knifes. That trade is too bad luck for me.*

Tell him he can have my knife and I'll throw in five dollars more, I said.

The trade settled, we led all our horses back to the rickety holding corral, lifted tule rope hobbles off the fence, and looped them around our ponies' fetlocks before herding the entire bunch out into the grass.

I was impressed how these Indian horses tolerated our working them without flinching. Socorro explained that a Chumash horse was seldom broken, only gentled from the moment it hit the ground. In response to Socorro's unmistakeable piston-arm message, signaling that his horse might mount the mares, Librado nodded in hearty approval. It was clear he liked the possibility of Socorro's stallion infusing good blood into their remuda.

By the time we returned from the corral, the village was in full preparation for a welcoming ceremony. A large fire was lit. We squatted around the circle of expectant Indians, sampling wild cherries, roasted grasshoppers, acorn soup that resembled sawdust, and chunks of a chewy shellfish eaten out of plate size silvery red shells. The meat was surprisingly satisfying and a nice change from the dried fruit, beans, jerky, and black coffee we'd been traveling on.

Several women arrived wearing layers of beads and buckskin aprons, and a few wore cotton shifts. One dancer taller than the others caught Socorro's eye, twice. When she retired from her dance, he got up and spoke to her.

The men were singing and dancing. They wore their hair loose and sported tall feather bonnets built up of white and black down topped by a sheaf of quills that I took to be eagle or possibly vulture. Everyone smelled of woodsmoke and the outdoors, a satisfying scent I'd long associated with a perennial fresh air existence.

Four men, three snapping wood clappers and one playing a bone flute, kept up a steady rhythm. Many of the circle took turns jumping up to stamp in unison and sing. A "stool" was carried out for Librado, an enormous vertebra, big enough for a man to sit on. Socorro explained the vertebra was from a *balleena*, a sea creature Chumash men risked their lives spearing from big canoes. He'd seen one of these monsters washed ashore *big as twenny horses an stink like twenny dead horses too.*

The locals kept up the dancing for hours. I got up once and stomped around in my boots, delighting the Indian children and bringing sideways glances from the men. Socorro was nowhere to be seen. I guessed he'd snuck away with the tall long-haired señorita. I'd watched him discreetly whispering to his cousin, who'd raised a hand to her mouth and then pushed Socorro away more in amused encouragement than warning.

Next morning I was roused by someone kicking my heels. *Time to get yourself a gorl now, jovencito.*

Rising to my feet I stretched like a lazy dog. *Looks like I better get to it before you do.*

Socorro rubbed his chest and tried to stare at nothing in particular. *She like my big knife,* was his reply, and as I bent to roll my blankets he gave me a hearty boot in the ass.

We sent an Indian boy to get the horses. Saddling them, we rigged a double blanket saddle and rope stirrups on the buckskin. When we were about to leave, Amada handed Socorro a water bag that contained manzanita tea and said it was invigorating. Librado held a bundle of lit sage and proceeded to swathe us in pungent smoke. Suddenly he looked up and raised both arms to the sky. Two enormous birds with ragged wings glided slowly over the village. Amada explained to Socorro that the arrival of these birds signaled good medicine, and although all the adults in the village had been forced to work for the mission and act like Catholics, these, the biggest birds of all, never killed anything, cleaned up the dead, and were as sacred to the Chumash as the white man's big God. We watched the birds glide into the distance before heading toward the cut in the nearby hill.

I was experiencing hope mixed with apprehension. For the first time in many weeks I felt Gaagii stirring in my stomach and was unsure whether my crow spirit continued to be in any way my helper. I'd felt at ease among the Chumash, especially in their sanctuary in these gentle hills. Now, considering the possibility of finding Dahlia, I felt pangs of restlessness and uncertainty about the prospect of settling down. My roving attraction to wilderness had been partially fueled by my mother's conviction that the human race will eventually die of civilization, a foresight I later discovered she'd taken directly from Emerson. What little I had seen of the onset of civilization was happening fast. Locomotives, ferries, material cargos on a grand scale, capital buildings, commercial agriculture, people ... lots of people.

Riding south, what I saw of California presented more than sufficient beauty to nourish my wildest and fondest dreams. But there was, in addition, another bounteous mystery to explore: the sea.

o

We determined to ride directly to Mission Santa Ines but rejected the idea of taking Dahlia in broad daylight. We expected there was little risk of gunplay from her guardians. Although we didn't know this for a fact, we certainly did not want to visit violence on the only undamaged Mission, one peacefully tended by resident Chumash, a few Californio elders, and evidently Dahlia, too.

We needed to make our play at first darkness when Dahlia's room would hopefully still be illuminated by lamplight. Fearing the noise our horses might alert someone, we decided to hitch them uphill from the mission quarters, go in afoot, and, if possible, carry Dahlia back out.

I decided I would ride the Chumash horse and Dahlia could ride Saloon because my mare's saddle didn't fit the Indian's buckskin. I lengthened the stirrups on the buckskin mare and shortened Saloon's to fit Dahlia's height. If it turned out Dahlia was too weak for a long ride we'd take our time, stop whenever necessary, and come daylight be back among the Chumash.

We took our time drifting through the hills toward Santa Ines, even stopping to brew some campfire coffee. On the wagon road we encountered a mix of stage coaches, ox carts, and one or two spring wagons carrying men in bowler hats and ladies holding parasols, both buggies closely accompanied by carts carrying I imagined whatever was deemed necessary to their comfort. I made a note of the two carts, admiring their light build and the high-stepping gait of their well-groomed horses.

By mid-afternoon we turned westward toward the coast, and by late afternoon, close on our destination, we turned into the yellow hills and hunted for a good place out of sight that would allow speedy access to the mission grounds.

The words *Dahlia, California, Santa Ynez*, a refrain whispered for almost a year, had become a prayer that surely was about to be answered. Alternately reclining on the oak mast or pacing like a captive puma, I urged daylight toward darkness with every step while Socorro either watched with amusement or dozed under his Californio sombrero.

When dusk came it lingered endlessly in grey half-light. Socorro insisted I hold on a while longer for full darkness. Finally, under the waxing half moon we spotted creases of lamplight under a few doors and from shutters in the row of adobe quarters below.

We collected our horses, led them under the oaks into a brushy copse, and picketed them. We followed a path that snaked off the hill through a low walls' opening onto the mission grounds. I stopped to survey the buildings and listen. Their silence was a good signal. I hurried ahead of Socorro toward the door identified by the Mission's understanding *abuelita*.

I don't recall my feet touching ground as I strode toward that mission room leaking light beneath its doorsill.

While Socorro kept watch I drew the bolt through its iron loops, pushed open the door, and slipped inside. Apart from dried flowers placed in an adobe alcove and herbs hanging from its rafters, the room was bare save for a bed, a three-legged stool, and small rough hewn table.

As my eyes adjusted to the glimmer of a recumbent girl, I was transported to the Taos granary. Apprehensive about disturbing her sleep I knelt by her bedside for several minutes. Dahlia's fragility, her gentle exhalations and warm scents of cumin and wool seemed too tender a rest to disturb.

This hesitancy must have troubled Socorro; it was his *tap tap* on the door that opened Dahlia's eyes. She lay still a long moment staring at my face, then, reaching wordlessly out of her blanket, drew me close.

Folded by my kneeling posture I surrendered to Dahlia's arms, relieved to feel the strength of her welcome embrace while still anxious in my desire for us to get away. *My friend is waiting outside*, I whispered. *Can you ride?*

Dahlia's response was to continue wordlessly holding me until she collapsed onto the pillow with a breathless sigh of relief. *I dream so much it happen an keep the lamp burning because you use to always come at night so I keep my clothes all in one pillowcase.*

As she swung off the bed and covered her shift quickly in a blanket, I grabbed the bag of clothes and passed them outside to Socorro. I scooped her into my arms and sidestepped through the door. Free in the night air I swelled with the exhilaration of carrying Dahlia across the threshold of our world.

Socorro hurried ahead to the horses. I passed through the stone wall and, stepping off the mission grounds, felt my boots shift from packed earth to weedy hillside. Cradling Dahlia, I asked again if she felt strong enough to ride. She murmured between kisses into my shoulder *Yes, yes if you rise me onto the horse.*

Just above the brushy copse Socorro steadied Dahlia's horse on a flat spot. He steadied Saloon while I helped her into the saddle and adjusted her stirrups. I Mounted and then guiding Dahlia's horse alongside Saloon, looped her reins toward Socorro so he could lead us. She was shivering as she gripped my horse's big pommel with both hands and leaned heavily forward. When I attempted to assist her she brushed my hand away.

We picked our way through the oak trees and followed the moonlit trace of the wagon road in the direction we'd come. Our horses had a firmer sense of where to go than we did and kept up a fast walk. After we'd cleared the mission enough to feel at ease, Dahlia took a long draught of the concoction Amada had given us. She attempted to stay my concern that our ride was too arduous, but I could see she was struggling to stay upright, and her assurances were barely audible.

We managed to travel a few more miles before Dahlia began to sway precipitously and had to be lifted down from the saddle. Socorro led our horses off the road and tied them to a tree. I carried her to a grassy spot and we huddled close trying to determine what next to do. I quickly retrieved our blankets, re-wrapped her in one, and helped her lie back against the other.

I go ahead, Socorro said, *an bring some rig she doan fall off.* With no further discussion he swung into the saddle and we listened as his horse's gallop faded away down the road.

Dahlia attempted to talk but I hushed her and drew close to provide warmth. Her shivering became intermittent and she drifted into sleep. Her shorn dark hair had grown back almost to the length I recalled. I nuzzled my face in the nape of her neck.

I kept so vigilantly still that I dozed off raised up on one elbow and awoke feeling its pins and needles. I listened to the irritated stamp of our horses and to the wingbeats of a covey of birds flushed from their roosting. Dahlia had fallen into a deep sleep. I hoped the steady rise and fall of her breathing indicated she was completely at ease with our clandestine rescue.

It was not yet dawn by the time Socorro returned with Amada and two Indian men, one of them leading a horse carrying two peeled poles and packing a rolled bundle of stained wagon canvas. Dahlia awakened at Amada's voice and was given more of the manzanita tea, which brought beads of sweat to her brow, making me suspect it was an Indian concoction administered to release toxins. Amada whispered in Spanish to Dahlia and rubbed her wrists.

We are going to a safe place and there is a doctor there, I told her. Forgetting that Amada did not speak English, I asked, *how is she?* Amada, grasping the essence of my inquiry, lifted her hands to signal there was little need for concern.

The Chumash men quickly tied the sapling poles to the buckskin's pommel so they trailed out behind the horse forming a "V" with the wide end dragging on the ground. After cinching two sticks across the poles with rawhide thongs, they tied on the thick canvas and created a drag, or "travois," as early French trappers had called this useful Indian conveyance. We arranged Dahlia's blanket on the drag and helped her onto it. Even comfortably wrapped she could still reach out to the poles and steady herself over any rough spots.

It was coming dawn over green hills and low-hanging oaks, and the pause between night and morning began to fill with light. Crisp air tasted of silver and the leaves were so still birds were hesitant in their songs, as if testing the possibility of another day.

For some reason the Chumash appeared anxious to get off the wagon-road, so Amada waved them ahead. I remounted Saloon and led the buckskin pulling the travois at a walk. Alternating leading and riding alongside Dahlia, we made steady progress, only having to dismount twice to lift the travois poles across bad stretches of ground.

Approaching the pinnacle cut, an Indian boy who'd been on lookout galloped back to the village consequently there were people waiting for us when we arrived.

Amada directed us to lower the travois and carry Dahlia into one of the beehive-shaped huts he'd selected for the healing.

I laid Dahlia onto a layer of deer hides and covered her with the blanket off the travois. As she sank into the soft bedding, Dahlia grasped my hand. *By night on my bed I sought him who my soul loveth,* she murmured with a faint smile before closing her eyes.

Amen, I whispered.

○

Kitsap Solares seldom stood still, and his right eye sat in milky-gray stillness while the other darted unpredictably, like a spirit arrow aimed to penetrate your being. The Chumash bear doctor had "flown" *there and back over the slippery rocks* so many times he was more concerned with pleasing some other-worldly star family than with the irksome chore of exorcising sickness. His task was usually just a matter of using his *seeing power* to exorcise demons and then applying some plant ally he'd learned to befriend a long time ago.

Old Kitsap Solares was thoroughly experienced and a long way ahead of confident. Kitsap's spirit "flew" wherever it chose to go, a journey usually initiated by smoke. Smoke was really all Kitsap needed to travel, especially the sweet smoke of white man tobacco.

His task completed the old man would return home to hibernate in an abandoned grizzly cave below K'ahus Rock above Matil'ha Creek. Recently two nosy white men in big laced boots, nipple-topped hats, and wire-rimmed spectacles had deposited a box of avocados at the entrance to his cave. They also left a jar of molasses, six oranges, a pair of pants, and four wool socks. He ate the oranges and was smoking their peels into coils of blackened charcoal to make a tea to quiet the war party in his belly after slurping all the molasses. Kitsap also sampled the avocado's pale green flesh and kept their big brown seeds in case they were to be eaten somehow as the seeds seemed too useful to throw away. The socks he used to store nuts out of reach of ground squirrels. Kitsap constructed a scarecrow stick man, dressed it in pants, mounted a deer skull for a head, and planted the figure at the spot where the men had turned up the trail. Then he collected a mound of bear shit deposited it at the base of his rickety sculpture, and walked down the trail for several mornings after to urinate on his stick man's blue trousers.

It worked. No one had come back.

It was apparent that Kitsap Solares was a man of considerable standing Everyone in the village walked by the wizened hermit with their eyes lowered, or delivered food offerings to the door of his healing hut or *ap* as the Chumash call their reed houses.

My first impression of him was of a wrinkled elder in a feather skirt with clay-painted rings circling his bony legs and a rattlesnake headband that he adjusted around his chopped grey hair. At work, he kept muttering and lifting his hands to the sun. He circled Dahlia's shelter, stopping to do battle with invisible enemies against whom he'd feign spear thrusts. Confronting tougher unseen challenges he'd chant spittle-lipped spells.

Kitsap Solares maintained these antics until food was set at his feet which he then devoured before curling up for a quick nap. Spotting bear paws tattooed on both Kitsap's soles, and recalling how the Navajo painted snakes on their moccasins to give their owner stealth, I pointed out Kitsap's feet to a woman retrieving his food basket. Shaking a finger, the woman muttered Chumash words for "bear medicine," *kahus atiswinic,* deep in her throat, and hurried away.

Kitsap did not want anyone too approach Dahlia's *ap* and had scraped a circle around it no-one was allowed to cross except women with food for Dahlia. Through unmistaken pantomime Kitsap had demonstrated how if anyone entered the circle a snake would bite them in a very sensitive region which would cause them to fall down and, after much tongue panting and belly agony, die. This warning was further punctuated by Kitsap sketching wriggles in the dust and hissing *qshap qshap* in a convincing imitation of rattlesnake displeasure.

I watched and listened obediently to all these decorums which humored me because I believe the ceremony only applied to local Indians who needed Kitsap's vision to keep the world running properly.

Just in case Kitsap might prove to be a crazy man rather than a doctor I persuaded Socorro to quiz Amada as to what was about to go on. She refused to say a word about the old man's intentions except to tell Socorro that Dahlia would be fine and that I should do exactly what Kitsap Solares demanded, offer no payment of any kind, and keep my mouth shut.

I was fine with evading Kitsap. I tended to expect that Dahlia was going to get well pretty soon anyway because I believed the medicine she really needed was the balance we created gazing into one another's eyes where there was nothing to break our fall and where time did not exist.

I was loafing about and day-dreaming when a Chumash helper arrived carrying a cluster of brown seed-pods and a small serpentine bowl which he took to the old man. I was dutifully squatting as close to Dahlia's *ap* as Kitsap allowed when Kitsap approached with jimson weed trumpet blooms stuck in his headband like floppy white ears.

Kitsap had me stand up so he could dip his fingers into a green soap stone bowl and smear a dark paste on my temples, muttering as he painted me for what I figured was some necessary extension of Dahlia's healing ceremony. *Momoy*, "medicine plant mother," he assured me wiping his slippery fingers on my shirt. *Momoy*, I repeated obediently. *Momoy*.

So far all I'd seen of Kitsap's medicine appeared reliant on spitting, babbling incoherently, punching invisible beings, overeating, falling asleep in awkward positions, and bear claw tatoos. I had no idea he'd anointed my temples with a jimson seed paste powerful enough to enable men to fly over mountains or at least imagine they could as I was beginning to rise, rise, captive of a gathering hum gaining intensity as though my skull imprisoned a host of voices gathering volume increasing in an excruciating pressure, until the

unbearable
BURSTS
into fields of light
a release
gliding
above a landmass resembling a turtle

and abruptly landing flat on my back I found Kitsap poking my ribs with his toe. Deciding his patient had returned alive, he left me to finish my journey.

Though I was aware of my location, the outer world approached me in colorful pinwheels. My limbs were immobilized and my eyes refused to blink.

Plumes of sage smoke billowed from Kitsap's healing *ap*. One plume billowed a lithe giggling woman fixing me with almond eyes big as canoes, her seaweed hair and nakedness elongating into a tangle of sea otters that vanished into a raft of kelp and then squinting smoke, smelling smoke, tasting smoke, I was up and running toward Dahlia's *ap* but Kitsap's helpers grabbed me and wrestled me down on sandy ground.

The sun was clawing my eyes and the old man was pressing bony knees on my chest as, fiercely awake, I knew Kitsap Solares had *seen* Gaagii Hasleen and that his men had come to help him take what had been seen, and that's how it was, that's how it was going to be, so I flailed and fought because they wanted to rip out feathers that bear mother on the banks of the Pecos shook down from a cottonwood tree and that the Apache medicine chief had stuck deep in me and I needed those wings a hell of a lot and so did all the crows following me, and I knew if old man Kitsap stole them I'd never fly again and lose my bridge to the other world and miss Gaagii forever because this Chumash far-seeing doctor kneeling on my ribs and gripping a soapstone chillum with stars carved on it knew as well as I did that he was about to snag Gaagii Hasleen a long way from his crow country, and he began to suck my feathers and crow power and spitting out any *momoy* that came out of me too and Kitsap knew I could *see* him too and knew I knew he'd get to strut under the stars, smile in his sleep and lift tobacco to the moon and feel kin to the smoking fissures of the earth that constantly dissipate poisons, so Kitsap Solares could enjoy following his own white smoke exhaled toward the other world where maybe all things are the same and maybe they are not.

Kitsap Solares was out to steal Gaagii Hasleen and that's how Kitsap wanted things to be because he was a hungry shaman and had been ever since as a young man who bragged he could eat four red *toloache* blooms and did and the plant had killed him and he was only revived by three naked Chumash girls commanded by the Chumash to ride him back to life but he'd come back with the soul of someone else, a grouchy loner with an insatiable appetite for power.

What thought had I given to how Gaagii Hasleen was created or destroyed? All I'd known was that I could see into people and sense death faster than Rusty Cuellar could draw and hear crows tell me Comanche were coming on the run, and had years stored in me by consuming books and had time beyond years forced upon me by crazy Apache medicine and from riding moonlit miles talking to horses and feeling wild as a runaway child crossing the whispering bridge that connects two legs to four.

But I kept holding on to Gaagii and they kept holding me down, four rock-faced Chumash wrestling me while the old man pressed his soapstone tube into my belly and inhaled through it. Every time Kitsap sucked, more darkness drained away, making me smaller.

I fought the pain, straining to keep those big flight pinions in my shoulder blades and to keep my crow feather's rainbow sheen, and I warned the Chumash to let go, to stay away from me, warned them my dance has invisible footsteps and my power eats light so perhaps they should not steal my feathers because even the morning star and the sun's rays would avoid them and they would never again know what a day was, and goddamn them all nobody listened and that wily old man who stank of sage smoke and moldy acorn soup kept ripping and spitting out feathers, puking frothy black bile, grimacing into my face with that lone milky eye, and leaping around, prancing like a scavenging rag-winged-medicine-sucking two-legged victorious one-eyed hop-dancing crow and left me there lying on my back until I heard Dahlia's voice and looked up to see her smiling.

Soon I was breathing easy again and my Navajo friends, killed by that antelope-headed Apache medicine chief back below the Pecos, had quit singing their death song into my skull so looking up into her eyes I could see all the way through Dahlia de Belardes and she could see all the way through me.

Next day it turned out Kitsap had left, through an assistant, a diplomatic and traditionally discreet and overly obsequious invitation to *consider arranging to provide a year's worth of the sweet tobacco, only a small year's supply of the white man's twist possibly to be provided near where he had come a very long way to see into human beings who happened to need his allies, so he had provided this small thing and had in some small way fixed the world.*

I gave twenty dollars to Librado to make sure Kitsap received enough tobacco twist that if a Kitsap Solares year was the same length as a Devon Young year, it would be acceptable.

Kitsap Solares had also left behind a version of what he considered to be a message passed through him from the star people. Amada told Dahlia that Kitsap's helper, another one of her cousins, told her Dahlia's illness grew from "sadness." Kitsap also advised we get plenty of sun because a *big man from another far-away tribe* had made us both sick. Kitsap said he'd fixed Dahlia strong enough to scrape skins and grind acorns for the rest of her life however no matter how much we did the *moonlight happy dance* children would never come to us because that big man's magic had made it too dark inside me for *new little people to find their road into the light.*

○

Dahlia's recovery was soon evident. Her voice regained the lilt I remembered and we spent our days walking in the green hillsides and chattering like the re-united lovebirds we were. She observed that I had matured in many respects and decided I was fortunate to have had Socorro by my side throughout my journey to California.

Dahlia's seclusion in Mission Santa Ines had been initially a bearable one as she had been permitted to work in the gardens and was allowed contact with the resident women who prepared food for the monks. However the recent months had become arduous after a new priest arrived to head the mission. The newcomer's strictures ran to required periods of fasting and an insistence that Dahlia prostrate herself for hours on the cold floor of the chapel which had made her sick.

After several excursions in the delightful country and time lazing around the Chumash village we decided it was time to leave. Dahlia considered it risky to linger close to Mission Santa Ines. She'd never received one letter from her family back in Ranchos but had seen the man who watched her regularly accept money from the new priest. The same father, observing Dahlia's love of reading, decided it was in the best interests of her soul to send her north to Grass Valley and take vows there in Mount St. Mary's Convent and Academy. When Dahlia attempted to resist his orders what few books she owned were taken away.

The night before we were going to leave, Socorro re-appeared after a five-day absence. He was accompanied by the tall dancer whose name was Candelaria. Socorro suggested he and I stroll down to the corral.

As we leaned over the corral gate, Socorro handed me his knife.

Socorro, you trying to give away your luck?

I got plenty luck. I got Candelaria. Tomorrow we move back with her family in San Buenaventura. These Chumash people are gettin pushed out. We get married down there.

Married? Lightning strikes fast.

Si, hombre, an then comes plenty rain.

Socorro pressed the knife handle into my palm and closed his hand around it. *A vaquero fren forge this blade out of a broken Spanish sword he pull out of a dead bear he come across. One day three men come to steal some horses we run down from the hills. I take that broke sword an stick one of them an break the other man's head with a rock. The las man stick me before Secondino shoot him. While I was laid up Secondino forge this knife an fix that nice bone handle to it.*

The man who make this knife name is Secondino Mora. Mebbe he is still in Lagonas. Show him the knife an right away Secondino is your fren same as I am your fren.

Where exactly is he?

You and Dahlia keep south on the Mission Trail close along the sea. Is mebbe three days from here to Ranchos de San Vicente y Santa Monica. Then you follow the trail along the sea toward Mission San Juan Capistrano. The place is call Lagonas. Lagonas is by the sea. The next mission from there is Mission San Capistrano but you doan go that far south.

Lagonas?

Si, Lagonas. You come down a long hill to the playa an there's a canyon that runs back in from the sea. You ride east down the canyon until you see a cliff got a coyote rock on top. Two rock ears stickin up, over a swampy place with plenty water. Secondino live back in there. If he still there you will see his calico horses, he always ride calicos. If Secondino is not there he must be dead so you go ahead an settle there. It's a good place, plenty water and good grass.

What do you want me to tell him?

Nothin jus show him the knife an he will know. I think Dahlia like Lagonas. Lagonas is muy muy bonita. If we doan stay up here with Candelaria's peoples in Buenaventura I bring her down there myself an maybe get some work on Rancho San Joaquin.

How long since you were down there?

In response Socorro exhaled like someone who'd been away from a place he loved long enough to feel the weight of absence. *Fifteen, sixteen years.*

Likely a lot has changed.

The country will be the same less a lot of people have pushed in. If Secondino is not still there, stay anyway. You got some money and that pretty girl. I see why you loco for her. It make me happy to watch you happy together. I got a nice woman too. Hope I didn't wait too long.

Too long for what? I grinned.

Socorro looked across the corral at the horses counting their feet and swishing their sticker matted tails. *Everything,* he winked, *eccept Candelaria.*

Our parting embrace suited the hesitant refusal of two close friends. Turning away and walking back to the adobe, I considered how across all kinds of country being myself alongside Socorro Alvaro Diego Requelme had proved to be the most natural journey I'd ever been privileged to share.

o

Dahlia and I started our horses south at an easy walk and arrived on the outskirts of Santa Barbara by late afternoon. On the way we discussed the idea of purchasing one of the spring wagons I'd seen on the road to Mission Santa Ines. Asking local growers, we were directed by one fellow to a cooper by the name of Wade Partington who fixed stage coaches and dealt in wagon parts. We tracked him down at his roadside operation, a yard cluttered with assorted axles and broken wheels.

We immediately spotted a pretty one-horse buggy, with smaller front wheels painted red, folding canvas hood and a high seat for two with enough of a bed behind it to carry saddles and a little more.

Partington, an amiable middle-aged man wearing a leather apron, was supervising one of his workers braze an iron hoop onto a red and yellow wheel. Under the slant roof of his blacksmithing shed another heavy-set man was working a forge.

What can I do fer you folks? Partington asked, observing our interest. *I traded that little rig from a lady come up from Los Angeles. She kept the horse but I got all the harnesses an the shafts is solid. Sell you the whole outfit for seventy dollars. Course you need one of your horses to pull that don't kick the traces. The buggy is a modified Stanhope rig. Lady said it come off a ship from back East.*

Partington demonstrated how to rig the harness and helped me bridle Saloon and back her horse into the traces. Saloon would have nothing of it and immediately started back-kicking and wrestling the harness. We walked her out of the sidebars and tried the buckskin. Dahlia's mare appeared unfazed by the traces and we walked her around in circles until she responded alertly to the reins. Partington climbed down, handed Dahlia a snapper whip and helped her up the step onto the seat. Might run you a split rail and rig it for two horses if you want, Partington said, but it don't appear the other saddle horse takes to it.

We watched Dahlia drive the buggy around the yard. She looked delighted to act the fancy lady clucking that little rig in a tight circle and reining her gentle buckskin to a halt.

More than sold on the purchase, I suggested sixty dollars.

Rig like that with harness would run you a hundred most places if you could find one this far west. Paid fifty for it myself packed the hubs, and cleaned it up too.

How about sixty five, I offered.

Partington gave me a wry smile. Where you in from son? You worked a herd or two by looks of that saddle you are putting back that mare. Where'd you git that coffin rig? Looks to be an old vaquero hull with that frying pan pommel. I ran plenty wild stock out of these hills when I was your age, dapped a long loop on a few myself.

I told him that I'd herded cattle on the plains, only recently rode clear down from Sacramento and planned to take his buggy south and settle along the coast. Amused by my background, Partington shared his memory of back in the fifties, when California offered plenty of opportunities to heap cowhides on its beaches and trade all manner of plunder from anchored schooners eager to carry tallow, timber and hides to foreign markets.

Where you going? Partington inquired.

Lagonas. We were told it's a cozy spot. Heard of it?

About a week's ride from here. Most of it was an old Spanish land grant. Had a Mex-lookin feller on a ribby cow horse come in not long ago seeking to have his cinch re-sewn. Claimed he'd worked down there. Stock paper has it some rich Irishman from New York bought the whole San Joaquin grant.

Partington went to narrate that he planned on closing out his own business and settling further up the coast, then angled that he'd consider swapping Saloon for the buggy and even throw in another fifty dollars. Appreciating the man's offer and eye for a good horse, I kindly refused. We settled on a price of sixty-five dollars for the buggy, although it appeared that Dahlia had already assumed ownership.

If Wade Partingon's easy manner and openness was any indication of what lay ahead, I was encouraged. He invited us to join him and his wife, and three workers over a glass of mission grape wine, cheese, and torn slabs of sourdough bread.

We re-checked the harness, hitched Saloon behind the buggy, loaded the extra saddle, accepted the leftover bread and cheese from Missus Partington, and, sitting side-by-side flicked our buckskin into a trot. Dahlia had decided to name her buggy horse "Dulce" and insisted with some pride on handling the reins.

Trotting out of Partington's gate into a California afternoon's expansive blue sky felt like an invitation to share an endless song. The air was crisp and salted by an ocean breeze. Riding our buggy above a wide beach and ochre cliffs, then through orchards and scattered red-tiled adobes, it felt saintly to be in the same world as everything else alive.

When came upon a roadside sutler above the settlement of Buenaventura we purchased blankets, sail canvas, an axe, rope, eating utensils, and a shovel. Dahlia picked through the aisles and selected some yardage, pots and pans, soap and various sundries essential *for a happy woman to make a happy man.*

During our three-day journey south we'd been advised to hasten through Los Angeles which a passing teamster claimed: *Ain't much more'n a boomtown pueblo of nigh five thousand people, half of 'em sour Messicans gettin pushed out by money grubbin speculators. Take care you don't git that horse an buggy stole. The place is growin wilder an faster than law can handle.*

We followed a coastal road past several canyons eroded into crumbling cliffs until it opened onto a sweeping bay that defined the port of Los Angeles. Our route continued above a steep palisade overlooking a wide beach fringing the bay where numerous ships lay at anchor. The hills to the north overlooked several run-down adobes and newer plank-built residences skirting the reach of a great swampy delta which showed signs of recent floods.

Despite the mud and rutted shambles of reeds, brush and flood plain detritus, a steady stream of wagons bypassed one another hauling cargo both seaward and ashore. We watched four uniformed men with rifles, escorting a shipment of silver bullion down to the pier. Waiting iron ingots, barrels of nails, grease buckets, shovels, pitchforks, plow blades, great rolls of wire, windows, packing cases, furniture and produce crates of all sizes were stacked in rows.

The roads inland fanned in random directions in their teamster's attempts to navigate around marshy potholes, broken wagons, and boats in various stages of abandonment, construction or repair. Here and there hucksters and assorted agents stood by signs advertising land sales, jobs, horses, quick cures for sickness, boat passage, currency exchange, fresh water and cheap lodging. Several places required us to navigate rickety duckboards and hastily built pilings jammed by brush, empty bottles, animal carcasses, and twisted tree limbs.

Continuing south along the coast and leaving Los Angeles behind, we camped in sandy coves and were relieved to find ourselves undisturbed. The coastal nights were cool but not uncomfortable. We searched for watering places to stop and camped on the sand below patches of salt grass for grazing our horses.

Creeks were sparse but sufficient. We'd camp early, rig our canvas across overhanging tree branches or the entrance of a sea cave, build a driftwood fire, and wander the shoreline barefoot, collecting shells and chasing long-legged shorebirds. We became more careful romping in the tide. After a crashing wave dumped us on shore, we settled for playfully darting in and out of its gobbling rush. Afterward, shivering by a fire, we'd kiss our dimpled skins and huddle in blankets, inventing a small secret language to name odd shells, drift wood shapes and strange fragments delivered by the surge.

Our clothes were sandy, our soles wrinkled, and our hair stringy from woodsmoke, salt, and sunshine. We felt happily marooned from other lives far removed from this haunting coastline of untouched beaches, rock castles and crimson sunsets. Our harmony with the eternal *croal croal* of an evening tide developed a dreamlike intimacy and sensual courage.

After uncounted lazy days we were running out of supplies and, clambered up from another beach to greet our horses standing expectantly in the saltgrass. We loaded our buggy and moved on, passing beaches below cliffs high and low, tracing a sandy wagon road, sometimes forced inland by wetlands or runoff canyons too steep to cross. There were no bridges, and twice our progress was side-tracked for half a day until we found a marshy crossing and a dry reach leading back to the coast.

Our horses needed shoeing and our wagon wheels were starting to wobble for lack of grease. Assaying our hunger and our rig's evident need of repairs, I looked at Dahlia and, half in jest, declared *Man can't live on love alone.*

Si. Man need someone to live with.

A man needs a bath, too.

I like you even when you stink worse than a horse.

A horse?

Hmm. Si, a dead horse.

What about you?

I can say you stink but you cannot tell that to me.

Why not?

A man never tell his woman she stink.

Whoa. We both stink.

No.

Even if you do?

Who wash your clothes?

I have always washed my own clothes.

No more. I will do that.

Okay. You smell like a rose.

You make a big lie Devon. An I believe you.

I'm confused.

What is "confuse"?

"Confused" means someone doesn't know what somebody else means.

That's good. I help you be confuse if you stink and I wash your clothes that smells like something die but I smell always as a rose.

Always.

Si, always.

Okay.

An we got to fix these squickie wheels.

We?

You think I jus wash clothes?

You can cook, too.

Good enough to make you fat.

What else can you do? I asked.

Dahlia snapped the buggy reins and smiled. *You a bad man, Devon Young.*

°

It took us eight days to reach a fishing settlement with a single supply store that doubled as a saloon festooned with nets, shells and ships lanterns. The driftwood ramada stood atop a grassy dune above a cluster of makeshift fishing shacks. Its proprietor, an ex-sailor wearing cut off trousers and a battered captain's hat, directed us to help ourselves from a barrel to dip water for our horses.

To our inquiry of if he had anything to eat, the man hefted a fish and proceeded to slice it into slabs that he then arranged on a bed of coals, directing us to turn them as we chose. He quartered some lemons, set some on a hatch-cover table, and dropped several more into a clay water pitcher. Meanwhile the man kept up hearty discourse on the benefits of citrus, certifying his health was evidence of a daily diet of fresh fish and complaining of the challenges of maintaining it fresh for more than a day in hopes that his sparse supply of paying customers might sustain his determination to live by the sea.

I had encountered the term "old salt" usually in books about ships adventuring to distant regions. Logan Pruitt was the first genuine old salt I'd encountered. He certainly appeared salty enough. His hair was a flecked grey and his salty speech would curl the ears of a mermaid on a ship's bow. His hands were freckled hams and his legs thick as spars. A gelatinous belly initiated every move toward a great mug of watered rum and he chewed smoked fish like tobacco while speaking to anyone in range of his salty tongue, which, while eating our grilled fish, we were. He'd signed on hide and tallow boats around the Horn until, he declared, *I got myself anchored to a tollable wife who laughs like a gull, seven mules an enough land to supply ten clipper crews.*

Paying up, I asked how far it was to Lagonas.

Around ten mile straight down the coast. You come to a long hill that goes all the way down to the beach. Hardly nobody living there. No harbor, pier an mostly a rocky shoreline but it's a real peach of a spot.

We gathered up supply of apples, beans, sugar, salt, coffee, and corn flour, shook hands with Logan Pruit and tucked everything in the bed of our buggy. A warm offshore breeze had come up that flattened the sea. The sand around the man's lean-to was littered with shells and either side of the path leading down to the road was lined with enormous bleached skulls, giant ribs and several vertebrae larger than buckets.

¡Qué raro! Dahlia exclaimed. *What are those bones?*

Whale bones, I'd guess.

Like the big fish eat Jonah? They live here?

Out in the sea. A whale is the biggest animal. Socorro says big as twenty horses.

Do people eat them?

Sure. Whale and beans.

Okay. When we are to Lagonas you catch me one.

They have teeth big as cow horns and sailors lost overboard swallowed by a whale can be spit out a thousand miles from where they started.

How do you cook the whale?

It takes enough timber to build a barn to make the fire then the meat is cut into slabs by ten men and served on corn tortillas wider than a blanket.

Dios. Nothin is wider than the story you tellin me.

I like you, I grinned. *The last time somebody tried pulling the wool over your eyes there was nothing left on the sheep.*

What is wool over my eyes?

It's a way of saying you are too smart to be fooled, the wool is … never mind, some things are tricky to explain.

I need to be explained.

Everybody needs to be explained, I said.

o

We followed the old salt's directions and within an hour started on the long downhill grade he described. Before reaching the beach we pulled over to admire a magnificent view.

A curve of hills sloped to a wide flat onto gleaming white beaches and kelp-strewn coves tucked between rocky points. A gentle surf was pushing foam onto a shoreline where numerous shore birds darted after sand crabs and seagulls mewed overhead.

Looking down at the sea's radiant greens and blues with nary a human in sight, I declared Lagonas *as pretty a place as ever was.*

An the air smell with flowers. Let us together close our eyes, Dahlia suggested. When we opened them the view was still there and we sat inviting its beauty.

As we reached the beach flat, there were no sign of houses nearby except one tiny clapboard shack perched on a headland a few hundred yards away. Directly before us was a shallow estuary, the outlet of a stream likely flowing from the canyon Socorro had described. Lagonas looked to be untouched its tranquility protected by an absence of a harbor and by its rocky shoreline.

Noting that we were almost whispering to one another, Dahlia covered her face and peeked through the rails of her fingers. *I think we are not suppose to talk so loud in this place.*

There is nobody is around to hear us.

Plenty peoples is hearing, Dahlia dropped her hands and nodded mischievously. *In the leafs, in the stones and in the sea.*

Dahlia's wild imaginings and playfulness reminded me of Emerson's claim that "nothing great is created without enthusiasm." *Hmm. Yes think I hear them. Mostly the voices of the seeds.*

Hear the seeds?

Yup. Beans talk loudest. They are telling me I'm so hungry I could eat my hat.

Dahlia picked up the reins and clucked our buggy forward. *I think you being too old for me Devon. If a man forget he was a boy he will not remember he is a man.*

Aren't you hungry?

Is so beautiful here nobody eats.

Then I need to see something ugly pretty soon.

Fumbling under the buggy seat Dahlia produced a green apple and handing it to me crossed her eyes and stuck out her tongue.

Taking a wicked bite I munched happily. *You're full of surprises. I had you figured as way too pretty to save my life.*

Curious to see if anyone occupied the headland shack we splashed across the shallow estuary, and followed an obvious track that meandered between dunes of rubbery plants toward the hut. Nobody was there although the shelter contained tent poles, a roll of canvas, and an iron grate leaning against one wall.

We decided to back track the estuary outflow and hunt for the spot along the canyon that Socorro had described. On the canyon's northerly side, rocky outcroppings rose among scattered flats and steep ravines. On the south side a creek-bed was defined by brushy copses of sycamore, box elder and alder. We unhitched Dulce and Saloon leading them across a field and through brambles into the line of trees. Beneath their dappled shade a creek ran clear and we startled a nice four-point buck.

Continuing through the canyon I began to look for the signs that we were close to Secondino Mora. Dahlia walked the buggy and I rode Saloon ahead along a sandy wagon trail, noting a few wheel tracks and hoof prints. Well over a mile in the canyon briefly broadened. The creek widened into a pond enough to narrow the road and red-winged blackbirds clung to tule spikes. A few hundred yards farther where a grassy field extended on both sides I spotted two-brown and-white horses grazing. On the opposite ridge-top stood a sequence of interestingly shaped rocks, some weathered with circular holes and one, poking two pinnacles from its crest, with ears.

I waited for Dahlia to catch up and we walked side by side until we came to a horse trail that snaked up behind a line of trees. The steep trail was just wide enough for our buggy before it turned and rolled gently onto a meadow grazing several calico horses. Slightly higher under a sheltering cliff, a tidy cabin nestled beside an open-front barn where a man was examining the hoof of another calico horse. Spotting intruders, the man let down the hoof and walked toward us.

Approaching him I stopped to draw Socorro's knife and signaling that I meant no harm tossed it at his feet.

He picked it up, studied me, and looked at the knife in wonder. *Socorro.* He exclaimed, *¡Su cuchillo!* His face shadowed. *¿Es muerto?*

No, he isn't dead, señor, I replied. *Socorro es un buen amigo.*

Yo soy Secondino Mora, he said and, handing back the knife embraced me as a long-lost brother then waved for Dahlia to receive the same welcome.

Mora was a wiry vaquero with small hard-knuckled hands. His eyes were steady but danced when he spoke of Socorro. I guessed Mora was in his sixties but he likely was older. His remnant Californio signatures were his pony tail, a silk scarf under a weathered poblano hat and wrapped leather leggings. Mora spoke English but not much of it so it was a blessing Dahlia could translate.

When we explained our desire to settle in Lagonas, Mora seemed delighted but concerned that we might be too unfamiliar with a coastal location given that we were used to wide-open spaces. He explained that the canyon was a collection of tight little places and though there were plenty of deer in and above its grassy hillsides they were scattered and the bears had pretty much been wiped out by vaqueros working the boundaries that formed the north side of the canyon. Mora explained that there were few local settlers but all manner of necessities and dry goods could be acquired from a mercantile a half day's ride inland.

I was eager to introduce the two concerns uppermost in my mind: land to settle and the availability of work.

Mora explained that he traded horses. He'd either catch them far back in the dry country to the east or buy problem stock from ranchers and gentle or doctor them. He also liked to tool leather and traded his workmanship wherever he could. He'd recently quit as a working vaquero for Jose Sepulveda, whose land grant was recently purchased by a rich Irishman.

Sepulveda's grant had been losing money for several years. All the land along the north side of the canyon had belonged to him. It grazed cattle and sheep, was partially fenced, well watered and had a fine hacienda on it surrounded by numerous run down worker's adobes. If the next owner retained the lead hand Mora knew, Mora said he could get me an introduction and thought I could get work especially because the new owner was an Irishman. Otherwise, he explained, it was a five day wagon trip to Los Angeles and if someone had a team there was money to be made hauling goods north and south.

Regarding local land Mora smiled as though he knew a secret. Everything north for twenty miles and inland for twenty more was part of one big ranch. However, sections that constituted the beachfront had never been appropriated. I explained that we weren't looking for a big piece, just a sheltered spot where we could have a garden, a small corral, and enough wood to keep us going.

Mora walked us into his cabin. It smelled of coffee, leather, and hay and was spotlessly tidy. It had no glass in its windows, only shutters and a stone fireplace, a single bunk, and three saddles straddling a porch rail overlooking the meadow. The walls were hung with tapaderos, reatas, manila ropes, bridles, and three rifles. There was a bearskin rug on the floor, another bearskin on his bunk and a cougar skin over a chair. On his table, leather-working tools were neatly arranged in wood compartments.

Over coffee Mora suggested that in the morning he'd show us a spot. So far the area was only beginning to attract a handful of summer visitors with supplies enough for a ten day round trip and leisure time to spend a week camped along the beach. Word had spread that the area's climate was an ideal location for people suffering from lung issues. But no matter who arrived Mora knew that once anyone saw Lagonas, it worked its own spell. With winter approaching, we'd be unlikely to see many people at all.

He was sure land uphill from the beach would go first, although, at the current pace of things, development was a few years off. If Lagonas did get surveyed and land was distributed the government would be involved. However regarding settlement inside the canyon, although it probably belonged to the Sepulveda grant, it had been mostly fenced off from the pasture above.

I felt hopeful that, just as in the rest of the West, a primary magnet for settlers would be quarter-section government allotments given on the condition that the allocation be developed in some way. As the canyon offered no obvious lucrative "resources" other than its water, we decided to chance staking a small claim under the law of first-come first-served.

The next morning we saddled three horses and followed Mora west along the canyon. About a mile in from the beach we pushed through a stand of willows and waded the creek. The water ran clear through a nice pool. Close up against a cliff overlooking Lagonas was a meadow big enough to summer graze at most two horses.

Mora showed us where he'd once started to split logs with the idea of building himself a cabin closer to the beach. The little flat was high enough to secure it from spring floods and open enough to allow plenty of sun. The stretch above it along the canyon supported a mix of buckeye, alder, cottonwood, maple, arroyo willow, sycamore, and assorted oaks, some stands quite large with plenty dead and down.

Pleased to see how taken we were with the spot, Mora suggested he wait for us and pushed through the trees back toward the road.

Dahlia sprang from her horse, shook off her boots, and, spreading her arms, spun across the meadow through beams of pollen dust before returning to pull me laughing from my saddle. Fallen side by side we lay in the grass with the sun on our faces.

Turning to Dahlia, I whispered into her hair, *Listen to the creek, it's whispering our names.*

Dahlia rolled toward me. *I am happy this place speaks with you.*

It's a little smaller than I imagined but it's all here. I pulled Dahlia to her feet. *Let's ask it if we can stay.*

It say we are marry in the meadow, to the creek, to all the birds and flowers an deers an the stones. Dahlia's eyes brimmed with tears. *So much times I have been far away from my life.*

Not from mine, I said.

Secondino had offered to show us more. Our horses retraced their steps to the road where he beckoned us to follow. After a short walk down the canyon we leaned our mounts up a knoll cresting a hill onto rolling pasture of the south west section of the ranch.

When we stopped Secondino noticed Dahlia's bare feet. *¿Su botas?*

I leave them back there, Dahlia smiled. *In our meadow.*

Si. Where they belongs. Mora smiled.

We rode further into the ranch while Secondino explained that when Jose Sepulveda had gone broke his tenant herders had abandoned several adobes. He showed us a cluster of plank dwellings and some stacks of logs already adzed into useful dimensions, window sills and leftover roof tiles stacked among the weeds. He assured us we could help ourselves. The ranch stretched north and east, expanses of graze broken by sculpted rock outcroppings and sparse cover of trees lining seasonal creeks in the canyons and gullies. We encountered signs of mountain lions and spotted three coyotes which Mora had once been paid to shoot in order to protect the sheep. Mora narrated how Sepulveda had lacked a handy market for his stock but now freshly built New Port provided a sheltered harbor, which meant ship commerce would be moving in.

o

The day Mora showed us this cozy spot marked the beginning of our days in Lagonas. We began with very little but made it through the mild winters very well, although Dahlia's health was a challenge whenever it rained.

The first two years I worked alongside Secondino either running horses or driving a wagon back and forth from the southern reach of Los Angeles. We'd free run a mob of horses from well inland until the wild stock disappeared altogether. On the return trips from town I'd bring tools and whatever was needed to develop our place. Much of the wood and roof tiles came from the abandoned tenant buildings on the ranch.

Dahlia grew a vegetable and flower garden. We planted two avocado, three orange, and two fig trees. Dahlia also kept chickens. I embellished our diet with venison, squirrels, and once in while a yearling steer. We were cash poor but seldom felt in need. By the third year people had begun pitching tents above the beach. We'd ride down to meet them with fresh drinking water and sell Dahlia's eggs, her tortillas, and sometimes grilled fish or an extra chicken.

Besides taking outlying supply trips, we scavenged the beach. Mora showed us how to collect abalone, mussels and clams. I enjoyed hand lining off the points for fish and frequently landed good sized rock bass. Still wearing my cowboy hat, though shed of my boots, I liked to think of myself as roping fish. When the moon and tides brought them in we'd go grunion hunting, collecting buckets of these shining wrigglers to smoke or make chowder. Beach combing provided a wealth of fascinating detritus much of it remnants of reefed ships. Our little timber-plank house began to resemble a ship's bridge, and our garden was embellished with mahogany railings, sun-bleached oars, thick cable rope and oak decking which I used to make a porch.

Dahlia had taken to selling herbs and flowers from a ramada I erected near where the canyon opened toward the beach. The government's Timber Culture Act of 1872 allowed a settler one hundred and sixty acres conditional to planting a hundred trees. Eucalyptus, an easy and fast growing shade became the favorite solution to fulfilling the government's requirement. I'd load up on seedlings we'd started and sell them in bundles of ten for a dollar. Some newcomers paid me to plant those trees, too.

The eucalyptus then became a weedy nuisance so a few years later I was being paid to uproot them or cut them down. In 1879 we acquired a quarter section on the southern edge of town that I planted. In 1882 I sold this grant to a Mormon by the name of Brooks for five hundred in gold, a fortune at the time. With some of this money I built a more permanent and pretty ramada for Dahlia. While she was waiting for customers she began painting small seascapes in watercolors many of them displayed on the walls of our house.

In 1876 Bill Brooks had started Lagona's first stagecoach line. By 1903 what was now a beach community called Laguna had a hotel and around three hundred permanent residents. The coast road is still dirt and so are the roads in town although they are regularly graded. Droves of artists started coming in to paint. More clapboard cottages began to spring up. Folks take the train to El Toro and then the stage through this canyon into Laguna.

Today our town has tripled in size, with John Nichol's Livery, a post office, a grocery, three hotels, and Elmer Jahrau's lumberyard. Elmer imports lumber on the *Emma*, a schooner that offloads wood and floats it in on the tide. The lumberyard enabled a building boom. The town remains picturesque, although because folks can't drink scenery, water had to be hauled in barrels as wells tend to salt up. In 1905 a pipeline was implemented to pull drinking water from the canyon, requiring me to dig a well that, so far, hasn't failed.

Dahlia's folks either never wanted to find her or maybe couldn't track her down. Rumor had it from Socorro that they'd left New Mexico but we never travelled there to find out. For years Dahlia remained stoic about ever seeing them again though she occasionally expressed curiosity over the fate of her aunt and her cousin Alicia. Dahlia became a voracious reader and although her English vocabulary grew sophisticated her accent and injections of *Almanac* advice endured. She gathered our pretty spot around us neat as a handwoven serape. I enjoyed hearing her talk to the flowers, to chickens, lizards, ants, bluejays even willow branches and broken pitchforks. Her grace and irresistible lilt seduced smiles from everyone she met. She attracted a handful of women friends who adored her to the last. Dahlia's spirit carries over to my own days blessed as they are by Lagona's beauty and by the affection we shared.

Socorro developed a horse ranch north of Santa Barbara, fathered five children and named his firstborn son Devon. Our annual summer visit gradually became less frequent given Socorro's failing health and the arduous distance between our homes. Last month his second oldest son drove down in a brand new Model T pleased that it took them only one long day.

As his son helped him down from the automobile, Socorro grumbled that he still preferred a wagon because horses, unlike automobiles, got tired and needed to rest. He still wore a vaquero headscarf although his long hair had turned bone white. The vaquero's weathered features were ravined, his eyes clouded with a blue mist, and his veined hands trembled. Although he'd aged noticeably since I had last visited him on his ranch, his alert presence endured.

As I guided Socorro toward a seat on my garden bench, he asked his son to roll us a smoke. *Nice little place,* he observed. *It always feel good here. Get to sleep easy an no Comanches.*

If I'd known who those Indians were I'd have thought twice about that cattle drive north with Jack Rice. You know, I never asked you, whatever happened to that big liver stallion?

Died a long time ago but some of him is still around. Threw fifteen foals look just like him. Sold twelve for good money. My childrens all ride. The youngest better than any of 'em. She never listen when her mother catch her jumping fences bareback. They all speak English. My daughter is always correctin, he shook his head, *correcting me.* Socorro pulled a flask of mescal from his jacket, unscrewed it, and passed it over.

I lifted his flask in an old cowboy toast. *Ride it like you stole it.*

Dipping his head in amusement, Socorro took another healthy swallow. *You never had no horse could beat mine.*

We both had solid horses and rode with some good men. Well, maybe a few not so good, I chuckled.

Whoever deal the cards threw down what they needed, Socorro concluded.

Maybe there's justice after all.

Justice sleep but it always wakes up. Socorro was pointing his cigarette toward my corral. *How much stock you got ?*

Just the two mares in there. Bred them out of Mora's calicos.

Findin any work?

Not much. I like to fish the sea.

My oldest takes his brothers fishing off Anacapa. Sometime they come home an say they got scared by a whale coming under their boat.

We see them spouting by in the winter. One washed up dead last year, I said.

Big, huh? Like I tell you.

I walked it head to tail. Twenty paces, seven horses long, but seemed like it might weigh a hundred horses. Stank up the beach for weeks.

We still got condors come over the ranch. My daughter found some feathers an Candelaria say she keepin them to get buried with.

Whatever happened to Kitsap Solares?

Nobody know.

After a pause I asked, *Where do you figure folks all go, Socorro?*

We're already there, was his reply.

We sat and yarned until his son returned. A handsome dark-haired kid wearing driving goggles, a canvas jacket, and a black tie, he had inherited his father's steady eyes and quiet manners.

After we'd embraced and Socorro had settled in his car seat we looked at one another through the window long enough to recognize that it was likely for the last time.

Fisting away tears I watched the Model T vanish up the canyon. Seized by inner voices, lowering my hands I studied the veined mortality of their life, a life I had dreamed until my will to imagine had been fulfilled by a world no less divine than a prairie sky, the Pacific sea, California's golden hills and Dahlia's family of tended flowers. In Socorro's departure I felt Dahlia's too as though lacking physical boundaries they had achieved a mysterious wilderness outside time. Standing in the road's dusty sunbeams my senses were wondrously charged by the conviction that I had left no part of myself unlived.

After Socorro's departure a weightier silence settled in the canyon. Evening re-awakened visions of Dahlia and, given the choice between writing or resuming another conversation with a fishing hook, both options won out.

The new summer sun reveals a dancing world
its light has made, windy willow branches
that rise to sway and sweetly take their bow.
In a dawn whisper of the eternal my horses
nicker at dusty sunbeam motes of souls
that drift the sermon of a crow, a croak
across dry plains calling life's holy
track beat-flattery of love and death
across earth's map of blood and breath
to seek a stolen lady whose dark-eyed smile
and mermaid lilt of Spanish charm
seduced so far west my absolute belief
under sunset reefs I became a fisherman
on a silver causeway moored upon the sea
adrift upon the salty tiptoe tide of destiny.

*To my immigrant parents
and their gift of America*

FIRST EDITION 2013
ISBN 9781562791377

Night Ride with Dahlia
PHILIP DAUGHTRY

MERCURYHOUSE.ORG